Lady in Red

MÁIRE CLAREMONT

headline
ETERNAL

Published by arrangement with NAL Signet,
a member of Penguin Group (USA) LLC.
A Penguin Random House Company.

First published in Great Britain in 2013
by HEADLINE ETERNAL
An imprint of HEADLINE PUBLISHING GROUP

1

Cataloguing in Publication Data is available from the British Library

ISBN 978 1 4722 0477 6

Offset in Times by Avon DataSet Ltd, Bidford-on-Avon, Warwickshire

Printed and bound by CPI Group (UK) Ltd, Croydon, CR0 4YY

Headline's policy is to use papers that are natural, renewable and recyclable
products and made from wood grown in sustainable forests.
The logging and manufacturing processes are expected to conform to the
environmental regulations of the country of origin.

HEADLINE PUBLISHING GROUP
An Hachette UK Company
338 Euston Road
London NW1 3BH

www.eternalromancebooks.co.uk
www.headline.co.uk
www.hachette.co.uk

For my mother, Kathryn, who gave me my love of writing and who always believed.

I miss you.

Acknowledgments

Once again, I have my favorite women to thank. Delilah Marvelle, I adore you, sister mine. Where would my writing be without you? Lacey Kaye, you are such a rock star and I'll never forget all your support for this series. Helen Breitweiser, thank you so much for always standing behind me, no matter how tough the situation, and Jesse Feldman, you've given my characters a home and made them stronger with your guidance. I can't say thank you enough.

Chapter 1

London
1865

L ady Mary, only daughter of the Duke of Duncliffe,
stood silently on the doorstep of the servants' entrance to one of London's many whorehouses and dared
herself to knock. It was no ordinary whorehouse. Oh,
no. This particular establishment was her last and only
chance at salvation.

The irony didn't escape her that most would consider this door the path to hell, not heaven. But thanks
to the machinations of her father, she was not most.

Cold, piercing raindrops slashed down on her raised
white knuckles. Her pale flesh glowed unnaturally in
the gas lamp light and pelting water. What little color
she'd once had had vanished due to her imprisoned
existence these past years. Weaving slightly, her muscles
burning with the ache of sleeping in roadside ditches
and on muddy fields, she braced one hand against the
cold white stone doorway. With the other, she grabbed
the brass knocker and rapped it against the polished
red door.

There was a scuffle of shoes against stone on the
other side and then the wide door swung open on iron
hinges.

A girl, her white mobcap fixed atop nut brown hair,

gaped. Her round brown eyes traveled the length of Mary's bedraggled frame, widening so far the orbs might have popped out of their sockets. A peep of dismay—no doubt from taking in her mud-stained skirts, the ratted quilt about her shoulders, and her hair, her shorn hair—passed her plump lips.

"Look 'ere, me girl," said the maid in her low, thick East End inflection. "We don't take in no common doxies."

Mary leaned against the frame. Now that she had finally reached her destination, all the strength she'd clung to seemed to be fading. "Please, let me in."

The rain began to pour down in furious late-winter earnest, slicking her short hair to the top of her head. Mary cringed against the icy assault, eyeing the space between the door and frame as if it were a portal to bliss.

The girl, most likely the scullery maid, started to shut the door, her round face creasing with disgust.

Oh, no, she would not!

Mary thrust herself forward, jutting herself between the door and the jamb. For one brief moment she was sure the maid would slam it against her, bruising flesh with no care for bone. Thankfully, the maid hesitated and Mary placed her hands on the rain-spattered panel. "I beg of you."

The girl shook her head, the mobcap fluttering. "I told you, I did. We only 'ave ladies of 'igh quality 'ere."

Mary drew herself up. "I am a lady. Born and bred," she declared, determined to convince the maid. "But even true ladies fall upon times of difficulty."

That much was true. Once, she had been one of the most pampered young ladies in Christendom and beyond, but few souls from that hallowed realm would recognize her now. "I have traveled a very far distance. Please, allow me to see Madame Yvonne."

The girl lingered in the doorway, her eyes darting around in indecision. "You do speak like a lady, but I can't let you in. I'll get the sack."

"You'll get the sack if you don't." Mary's patience swiftly disappeared as that last vestige of strength she'd summoned sputtered out. She'd come too far to be turned away at a servants' door.

She attempted to suck in a steadying breath, but coughed instead, a harsh rumble. Each laborious breath she took strained her chest, but she threatened all the same: "I'll call upon the m-main entrance if you prefer."

The girl's mouth dropped open, her face paling at the very idea. "You wouldn't dare."

Mary glared back at her, teeth chattering. "I have nothing to lose," she said through numbed lips. "Can you say the same?"

The maid seemed about to protest, but then her gaze hovered over Mary's face.

Mary lifted her chin. "Will you keep a lady standing in the rain?"

The kitchen servant shook her head and backed out of the doorway.

Without waiting upon ceremony, Mary stumbled in. The amber light and blooming warmth of the kitchen greeted her, its pleasantness bringing a smothered cry of joy to her lips. It was so splendid to see something—anything—that reminded her of what she had once had: a home.

Even if this was only a servants' hall in a brothel.

A fire burned brightly in the great cooking hearth, decked out with iron pothooks and a steaming kettle.

Carrots, potatoes, turnips, and leeks ready to be peeled and chopped lined the long oak worktable. It was the most perfect thing she had seen since the day before her mother died.

She didn't dare to blink. If she did, this moment might vanish like the laudanum dreams that came and went with the roll and fall of one's thoughts.

A cat lay curled up on the stuffed dark brown armchair before the fire, his tabby stripes rumbling ever so gently as the contented animal purred. She couldn't recall the last time she had seen a civilized cat. She had become all too accustomed to the yowling beasts that hunted down rats, hissing and spitting if you tried to touch them.

"Now, miss, as you can see—" The maid smoothed her reddened hands down her crisp white apron and kept several paces from Mary. "I've got me a bit of work to do. So you sit your bones there." She pointed to a hard bench far from the fire. "And I'll send up word." The maid eyed her warily, clearly unsure what to make of Mary. "What name shall I give 'er?"

"No name." Mary's fingers twitched at the end of her ratty quilt, water dribbling along her skin. No one could know her name. She didn't even like to recall it herself. "Convey merely . . . that it is Esme's daughter."

The girl stared blankly, thankfully not recognizing the given name. "A-are you in trouble, miss? Madame Yvonne won't want trouble."

Though it took far more of her reserves than she could spare, Mary called to mind the attitude she had taken with all her father's servants, a kind, firm authority. "What is your name?"

"Nell."

Mary nodded once. "She will wish to see me, Nell.

Now go find a footman and have him tell your mistress."

Assured at Mary's tone, Nell turned on her heel and headed up the narrow stair.

Slowly, her body as frail as an old woman's, Mary lowered herself into a chair across from the worktable. It was hard and straight backed with no armrests. She would have liked to sit closer to the fire and the cat but was simply too exhausted to move again. Her clothes and thin quilt, pilfered from a farmer's drying line, were soaked. She couldn't remember the last time she had felt warm.

Nor could she stop shivering.

For the first time in what felt like days, Mary allowed herself to sigh and close her aching eyes. That serving girl had looked at her as if she were a spirit escaped out of damnation. A far cry from how servants used to look at her, with smiles and the desire to please.

She probably did look a hideous fright. More than a fright. She most likely looked like a hag—no mean feat for an eighteen-year-old daughter of a duke.

She drifted momentarily before something jerked her out of repose.

In the distance, the clattering of steps, muffled voices, and the bustle of quick movements down the stairs drifted into the peaceful kitchen.

Mary's eyes flew open and she jumped quickly to her blistered feet, ready to flee in case it was a group of footmen set on kicking her out. Surely her mother's friend wouldn't . . . But she'd learned there was no one she could truly trust. Even her own once beloved father had turned against her.

"Mary!" a voice cried from the servants' hall. A deep, rich voice meant for the pleasure of a man. A tone so ingrained that such a temptation would always be in it. "Mary?" it called again, full of disbelief and shock.

A shuddering breath left Mary's chest. *Hope.* For a brief moment, she let herself hope. Her fingers trembled as she wound them in the torn quilt tucked about her frame. "Yvonne?"

Yvonne swept into the room, her dark violet skirts so wide she could barely pass through the doorway. She glittered like the dew under the sun. A thousand rainbows clung to her wrist and throat and her fiery tresses were laced with diamonds and amethysts.

Mary had never seen anything so beautiful. Not even when she had watched the ladies of the court from the balcony of her own home. Those memories paled against this glorious moment. Yvonne was a living, sparkling angel come to sweep her to safety.

Yvonne stopped suddenly, her full skirts swishing about her legs. Her lime green eyes widened as her face tensed with horror. "My *god.*"

Her delicate hand flew to her rouged lips. Blinking fiercely, tears sprung to her eyes. For several moments she only stared, as if paralyzed, until at last she said in a hushed voice, "You look so much like Esme."

When she was small, everyone had delighted in telling her how she was a miniature reproduction of her mother, but she'd assumed that the resemblance would diminish as she grew older. To hear such a thing today, when she felt but a mere shadow of herself, was a rare boon. "Do I?"

Her own throat closed as unbidden thoughts of her otherworldly mother flowed into her heart, warming her as no fire could. "Do I really look so much like her?"

Nodding, Yvonne hurried forward. Even though she

was wearing a gown no doubt worth more than most men could make in several lifetimes, she swallowed Mary up in a soft embrace of roses and sweet-smelling powder.

Mary stiffened under the touch and kept her hands down at her sides, her fingers clutching at her muddied rags. How she wished she could reach out and embrace Yvonne . . . or cry with fury or relief. But no tears remained.

Those tears had been cried out in her dark, freezing room in the asylum where her father, the world, and God had abandoned her. There was nothing left to her now. No emotion except the will to survive. She continued to stand woodenly in the embrace, half afraid that if she moved she would awaken and find herself sleeping in a ditch somewhere between Yorkshire and London. Or, worse, on her filthy, bug-ridden pallet under the watchful eye of the keepers.

There was also the possibility she might start screaming. She hadn't been touched by anyone but . . . *them* in three years.

"Charles!" Yvonne moved slowly away, her soft hands gesturing with the same fluid animation as her features. "Carry Mary up to my apartments. Use the back stairs and ensure that no one sees you."

The footman lowered his gaze. Consternation creased his young brow while he studied his white-gloved hands. "I—"

"*Now.*" Yvonne's face remained beautiful and cool, like a painted Madonna dressed in gilded robes as she gave her orders. "And tell the cook to send up broth and wine. A good bottle of wine to fortify her." She stepped back, giving the servant room. "Don't tarry, Charles. Go on."

Charles gave a curt nod, then stepped forward. His

footman's livery moved gracefully over his young, muscled body as he lifted his arms to carry her.

Even with his kind face, neatly combed blond hair, and gentle movements, her heart skipped a beat at the thought of his hands anywhere near her. An animal cry escaped her lips before she could stop herself. "Don't touch me," she hissed.

Charles froze, his ruddy cheeks tightening as if she'd slapped him. "I'm sorry, miss. It's only what Madame—"

"No, Charles." Yvonne's own face suddenly strained with concern and a slow understanding. "I'm certain Mary is desirous to walk of her own accord. Is that not so, Mary?"

Mary noticed the coaxing note in Yvonne's beautiful voice. It held that same tone the keepers had used on new patients. Only the keepers. *The keepers . . .* Mary blinked fiercely, refusing to think about those brutes of men and how simple coaxing had turned to brutal confrontations.

"Mary?" Yvonne said so lightly it might have been a whisper. "What do you wish?"

Mary nodded absently, trying to focus on Yvonne so she could leave the asylum behind her. "Yes. Myself. I'll take myself."

"Of course, my dear. And I shall go with you." Yvonne stepped forward, her gown shimmering the deep glow of amethyst in the firelight. Carefully, she extended a white-gloved hand adorned with jewels. "Come."

Mary stared at it for a moment. She'd trusted only one other person in the last years. Another girl in the asylum, Eva. Though she wished she could reach out and take Yvonne's sweetly offered hand, she knew it was best not to attempt it. She shook her head gently. "I cannot."

Yvonne lowered her arm and a sad smile flickered at her lips. "Of course. I shall lead and you shall follow."

Mary nodded, the only action she seemed capable of without shattering to pieces.

"Oh, and, Charles— Send up hot water for a bath." Yvonne's eyes trailed over Mary, a pained expression darkening her eyes. "I think we will need quite a lot of it."

Yvonne edged carefully around her, chose a lit candle in a brass holder from the side table, and then took to the back stairs, her steps brisk and firm. Mary followed her, taking each pace with as much care as she would over burning coals.

She had to stare down, careful not to step on the folds of Yvonne's stunning swaying skirts. They climbed the steep, narrow stairs in absolute silence. The silence grew heavier with each step and Mary's heart beat harder against her ribs. Unspoken secrets hung around her like murderous ghosts, each one threatening to steal her life or mind away if she betrayed them.

When they reached the landing, Yvonne whisked down the cream and gold hallway. Everything was gold. Swirls of it climbed the walls and snaked across the ceilings. And mirrors.

So many mirrors. Mirrors upon mirrors lined the walls like empty and ever-changing family portraits.

The faint light of the candle illuminated Yvonne's beautiful figure, and, ever so slightly, Mary spotted her own small shadow following like some twisted creature.

Mary stopped. Her heart slammed against her ribs as she slowly turned her eyes to the mirrors to her left and met a pinched face with hollow, darkened eyes. A strangled gasp escaped from her lips.

Yvonne whipped around. The candlelight now shone fully on Mary's face.

"No no no no," Mary babbled. She looked . . . exactly like her mother. Exactly as she had been at the end. Gaunt, beaten, bruised. A face without any vibrancy, only horrid shadows and emptiness. Slowly Mary lifted her hand to her face. She traced the bones, staring wide-eyed at her ghostly reflection. It was all there. The dark hair, only far too short. The extremely high cheekbones from some French vicomtesse in her distant past. And the eyes. Almond shaped and bizarrely violet. Kashmiri eyes. A gift from her maternal great-great-grandmother, a shocking woman, she'd heard.

She'd never thought it possible. She'd been determined that she would be stronger than her mother, but her father had truly won. Two women beaten, one in the grave, one dead in so many ways yet still traversing the world.

"Mary?" Urgency tightened that beautiful voice. "When was the last time you saw a mirror?"

Mary blinked and lowered her hand from the horror before her. "I—"

Her brow furrowed as she tried to recall the large London town house on Wallace Square. That house had had hundreds of mirrors. Even more mirrors than those around her now. Mirrors her mother had danced and preened before while her husband had lounged against a silk chaise, smoking his cigar, drinking his French brandy, enjoying his pretty toy of a wife.

Yvonne glanced from Mary's face to the reflection. "It has been some time, I should think."

Mary held her own wounded gaze in the mirror. "It has."

"Come." Yvonne held the candle back toward the

empty hall, the glow flickering in the mirrors. "We must speak and not in the hall."

Mary glanced about and sucked in a harsh breath. If she listened carefully, she could just hear the voices of men and women drifting from the bedrooms and up from the salons below. Although she had never been to Eden's Palace, she did know it was frequented by the wealthiest men in London.

Men who might know her father.

Yvonne bustled down the hall without another backward glance. Mary scurried after her, her own tired legs protesting every movement. At last, they reached a tall set of double doors, carved with a beautiful pastoral scene in which naked men and women lay entwined in the fields.

Yvonne pushed the doors open and rushed in, quickly lighting the many candelabras placed strategically about the large blue and gold chamber.

Mary turned and closed the tall doors herself, the panels almost too heavy for her to shut. She hesitated on the edge of the room, feeling utterly out of place in this lush chamber.

"Sit there before the fire," Yvonne insisted, pointing to a pair of delicately embroidered slipper chairs before the hearth.

She had no wish to catch her own reflection again in one of the many mirrors about the room, so she glanced down as she hurriedly crossed to one of the chairs Yvonne had indicated.

The heat penetrated her body with a delicious caress and she was tempted to relax just a little. It had been almost three years since she had sat before a fire so large, or with such exquisitely carved pale stone about it. Three long years since she'd felt any measure of safety or peace.

Several moments of prolonged, tense silence—which neither she nor Yvonne attempted to break—passed before Charles entered with a large tray. Three other footmen followed behind him, one balancing a hip bath and the other two carrying large buckets of water.

Mary recoiled on the chair. Every muscle in her body locked with stillness, as if she could render herself invisible.

With silence and ease, the servants moved about in a ritualized dance. Charles placed the tray on a gold-rimmed marble table near the empty chair across from her.

While the footmen worked, Yvonne poured out two large glasses of red wine, the liquid sloshing loudly in the glasses.

As soon as the servants had silently disappeared, Yvonne handed one of the crystal goblets to Mary.

Gracefully, she lowered herself into the chair opposite Mary, her amethyst skirts settling about her as if she wasn't wearing hoops beneath the silk at all.

Mary clutched the glass in her hands, waiting for the interrogation to begin. Dreading it.

"Drink," Yvonne ordered.

Dutifully, Mary lifted the glass to her lips and took a sip. The heady wine was almost too much flavor for her deadened palate. It burst across her taste buds, filling her mouth with an earthy delight.

"Your father said you had passed away." Yvonne toyed with her own glass. "Did you open your tomb and come forth to haunt us?"

The wine sputtered out of her mouth. Mary gasped and coughed as it stung her nose.

"Don't waste it, Mary dear. You need every drop."

Mary didn't bother to pat at the wine on her frayed

clothes. Instead, she wiped the back of her hand over her mouth, drawing red liquid from her lips. Red, the color of watery blood, now trickled down her hand. Only it wasn't blood. Indeed, it was not.

She kept her eyes wide, determined not to think about blood, or the way it slid along stone floors.

"You are surprised to hear of your death?"

Mary laughed, a short, horrid little bark of sound. "It is news to me, I must confess. Unless, of course, I cannot recall my own funeral and Christ has ordained another Lazarus."

Playing her fingertip along the crystal rim of her glass, Yvonne said, "When the footman told me you were downstairs, despite it being against all possibility, I somehow felt sure it was you. I had always wondered, you see. The timeliness of your death after your own mother's demise . . . always struck me as overly coincidental. Your mother had mentioned a few things about your father's behavior. Before the end."

Perhaps Yvonne would believe her if she told her the truth. But she bit back the words so ready to flow from her lips. She couldn't trust anyone. It wasn't safe. Not if Yvonne truly was going to give her refuge.

"We should go and see your grave. We could place flowers on it." Bitterness laced Yvonne's words. "I have these last three years. It is suitably by your mother's."

"My father is a monster." It seemed the only thing to say short of starting a discourse of anger that might never end.

"God, I am so glad you came to me."

"You were the only person my mother truly trusted."

Yvonne smiled sadly. "She was kind to me. Even when your father demanded she give up seeing me, she'd come in secret."

Mary fidgeted. It was hard to speak of her mother

after what had happened, but Esme Darrel had spoken quietly of Yvonne, of her goodness. As if somehow her mother had known something was going to befall her and knew that Mary could go to the madam if she ever needed help.

Yvonne leaned forward, her face determined. "What happened, Mary?"

Mary swallowed down the desire to confess it all. But there was so much she couldn't speak of. Never could and never would. "I—I can't say."

Yvonne let out an exasperated breath. "Then at least tell me in what part of the country you have been?"

"North," she croaked. She took a long, fast swallow of wine, unwilling to let herself taste the rich liquid lest she cough it up again.

"I see." Yvonne leaned back, clearly not satisfied with this brief answer. "Does your father know you live?"

She wished her father did think her dead. At least then he would have no reason to seek her out and condemn her again to unrelenting misery. Mary glanced down, her chest tightening at the very thought of him, before she forced herself to meet Yvonne's eyes and finally admit, "He was the one who sent me there."

"Where, Mary?" Yvonne's fingers tightened around her glass, whitening at the knuckles. "Where did he send you?"

Mary shook her head and tore her gaze away. It was as if she was being sucked back into memory and she couldn't bear it. Her eyes glazed over till the room was but a blur.

"I'm not going to harm you. No one will, not ever again."

Mary stared into the fire, not truly seeing the blazing light. Her eyes burned with the terrifying recollections of that place. Of her mother, of her broken body at the bottom of the stairs; of her father, remorseless and cold. "He sent me where I would be forgotten," she said simply, the words unleashing a jagged slash of pain, twisting her face as if she might cry. But no tears came. "A madhouse, Yvonne. He sent me to a madhouse."

Chapter 2

Edward slowly lifted his gaze to the plasterwork ceiling, wishing he could sink into the cushioned Chippendale chair. He was just as empty and desperate for any sort of meaning in his life as when he'd begun the night's revelries. He shouldn't have come to Madame Yvonne's.

He'd finally learned that there was no real peace against the past. Not even the usual choices a man might make to launch himself into mindlessness were taking their effect.

A scream tore through his head and stole his breath away. Holding his body still, he willed that girlish cry of terror ricocheting through his mind to dim. Would she never cease? Would she never let him forget?

Edward reached for the brandy on the mahogany table beside him and allowed himself to distance his thoughts from memory. He focused on the drawing room and its striped ivory silk walls. A young blond woman eyed him from her perch on the settee at the far side of the chamber. She shifted slightly, plumping her full breasts against her low-cut saffron silk gown.

She had yet to find a companion tonight and he was not going to be it.

He sighed. Once, such a sight would have distracted him. Now, the idea of another empty night just left him . . . well, empty.

There was no escape from his pervasive certainty that he was a hollow and disappointed man. A man who would never make peace with his failures. Still, the feeling wasn't quite strong enough to make him regress to a hermit's existence. He grunted to himself at the thought of being his sole companion.

His mother's own attempt at an opium-induced death was proof that solitude was not the answer to trouble such as his. At least he'd had the good fortune to learn from one parent's mistakes.

The blond sauntered toward him, her skirts swishing, curls bouncing about her lightly rouged cheeks. "Would you care for company, Your Grace?"

It was strange that all the girls knew him, as if his reputation passed always before him like a damnable shadow. But his past generosity to the women of this establishment had made them eager for his company.

She stopped before him, her full skirts lightly brushing his knees. Before she could utter one more word, another light-o'-love slipped up beside her compatriot. This one was a brunette, her russet hair curled softly about her face. She gave him a slow smile and said huskily, "Perhaps Your Grace would care for a good deal of company?"

At one time he would have said yes. That now seemed like an age ago. "I don't . . ."

"Or would you care for a private room to smoke one of these in?" The blond reached across the table to an opium pipe, which the young woman lit with an excitement that surprised even him.

He loathed opium in all its forms, but even so, he understood its power and siren call. It had never once passed his lips.

The brunette leaned toward her friend, lifted the

carved ivory opium pipe from the blond's hand, and drew a delicate puff.

Smoke wafted around them, dancing like demons in the gaslight.

Edward stood, suddenly unable to bear another minute of it. Why the devil had he thought this place might ease him? It was all so brittle, so false, so utterly without meaning.

Both girls smiled, assuming he was about to join them. Instead, he shook his head. It *had* been a mistake coming here. As kindly as he could, he tilted the blond's chin, angling away from the opium smoke. First he pressed a kiss to her powdered cheek; then he turned, took the brunette's slender hand in his, and offered a gentle kiss to her palm. The acrid taste of destruction was on her fingertips, but she took the sweet offering as it was meant. A comfort in the cold, hard world.

"Your Grace," one of them called coquettishly. "You cannot possibly be finished for the night."

"Not a man like you," the other purred.

Their uninventive speech only made the evening's unsatisfactory end worse.

Heavier tendrils of opium smoke spilled about the air, caressing him with its sickly sweet scent. The noxious stuff reminded him of his mother's lingering descent and he needed to escape from it.

Pretending he was perfectly at ease was too tiring. He was exhausted by pretense.

Yet most of his life was just one great show, a show of defiance against every person who stared at him and thought of his father.

Himself included.

"Ladies—" He didn't smile. It wasn't something they required, nor likely had been led to expect from him. "You are both lovely, but alas I am tired. However, I shall sing your praises."

And he would. He wished them well and hoped that one day they'd find protectors to pull them from this position that drove women into early graves. He doubted they would. Still, he hoped all the same.

"Until we meet again," the blond said with what she no doubt thought was temptation itself.

Edward inclined his head, a courtly gesture he'd give to any lady, then turned on his booted heel and headed into the quiet hall. Striding down the wide way lined with mirrors, he was very careful not to look at his own reflection. He walked quickly, purposefully. Attempting to outpace his perpetual feeling of defeat.

Once again, London had become an endless, ongoing parade of empty pleasures. Each more debauched than the last, even as his hostesses attempted to freshen his experienced palate. What if nothing could? Is that what had happened to his father? It would certainly explain the old man's turn to twisted play.

Perhaps he simply needed a sympathetic ear to ease the growing pressure of his demons, and only Yvonne could give him that. The woman truly was a genius of the boudoir, and if she had let him, he would have taken up residency in her room years before. Such a female would have held his interest for some time. But she no longer entertained men, as far as he understood.

It was just as well. Madame Yvonne was one of the few people he actually liked. Woman of the night though she was, he admired her pragmatism, her shrewdness, and her unwillingness to be bought. In *almost* any capacity.

He didn't knock on the double doors; he was too important a client to give way to ceremony. The lights flickering about the room were seductive and warm.

The big bed, laden with red and white silk pillows, was empty.

The surprising lap of water drew his attention. He turned toward the fire with its amber glow. And there— Holy god. There was hell in the firelight, beckoning even the best of men.

A creature of pure beauty.

Her short black hair, terribly unusual, fluffed about her elegant aristocratic face. A face that was far too thin, yet luminescent for that delicacy. Her neck seemed impossibly slender and quite too fragile to hold up her head. The slim lines of her throat tapered to a collarbone so beautiful it was all he could do not to reach out to trace the fine-looking bones.

Her breasts, small yet rounded perfectly, the nipples pink and hard from the bath, were visible. The shallow water barely covered her hips. If he took a step forward, he would be able to see her mons.

He didn't. His interest was far from lust. Her very presence held him with a force that knocked the air out of his lungs.

Her knees poked up from the water, oddly girlish, like a filly's. And the longer he looked at her, the more he realized it was not her undernourished body that pulled him into the calm eye of a storm, but the spirit that fairly shone from her.

"Hello, my dear," he ventured gently.

Her piercing eyes took him in with wild alarm. She shrank for a moment before grabbing the sides of the tub. "I am not your dear."

Edward blinked, abashed by her standoffishness. He'd expected the practiced and sultry voice of a whore or a whore in training. Her very presence in Madame Yvonne's bedchamber declared she'd been selected from a likely hellish life to be trained for pleasure.

But unlike the other women who were just brought to fill the rooms and halls of Eden's Palace, this woman's voice was sharp, abrasive . . . and most certainly afraid.

It was also cultured.

Edward held her gaze. Would she stare him down? He was not certain. There was no promise of pleasure in those shockingly beautiful orbs. *Fear.* Fear widened her violet eyes. Perhaps she had come from a place too damned for most mortals. Her perfect elocution eliminated the possibilities of St. Giles or Whitechapel.

For the first time in as long as he could recall, he was at a loss for words. One did not usually find frightened, naked young women in Madame Yvonne's room. Especially not frightened, half-starved young women who glared with defiance etched upon every feature.

"Go." Her pale lips parted, exposing white teeth.

"If that is what you wish." Yet he found his boots unable to move and do her bidding. It was as if she were a snake charmer upon the dusty street, playing her tune to keep him mesmerized. A strange stirring he hadn't felt in an age kindled inside him. Not desire, but . . . interest.

"Go," she snapped again, breaking the thrall of her gaze.

In one shaking sweep of motion, her hands tightened on the copper tub and she pulled herself from the water. She didn't even try to cover herself but stood fiercely, her defined, lean muscles tense. She was most definitely accustomed to being naked before men. But from the anger and apprehension crackling from her, he could tell she despised every moment of it.

He should have left. Immediately. He was not one to force his company on women, especially vulnerable ones.

But nothing could make him leave, not even if the building was burning to ash around him—not when he had to know who she was and why she was here. And he did *need* to know. The very demand echoed in his bones.

Water sluiced her small frame and he winced at the austerity of her body. Damnation, she hadn't been eating enough. Delicate was one thing . . . this was emaciation. And then there were the telltale chartreuse signs of healing bruises on her forearms and ribs.

The sight filled him with anger so intense he had to close his eyes briefly and force the fury to still so that he wouldn't frighten her.

She vaulted out of the tub and darted toward the fire.

It took him only a moment to realize she was going for the poker. But before she could reach it, her wet bare feet slipped on the marble before the grate and she plummeted forward, arms flailing as she desperately tried to catch herself.

Edward sprang across the room. His arms circled her just as her head narrowly missed the iron grating that would no doubt have left her severely unconscious if not dead.

The warm water soaking her body dampened his shirt and he could barely get a hold on her sleek skin. He held her carefully, his hands pressing into her back and taking all her weight, though her toes still skimmed the ground. She kept her hands folded protectively over her chest, not daring to touch him.

Her violet eyes widened, wounded and old for a woman of her years. "Are you going to hurt me?"

Her pulse thudded wildly, tangible beneath his fingertips. Her face had the aspect of a doe right before the hunters moved in for the final kill.

The muscles along her neck strained as she attempted to keep her head up. Before she could protest, he slid one of his hands up to her nape and cupped it carefully.

Two warring emotions brewed riotously within him. Sadness that her life had been so bleak and a sudden spark of hope. Perhaps she was the one who could shake him from his darkness. The one who could finally see justice done.

"No," he whispered, his voice rough to his own ears. "No harm will come to you by me. By anyone. Not now, not ever again."

"I don't believe you." The brittleness in her speech suggested she had had enough experience with cruelty to expect him to declare one thing and then do the very opposite.

Rigid as the poker she had sprinted for, she remained frozen in his embrace. The only sound in the cavernous room was their breathing, ragged and sharp.

Her words somehow found his heart. A heart he'd been so certain had vanished. She was a wise woman to be untrusting, but her wisdom had come from fear. Perhaps he should have let her go, but he needed to see her, to see deep inside the woman who had hypnotized him with her spirit. Nor was he ready to sacrifice this moment in which he suddenly felt so intensely for someone and it had nothing to do with sex.

Though the ache in his chest commanded him to hold her for eternity, if he was to gain her trust, he had to let her go.

Gently, he righted her so that her weight was evenly placed on her feet. He stepped back, restraining himself from trailing his fingertips over her soft skin. Though he wished to give her assurance with the stroke of his hands, more touch would most likely send a woman of her experiences lashing out in fear.

So, instead, Edward Thomas William Barrons, Duke of Fairleigh, a man whose morals were as pristine as a London cesspit, turned away from her and lowered his gaze to the now wet, ornately woven cream-colored Persian rug. "I mean you no injury."

She didn't reply. There was the slight clink of metal, then the padding of her feet along the rug. There was a faint rustle of fabric, and then silence.

He waited, his curiosity escalating by the moment. She didn't really expect him to leave without saying anything, did she?

"May I turn?" The unfamiliar words almost stumbled upon his tongue. Men such as himself did not utter the phrase *"may I?"* But for her he would. For her, he would do many things.

"You *may* not."

"What *may* I do then?" he teased, hoping to draw her out to see he could be trusted, at least to some degree.

"You *may* go," she ordered with a surprising amount of authority.

That voice of hers struck a chord within him. Very few of even the most practiced courtesans could replicate the accent and cadence of the most elite of classes. His class. Which indicated very clearly that she must have been born into a home of note. "If you wish it, then I will go, but first you will tell me your name."

"I will not."

He shrugged, giving off an air of ambivalence that he did not feel. "Then I will stay."

"Why do you insist?"

God, how he longed to turn and see her. But he was

testing her trust now, by merely staying in the room and not obeying her command. "Because it is what I wish and I always obtain what I wish."

Another protracted silence was her answer.

"So you are aware, I never jest." He inched his torso a little to the right, daring to glance back over his shoulder. When she still didn't respond, he turned a little more until she was finally within the realm of his vision. One of Yvonne's red silk sheets was wrapped tightly about her. A delicate hand grasped it closed just above her breasts. She stood like a warrior. A frail, desperate warrior. Chin high, but with a look that knew what it was to be conquered.

The rage that he'd pushed into the depths of his soul fought to return at the thought of her struggle. This woman had been used. And used again.

"You have no need to know my name," she gritted.

"How can I aid you if I do not know your name?" he asked softly.

Her brows drew together and she brandished her captured poker. "I do not wish your aid."

His little warrior held that weighty iron with her thin fingers wrapped about it in a death grip. It didn't matter that the thing probably weighed more than both her arms together. "And what will you do with that?" He nodded toward the black rod. "Crack my skull?"

She whitened, her face twisting with distress. "If—if you force me, yes."

Edward hesitated, sure he had somehow hit a sensitive spot, one he had not meant to probe. Perhaps no one and nothing could reassure her, but that would not stop him from trying. "I promise, the poker is not necessary."

She lifted the poker higher, her arm shaking. "I don't believe in promises."

Edward held out his hands slightly, the universal gesture of supplication. "Nor do I."

She lifted her chin defiantly. "Then why make one?"

Why indeed? He sighed, wishing his answer wasn't so simple. "Because I wish you to do as I want."

Her arm lowered ever so slightly. "Why are you being so honest?"

"Because you would not believe my lies."

She hefted the poker up again. "You are correct."

A tired wave of frustration hit him. Trust was not achievable tonight. Not now—possibly not ever. This was unlike anything he had ever experienced. At least, not with a human. He'd seen that haunted look before in animals beaten so cruelly by their masters that they were past any sort of taming. "If you will not give me a name, little warrior, I must give you one."

She shifted on her feet, her wide eyes darting over him, trying to understand his interest. "Will that satisfy you?"

He inclined his head, determined that she would see he respected her. "For now."

"Then name me and go."

It would have been amusing, the queenly nature of her fear, the way she ordered him as though he were naught but a serving boy, if it weren't for the panic still ruling her.

The name hit him like a chunk of star falling from the sky and he breathed it without hesitation. "Calypso."

The poker in her hand lowered in slow degrees until its point aimed at the floor. Her mouth worked tentatively, as if she was biting back a whimper or a cry.

He smiled, a smile he knew didn't reach his eyes. None of his smiles ever did. Yet he felt a moment's warmth. He'd moved something deep within her. Something meaningful.

It was the perfect name.

It was also the perfect time to leave—just when she was intrigued. He didn't know what gods he needed to thank, but finally he had found the answer to the screaming girl inside his head. Though he longed to stay, he would go now. At long last, he'd finally found someone to save. And once he had, he'd be free.

Chapter 3

Calypso. Goddess. Daughter of the gods. Cursed. Mary lowered the poker and stared at the strange, hauntingly beautiful man across the room. How could he know? How could he know that she had been cursed for making a fatal choice? Was it possible that, like Calypso, she should be bound in agony for the rest of her days?

"It is an apt name," she replied, her voice as strong as she could remember it ever being, though she could scant draw breath as she studied him.

Dark hair, darker than hers even, fell lightly over his forehead. The effect should have been playful. It was not. Playfulness was absent from his person. Two black slashes served as brows above eyes as empty and cold as an undiscovered cavern. There wasn't an ounce of extra flesh to him, not even in his face, which was drawn as if he, too, dwelled with never-ending pain.

And it was his pain that tempted her to suddenly open her caged heart and spill her secrets. She had never seen pain the likes of hers on a male face—until now.

Perhaps he was as broken as she.

The thought was preposterous. Men could never be that broken. They, at least, would always have some semblance of power, no matter their status. Didn't even the poorest men have power over their wives and children?

But this man was not poor. Quite the contrary. From the cut of his black evening coat, his slightly creased white cravat, and the black trousers that clung to his powerful legs, she could see he was a man of wealth. Self-assurance and inherent power rolled off him with the same kind of authority that her father had possessed. Yet for all his hardness, there was a boyish vulnerability to him, as though long ago all his hopes had been crushed like a toy, broken beyond all repair.

She shook off such foolish sympathies and mustered up the remaining arrogance she'd once possessed as a pampered child. "And your name?"

He angled his head to the side, still assessing her as he had done from the moment he had entered the room. "You are interested in it?"

Quickly, she stepped back from the unwelcome question. Why had she asked his name? She didn't want to know. Did she?

"My name is Edward." That deep voice, which could have urged water from a stone wall, caressed her cold skin, heating it with a foreign warmth. "Edward Barrons."

He bowed once again, only this time it was a deeper, more courtly gesture that should have seemed mocking but escaped any sort of insult. "And now, Calypso, I must leave. I have imposed on you long enough."

Oddly, she didn't wish to be left to herself. It didn't matter that, again and again, she had told him to go. She had been left to herself time out of mind.

But as far as she could surmise, there was not one man in this world who could be trusted, not even this one. So instead of begging him to stay and keep her thoughts harbored in safer meanderings, she lifted her chin and said, "Good-bye."

He didn't answer but turned without ceremony and left the room almost as quietly as he had entered it. The tall, gold-embossed door closed softly behind him.

She stood in the same spot for several moments, gasping. His very presence had changed the way her body felt. She no longer felt battered or afraid. She felt strong, alive. How had he done that?

Was there any possibility that she had dreamed the entire exchange? Considering her dependence on laudanum, it would not have been out of the question. But his commanding presence lingered in the room, surrounding her in its powerful embrace.

She stared at that golden door, one hand still firmly locked about the crimson sheet, the other gripping the lowered poker, as she attempted to make sense of him. She'd been so terrified. But he had not hurt her. Contradictory to all her expectations, he had even saved her from hurting herself.

While it was clear Edward Barrons wanted her for something, base rutting was not it. His consideration for her feelings and careful distance from her person seemed to confirm that.

"Mary?" Yvonne called tentatively from behind the closed door.

Mary rushed to the fire and replaced the poker on its brass hook. "Yes?"

Yvonne whisked into the room. As she pressed the heavy wood panel closed behind her, her skirts whirled out ever so slightly, the hue catching the firelight. "Are you well?"

The question was ridiculous and not easily answered. Her fingers crushed the silk, bound with her fingers at her breast. How could she give an answer?

Yvonne's painted mouth dropped to a ruby O as she spotted the pooled water about the bath. "Did you meet the duke?"

"The duke?"

Mary stared at Yvonne, barely able to take it in. Were the heavens laughing at her? Was she to be surrounded by dukes? First her father and now . . .

Yvonne arched a red-gold brow. "Edward Barrons, Duke of Fairleigh."

Edward.

"Yes," she murmured. A duke? Her father was a duke, and there were slight similarities between the men—confidence and inherent command—but that was where their commonalities ended. Barrons was as powerful as her father, and born to it in the bargain, but there was no edge of simmering cruelty in his eyes.

Yvonne rushed forward and reached out to take Mary's hands. Halfway through the gesture she hesitated, then pulled back, recalling clearly that Mary didn't care to be touched. Those empty, elegant fingers were now folded before Yvonne's waist. "He didn't . . . upset you, did he?"

She couldn't describe the bizarre complication of emotions the man had stirred within her aching heart. "No," she said.

Relief eased Yvonne's features. "He mentioned you."

Mary aimed her gaze toward the fire, feeling more confused than she had in days. Which was truly an accomplishment, considering the last days had been spent in roadside ditches and back country roads. "Did he?"

"He did. He suggested that you were a fascinating young woman."

Fascinating? Why in heaven's name would anyone deem her fascinating? A night specter perhaps. A madwoman. But not someone who could intrigue such a man.

"Yes." Yvonne closed the gap between them, leaving only enough room for the full crinoline covered in gold-shot silk. "And I think I may have the answer to our dilemma."

Mary clutched the sheet more firmly about her, a flimsy shield against the strangeness of the night's events. "I don't understand."

"You can't stay here, Mary."

The breath withered from her chest, replaced by gripping panic. She desperately searched Yvonne's face. Sincerity marked it. There was no hint of jest in Yvonne's declaration and that meant only one thing. The streets. And all the dangers it possessed. "Please—" She choked. "I'll do whatever—"

"It is not that I wouldn't protect you. I've cared for you all your life, and even if I had not, your mother's loyalty to me would have bound my heart to you. But your father . . . This is one of the first places he will look. He knows of your mother's and my affinity." Yvonne paused. "Am I right to think he will seek you?"

Mary's knees buckled and she crumpled to the floor. Sitting naked in a pool of sheets so soft she wanted to bury herself in them, she swallowed back the realization that she had traveled for days for nothing. Foolishly, it hadn't even occurred to her that her papa, the Duke of Duncliffe, would find her. Not when all she'd had on her mind was escape and getting here to Yvonne, her mother's only true friend.

How utterly stupid. How very, very stupid. *Of course* he would pursue her here. The moment he learned of her disappearance, he would hunt her down like a base criminal. When he found her, he would send her back. Back to that place where each day had been a nightmare of pain.

"What is this plan of yours?" she whispered, though at this moment she couldn't imagine anything that would save her.

Yvonne crossed to a pink-marble-topped table, laden with crystal-cut bottles of liquor. She poured amber liquid into two matching stout glasses. Holding her counsel, she crossed her chamber. As she lowered herself before Mary, the folds of her gown and hoops whooshed over Mary's legs.

"Take it." Yvonne held out one of the glasses.

Mary clasped the cool crystal in her hand. "What do you propose?"

Studying her glass, Yvonne cleared her throat. "Mary, my dear, I know you have been through a great trial, but I must ask—" She took a long swallow of her drink. Once she had eased the snifter to her lap, she inquired bluntly, "Do you think you could bed a man?"

Mary flinched. An image of large fists hitting and yanking assailed her. Then searing pain. She forced the nauseating recollection back into the trunk where she kept all such terrifying memories. Before they could come to full life.

"I can see that you have been forced into pleasuring others with your body."

What on earth was she to say to that? That, yes, she had been degraded and treated as less than human? The words wouldn't pass her lips. Not ever. If she didn't speak them, perhaps one day she could truly come to believe they weren't true.

Mary lifted her own glass and swallowed. Hard. Several swift gulps allowed her to savor the heat of the spicy brandy trailing down to her stomach. "It was horrid," she said simply, then added, "It was punishment."

"I am sorry. Though most likely not to the same level of hurt as yourself, I, too, have been forced." Yvonne laughed hollowly, her eyes haunted with imprisoned memory. "In my profession one cannot go long without receiving . . . unwanted attentions. Especially when one is first starting out and must subjugate oneself to a pimp."

Mary frowned at this revelation. If Yvonne had been . . . "How can you do what you do now, then?"

Yvonne raised a hand and brushed it gently over her lips, possibly ridding herself of the bad taste of unpleasant memories, before she smoothed that hand along her softly curled hair. "I was fortunate. I found a gentleman who worshipped me, set me up, and then gave me this house." The displeasure that had painted her features turned to a gentle fondness. "He was very kind. He taught me that I could enjoy my body again. He liberated me from fear and pain."

Mary could not imagine such a thing. The best she hoped for was to never even think about being near a man's body again. Perhaps then she could be happy.

Yvonne eyed her carefully. "I think the Duke of Fairleigh could be *your* liberator."

Was Yvonne mad? It was a word she didn't use lightly, having been declared *mad* herself, after all. Still, her proposal seemed nearly lunatic. Mary had no wish to be liberated from the fear that kept her in the constant—and justified—awareness of men's dangerousness, brutality, and capacity for the utmost trickery. "I do not think that likely."

"You feel this way now, Mary. Of course you do—"

"I will always feel this way." Her hand, still holding the sheet in place, dug through the silk until the bite of her nails pierced her palm. "Why do you think *he* can steal my fear away?"

"There is much scandal surrounding his family and his cold demeanor is his answer to the disdain of the world. But he is a duke, Mary." She paused, letting the information sink in before adding, "And exceptionally wealthy. Such a man—"

"Could protect me from my father," Mary finished, a dull acceptance seeping into her heart. Edward had made her feel something she'd never felt before: *powerful*, herself.

"If your father comes here, I will lose you within moments." Yvonne allowed no kindness in her countenance to ease the painful truth. "But if you were to go to the Duke of Fairleigh as his mistress, he might be able to keep you hidden and, if it came to it, safe."

Once again, she would be putting herself into a man's power. The world was such an unjust place. Could she never save herself? Could she only throw herself from one man's whim to the next?

Mary squeezed her eyes shut against the anger inside her. No matter how hard she wished it, this world didn't belong to women and she did indeed need a man's help. Edward's help. "How can you be certain he'd wish to keep me?"

"Because I have not seen him so curious about a woman in the years that I have known him."

"You will tell me what I must do?"

"Of course."

"I don't know if I can—" She grimaced, searching for words that would be acceptable to her ears. "Couple with him."

"When the time comes, I will ensure you will be able to. And he will not force you. He is not that kind of man. Quite the opposite, in fact."

"Fine, then." Even as she spoke, Mary couldn't quite hide her fear. He hadn't hurt her. In fact, he had seemed fixated on assuring her she was safe. But he was still a man, and a stranger. And despite the unfamiliar feelings he had evoked, she cared for neither.

But to keep herself away from that place . . . from her father, she would go to Edward. What choice had she?

Still . . . she had to admit that even though she had no choice, there was something about him. Something that tempted her to get to know him better.

Yvonne took her empty glass. "Good, then. I shall arrange it. I'm sure we can find you a pleasing frock somewhere. And in the meantime, let's drink to the moon, eh? And to your protection." She leaned forward, her eyes full of hope. "I am so glad you shall be safe."

Mary no longer trusted hope. It was a fool's emotion and she was tired of being a fool, as her mother had been.

Somewhere in the back of her memory, she could still hear her father shouting, *Whore. Just like your mother. You shall be a whore.*

And she would be. How amusing that, of all people, it was her father who had made her one.

Chapter 4

Mrs. Palmer stood in a small room in the Duke of Duncliffe's house, waiting. Waiting was something she didn't do well. She was the mistress of her own establishment, the Palmer Asylum. When she spoke her workers jumped.

And with every moment that passed, her fury grew.

She understood a duke's home was different. She supposed she was lucky to have been allowed through the front door and not forced up the back staircase.

She stood by the fire, digging her nails into her palms. Waiting. The news she had was not good. It was, in fact, abhorrent. Her world of control had fallen apart in recent months. Two girls had escaped her grasp and Mary was the force of it all.

She should have killed the girl months ago and put her in the ground with so many others that had tried to slip away.

She dug her nails deeper into her skin to quell her anger.

That damnable creature had assisted another girl, Eva, to escape, and then she herself had vanished. This might not have been such a catastrophe, except for the fact that her father was a ridiculously powerful man.

She waited.

Mrs. Palmer stared at the door, willing it to open.

It did not. She glared at the offending piece of wood. So much of her younger life had been at the whim of others, and now the threat that all she had worked for might be taken away burned like liquid fire in her veins.

Swallowing, she glanced around at the ruby-colored walls bathed in shadows from the fire. She'd never known such uncertainty. Always, she'd been in complete control of her asylum, guarding the secrets of the men who had placed their wives, daughters, sisters, and mothers in her care. *Control*. It was a trait she had admired so much in herself.

Somewhere along the way, though, she'd lost that control. All because of two women. Mary, of course, was the worst. An obstinate girl who needed serious discipline to keep her under her jurisdiction.

And now? Without her control, what did Mrs. Palmer have? Nothing. Soon, word might escape to the other gentlemen who'd hid their women away that she was not to be relied upon. That could not be allowed to happen.

The door swung open and the Duke of Duncliffe strode through, dressed for the evening, an orchid in his buttonhole. "Well?" he said.

She pressed her lips together, fighting harsh words. With this man she had to remember her place, even if she wished to lash out.

Duncliffe paced a moment, then stopped, his dark eyes harsh. "Tell me she is dead. That is the only reason you can be here."

Drawing herself up, she met his gaze. "I cannot, Your Grace."

He stared at her, a dawning sort of horror marring his handsome face. "No?"

She narrowed her eyes and said clearly, "She is escaped."

Chapter 5

The bed swallowed her up in a glorious embrace. She was floating, high and light. Her lids fluttered as she tried to open them, but she didn't quite have the strength. So she let them stay closed to reality.

Offering herself up to the feeling of rolling, she drifted up and down, up and down. It was wonderful, not existing. There was no pain to feel or body to experience it. If she could just let go, there would be no recollection of pain, either. Oh, how she had missed forgetting. It had been the only good thing in the asylum, the moments of complete escape from the world and the horrors in it.

"Mary?"

She flinched. It was a beautiful voice that penetrated her reverie. A voice like her mother's. She rolled onto her side, curling into a ball. Her thin chemise twisted about her legs as she buried her face in the thick pillow. She didn't wish to think of her mother. If she did, the great abyss of memory would open and she'd be lost to it. It was so much better to just dwell in nonexistence.

"Mary!" This time the voice came harder. Sharper. The same way her mother sounded when Mary had smudged her stockings or ripped her frock.

"You must rise."

"No," she protested weakly. She'd finally secured a semblance of peace. Rising would dash that small feeling of relief away. She knew it, knew it the same way she knew that men's souls were black and vacant.

Chill night met her body as the blanket was yanked away, accompanied by the whoosh of fabric. She snapped her eyes open and gasped. To her frustration, her errant arms moved with only sluggish obedience as she tried to clasp them about herself.

On a slow tide, the blur of darkness receded. And the entire bedroom seemed to ripple before the sharp edges of the burgundy walls, mahogany tables, and velvet chairs all melded into recognizable shapes.

"Chloe shall see the streets this night," that lovely though chastising voice snapped.

"Chloe?" *Who was Chloe?*

"Yes, Chloe. I'm going to crack her damned opium pipe over her head."

Hands grasped Mary's shoulders, then pulled her swiftly into a sitting position.

"I didn't s-smoke—" She struggled to form words on her clumsy tongue and numbed lips.

"The devil you didn't," the woman—*Yvonne. Yes, that's right, Yvonne*—said.

Yvonne!

Mary tried to jerk her head up to look at her mother's friend. Oh, but her head was far too heavy. "I'm so sorry—so sorry."

Panic was a familiar emotion, though it had been some time since she'd felt wretched, soul-scouring guilt at her addiction. Opiates had been force-fed down her throat for such a long time that it had been impossible to feel guilt or self-loathing. She'd been so lost in the medicine for those three years it was impossible to know shame. But now?

A gentle hand caressed her head. "I know, sweetheart. I know you're sorry."

"I d-didn't smoke. Laudanum. I—I took laudanum." Mary swayed, her body as heavy as bags of sand. It took considerable effort but she finally lifted her head and blinked up at the person forcing her to leave her comfort and forgetfulness behind. She'd been at the house now for two days and had been struggling to stop drinking laudanum. This morning she'd seen the bottle on one of the other girls' dressers and she hadn't been able to stop herself.

Now she had to wake her mind. Mary squeezed her eyes shut, then forced them open. Yvonne, standing before her, came into focus, outlined by the sharp shapes of the room.

Rich red hair curled about her pale, worried face. "We must have you up and about."

"Is he coming?" Her fingers scraped at the sheet, worrying the fabric with her short nails. Yvonne's own fear seemed to pass over to her. It was all she could do not to spring to her feet and run mindlessly into the night . . . or reach for her laudanum bottle. "Papa?"

Yvonne's brows came together, her face tense. "No. Not your father."

Mary nodded absently, even as her innards echoed with terror at the mere thought of the man who had condemned her to hell. Would she ever be without fear again? She doubted it very much. For that alone, she would never forgive her father.

"We need to ready you for the Duke of Fairleigh. Don't you recall?"

Mary gripped the edge of the bed. "So soon?"

She wasn't ready. This was all happening so fast she could barely make sense of it. Hadn't she arrived the day before yesterday? It was two days ago when she had set eyes on that hard, empty man who'd held her with such care, wasn't it? And now she was going to be his mistress.

"The sooner the better, Mary. You know that." Yvonne's beautiful, slender hands took Mary's small ones in hers and tugged her to her bare feet. "The longer we wait, the greater the risk you're in. And he has agreed to take you unto his keeping immediately."

Mary only half listened as the world spun. It took every ounce of her will not to fall onto Yvonne. She swallowed back a fresh dose of anxiety. What if he tried to be intimate with her this evening? What if he expected her to—? Cringing, she closed her eyes tight and banished the thought. She couldn't think about a man's hands on her body. Not without pain. Not without a sharp sensation of losing herself.

Yvonne let go of Mary's hands, then hurried toward the door. "Do not sit. I will find a corset and frock small enough to fit you. Once you are under the care of the duke, you shall be able to visit the stay- and dressmakers to purchase whatever you shall need."

Mary kept herself still, pressing her toes into the thick woven rug. It was a difficult task, willing herself to stay in the present moment and not let herself drift into memory . . . or even flashes of the evening to come. The air felt palpable to her skin as she stood with pokerlike immobility. If she did not hold tight to what little strength she had, she'd fall straight through the floor.

"Mary?" Yvonne tested, as though Mary had fallen asleep standing up. "Walk about the room. Whatever you do, don't sit and don't lie down. I shall return in a moment."

"I promise." Mary stared at the opposite wall and refused to blink.

"Good." Yvonne's delicate footsteps echoed down the hall, leaving Mary to herself.

She stood by the bed. Every bit of her being commanded she fall back onto the snowy surface and let herself glide away again. But she'd promised. With some concern about her ability to stay upright, she took a step forward. Thankfully, her bare foot slid easily along the smooth fibers of the rug.

As she took another step, the room swam. Mary stretched out her arms to improve her balance, which led her to another step, this one easier, more confident.

The sun had set. Most likely hours earlier, while she had been in a state of laudanum-induced slumber. Curious as to the place Yvonne had put her, she glanced about. Several candles bathed the room in an amber glow matched by a jauntily crackling fire. But beyond the ebullient hearth, there was no warmth. Not a single sign of occupation marked the room. No pictures or garments. No forgotten bit of embroidery.

Yet the chamber had been readied for use. Near the three tall windows was a carved black lacquered table, edged in gold. It bore a silver tray, graced with a crystal decanter of bloodred wine and two empty goblets.

Without any thought, she wandered toward it. She couldn't let herself think. For if she did, she'd think of lying under Edward Barrons, Duke of Fairleigh. Perhaps, once, she might have relished such a thought. A young girl, chosen by a beautiful man. But those days had long since died. No matter how beautiful or strong he was, she felt only fear at the idea of his body over hers.

It was something she would have to do, but she didn't have to contemplate it. Survival. That's all she would focus on. She had survived so much already. And she would survive this.

Her fingers grasped the ball-shaped stopper and pulled it free. Carefully, she hefted the decanter in her right hand and tilted it until the liquid poured freely into one of the goblets. She poured and poured until it sloshed near the rim.

Greedily, with both hands, she lifted the glass and drank. The heady wine, spicy and rich, slid over her tongue. It dashed straight to her belly, filling it with a pleasantly heavy sensation. She drank and drank, not pausing until she'd consumed half the glass.

Trembling, she lowered it and gazed down at the red liquid coating the crystal in minuscule rivulets. If she could just drink enough, perhaps she would feel nothing. She would not have to experience the degradation of selling herself for freedom from her father and the place he had condemned her to.

The door clicked open. Madame Yvonne entered swiftly with a lady's maid scurrying behind her.

Mary quickly lowered the glass to the tray. It clunked harshly against the silver.

Her mother's friend stopped, her sapphire blue skirts swishing back and forth just like a ringing bell. She eyed the half-empty glass and Mary's rigid stance. She let out a sigh, then nodded to the serving girl standing beside. "Pour me a glass as well."

The tumbling of the wine into the glass only seemed to intensify the tension in the air. Diverting her gaze, Mary took a more modest swallow of her wine.

She stared at Yvonne for a long moment, then wrapped her arms around the woman. Forgetting her glass of wine, forgetting her dislike of touch. At this moment, she longed for the comfort of her childhood. A childhood lost.

How she wished she could sink into Yvonne's loving embrace. "Thank you," Mary said. "Thank you for your help. I don't know what I would have done."

Yvonne held her carefully. "You will always have my help. I hope it will be enough."

Mary nodded, then pulled away. She longed to drink her wine to the dregs and pour herself another glass, but she wouldn't. Not now. Not before Yvonne. She'd wait. Until she was alone. When no one could see what she had truly become.

Chapter 6

Bone weary, muscles protesting as if he'd run from here to Dover, and brain as twisted as a wet cloth wrung by an overly vigorous washerwoman, Edward climbed down from his black lacquered coach into the dense evening fog. He contemplated offering up thanks that he had survived attending to his mother and the subsequent trip back to London. But his belief in a benevolent god was negligent, so he abstained.

Visiting his mother always drained him of any real will to do anything but sleep.

He mounted the waterfall-like crescendo of granite steps to the towering family home overlooking Green Park. He often felt he should have burned the place down until it were naught but Pompeian rubble. Only bad memories dwelled in this place. Bad memories . . . and himself.

The tall, elaborately carved double mahogany doors opened smoothly before him and a beacon of golden gaslight illuminated the steps. His boots and pressed trousers were immediately bathed in its infuriatingly cheery glow.

Grieves stood at attention, his black suit, stiff white collar, and starched cravat more perfect than those of even Her Majesty's own majordomo.

Edward entered and passed his heavy black cashmere coat and beaver hat to his waiting butler. He needed a hot bath. The scent of his mother's opium was on him and it left a vaguely sick sensation at the back of his throat.

He strode to the wide, curved staircase at the end of the Italianate foyer, more than ready for a strong drink and his nightly bath.

"Your Grace?"

Edward halted and waited for Grieves to unburden himself of whatever could be so important as to disturb his usually undisturbed progress.

"There is a young woman upstairs." Grieves hesitated. "I believe she is expected?"

Edward blinked, the words processing through his fatigued brain. She was here. Calypso. Mary, according to Yvonne. Whatever she was called . . . she was *here*. As if the fates had heard his plea the other night, Yvonne had come to him with a proposal, and Calypso was now his.

Edward stormed the stairs, not acknowledging Grieves. As he took the steps two at a time, he couldn't decide upon a scowl or a grin. A scowl felt more appropriate, given the afternoon's frustrations, but the feelings flooding through him bested such dismal emotions.

In the general displeasure that surrounded his visits to his mother, it had escaped him that Calypso was to arrive this evening. He'd thought about it all morning, deciding his home, while not the usual place for a mistress, was the best place to ply her with food, wine, and perhaps some conversation if she proved willing.

He'd looked forward to being in the presence of her broken soul, the broken soul he was going to repair. Now that she was here, he wasted no time getting to Calypso.

His boots ate up the long, dim hall. The room he'd

arranged for her was next to his, connected by a door and a small sitting room. The room, in fact, had been meant for his duchess, a duchess that would never materialize. It was perfect for keeping Calypso close, especially if she was in danger as Yvonne had suggested.

For the first time he could recall since childhood, Edward paused before a woman's door. Excitement and doubt, a torrid mixture of emotion in his usually stoic being, was marvelous and unfamiliar.

He opened the door and quietly stepped in.

Deep, frighteningly large traces of opium drifted toward him, blooming forth just like the lush smell of an exotic flower on the night wind. Only . . . only this scent meant death. Panic grabbed his guts as he desperately glanced around.

Where was she?

Gas lamps lit the large room, but she was nowhere in sight. The Chippendale chairs were empty and the cold pheasant on the brocade-draped table by the fire hadn't been touched. The carafe of wine, on the other hand, had been dipped into, a good measure of it missing. The crystal stopper lay abandoned on the emerald carpet.

Christ. Wine and opium. Did the woman wish to destroy herself? He swallowed back the nasty thought . . . *As my mother tried to do*.

Dread drove his every step toward the bedchamber. What had she done?

"Calypso?" he ventured.

There was no answer and he forced himself to take another step into the adjoining room. His eyes trailed to the four-poster bed draped in champagne silk and azure curtains. A large swath of purple silk draped over the rich coverlet.

There on the bed lay his warrior.

"Mary!" Childhood fear churned his innards as

memory stormed upon him full force. He could see his mother stretched out facedown before the banked fire. The same alluring scent of opium. Only mixed with blood . . . So much blood his boots had squelched in it.

Edward swallowed back the unbidden specter before he darted to the bed. His Calypso was in serene repose on the velvet counterpane. Maddeningly beautiful, even with her eyes closed, her black lashes dusted blue-tinged cheeks.

A gown of purple silk wrapped about her slender frame. It billowed out about her lower body, creating the illusion she was merely sleeping. But he knew that sleep.

He'd been here before. He'd been in this moment. The moment of knowing that hell was very real.

Her pale arm dangled over the side of the bed, the diamond bracelet he'd given to Yvonne to bestow on Calypso shimmering in the candlelight. Her delicate hand was stretched open as if holding something.

As he moved through what seemed to be mud thick enough to imprison his legs and arms, he took in every detail with rapid glances. A small clay vial lay on the floor. Shards of a crystal goblet, tainted with the faint red hue of his favorite Bordeaux, were scattered on the carpet near the bed. The jagged pieces sparkled like errant tears.

Dread gripped him to the point of strangulation. He shouldn't feel so powerfully for a woman he didn't know, but he did. His own life was in the balance. And somehow she'd put him there. He wouldn't be able to bear it if she'd chosen to end her life.

Finally, he pulled himself free of the paralyzing emotions and darted forward, grabbing her with both hands.

Faint, rough breaths lifted her chest. He nearly cried with relief. Then he realized she was just clinging to life, each rise and fall of her breast a tortured wheeze.

She was not safe.

"Mary?" he demanded, his voice harsh with horror and white-hot anger. "Mary?!"

She remained limp, her body a rag doll under his jerking hands. Her head, with its short black hair, lolled about her shoulders. Her eyelids were violet with the bruised look of the dead.

Edward released her. Wheeling around, he dashed from the room. His legs pumped so fast it was a miracle he didn't skid along the silk carpet runner. The tapestried walls blurred around him as he raced back down the hall to the stairwell. At the top of the landing, he ground to a halt.

There was no time. No damned time.

"Grieves!" he shouted. Leaning over the balustrade, he scanned the mosaic floor below, willing the butler to come. "Grieves!"

Footsteps clattered on the tile and then the butler's white hair came into view. The old man craned his head back. "Your Grace?"

"Send for the doctor! And bring up water and soda."

Grieves's myopic blue eyes widened so abruptly with shock it was a miracle the orbs stayed in his head.

"Now, damn it!" Edward boomed, his own voice ripping at his throat.

Though Grieves's face twisted with fear, he didn't reply. With surprising agility, he bolted through the narrow paneled doorway leading to the servants' hall.

Edward sprinted back to Mary's room. He didn't stop running until his feet scrambled to a halt before the wide foot of the bed. His chest thudded with each racing beat of his heart. Once again, his gaze darted over her body. She was still breathing. But each breath was a struggle.

Without thinking, Edward reached forward and grabbed her purple silk bodice with both hands. In one quick motion, he ripped. The shimmering fabric tore raggedly, threads of soft silk flying like miniature streamers into the air.

He yanked the fabric free of her body, then stared down at the tightly laced corset. Ivory silk edged in Venetian lace peered back at him with the clear intent to tempt a man with wicked innocence. Right now, it was only crushing his Calypso's ability to breathe.

Mercilessly, he flipped her onto her stomach. The long swaths of her skirts tangled and her wooden hoops banged and cracked like old bones.

A groan slipped from her lips.

"That's right," he growled as he yanked at the ties. "Wake up."

He pulled the ribbons through the metal grommets. Years of removing corsets from countless women had prepared him for this moment. His fingers flew, but it took him far too long before he could pull the slick fabric free from its last loop and peel the corset from her chemise-covered flesh.

Without hesitating, he jerked at the tapes of her skirt and hoops, working them free of her lower body. He moved carefully now, to prevent cutting her legs with a broken crinoline.

Just as he slid the massive swath of skirts free, Grieves's solid footsteps thudded into the room. Edward didn't look away from his task as he threw the ruined garments to the floor.

Out of the corner of his eye, Edward spied Grieves

rush up beside him. He presented a frothing glass upon a silver tray.

"Here," Edward snapped, still half kneeling on the bed.

Grieves thrust the tray forward, his wrinkled forehead as creased as a sandy beach after the tide. "What's happened, Your Grace?"

Edward ignored his butler's question and snatched the glass from the tray. "Do what I say."

Grieves nodded, his mouth agape.

"I'm going to hold her still." Edward shoved the crystal glass into the butler's hand. "You're going to force this down her damned throat."

Grieves's eyes flashed with alarm, his gaze traveling from the fizzing glass to Mary's prone, half-naked body. "Your Grace?"

Edward mounted the bed, positioning himself against the pillows and headboard. With more roughness than he'd intended, he grabbed Mary's upper arms and dragged her weightless form up the length of his body. Sucking in slow, sure breaths, he rested her against his chest so that she sat upright. He could feel her delicate bones against the muscles of his chest. He found himself willing his own ferocious capacity to live into her. "Do it."

Grieves flinched, then edged up to the side of the bed. He dropped the silver tray to the floor and the dull thud echoed through the room.

Edward curved his palm against the base of Mary's head, bracing her so she could slide neither right nor left. Then he gripped the nape of her neck, tilting her back.

With a look of pure determination on his face, Grieves opened Mary's mouth and pressed the glass to her lips.

"Drink," Edward whispered against her ear, aware of the way her silken hair felt against his lips. Even the scent of laudanum and red wine were not enough to cover the faint touch of tea roses emanating from her soft locks. For some unfathomable reason, it was this simple thing that ripped him apart with the desperate hope she would survive this.

The bubbling soda water flowed into her mouth. The liquid merely spilled from the corners of her lips and dribbled down her cheeks.

Grieves lifted his gaze to him, dismayed.

"Pinch her nose," Edward ordered, his heart slamming like a hammer against his ribs. There was no way in hell they were giving up.

Grieves didn't wait. His white-gloved fingers pinched Mary's small nose and he kept pouring the drink into her mouth as if he could somehow will her to come to.

At last, she swallowed in one great, tortured gulp.

Her body jerked against Edward's. She gagged, then coughed. Shaking against him, her chest expanded in a huge gasp. She flailed her arms, struggling weakly to get away from his demanding grip and Grieves's unrelenting pouring.

Edward didn't let up, nor did he feel relief. They were a long way from safety yet. "Give her a moment to breathe. Then do it again."

Grieves pulled back, his worried old eyes flicking over her. He held the glass at the ready, and as soon as Mary had stopped gasping, he pressed it back to her lips and pinched her nose closed again.

She drank. Her body convulsed around each swallow.

Grieves didn't relent until every last drop had been forced down her throat. When the glass was empty, he stepped back. "Now what, Your Grace?"

Edward rocked Mary carefully against him, imploring her to stay with him. "We wait." Edward grimaced, willing her to respond. "And grab the chamber pot."

It was only a matter of moments before she jerked, her throat working as her stomach rebelled. Quickly, Edward turned her. Grieves was there, the chamber pot ready.

The poison came out of her mouth in one fast go.

"There you are, Calypso," Edward said gently, his hand stroking her back. He wished he could tell her the worst was over, but he knew it wasn't so.

She shuddered and groaned.

Gently, Edward pulled her back up and rested her against his chest. He whipped a handkerchief from his pocket and wiped it softly against her mouth. He longed to wrap his arms about her and clasp her to him in a vise, but that would not aid her fragile body.

"Will the young lady require water, Your Grace?" the butler asked with surprising calm.

"Certainly." Mary was not going to want to ingest a damned thing, but water was the only thing that would help her now.

The butler took a step back, transfixed by Mary's still form.

"Grieves." Edward stayed his butler, rocked by a level of gratitude that astonished him.

"Yes, Your Grace?"

Edward paused for a moment, aware that he might have never before said these words to a servant. "Thank you."

Grieves's brows lifted slightly in shock. "Of course, Your Grace." The older man bowed, then headed out the door at a brisk clip.

As soon as he was gone, Edward allowed himself the brief luxury of closing his eyes. He savored each strong breath Mary drew in. He hadn't been mistaken. His Calypso hid a depth of experiences and emotions that it would take a lifetime to uncover.

Any man in his right mind would drop her back on Madame Yvonne's doorstep.

Any man would have judged her beyond saving. She had been at death's door, knocking determinedly for hell to let her in. Perhaps she had no wish to be saved. If that was the case, could he still manage it? Could he force her out of hell?

As he stared down at her, his need to keep her close was so fierce he burned. He brushed his fingers over hers, needing to believe she hadn't tried to kill herself. Not like his mother. He'd seen Calypso's strength, and those tempered by such determination didn't try to take their own lives. But what if she had?

Edward closed his eyes, and for the first time in years, he prayed to a god he didn't believe in. He prayed with all his might that she longed to live.

Chapter 7

"Can you tell me her family name?"

Mary felt herself pulling away from the safety of her dreamless void. Fractured and in shocking pain, a healthy dose of panic laced through her as voices murmured in the shadows of her mind.

She held absolutely still, not sure whether she was truly hearing this muted conversation or whether she was just imagining it.

Dear lord, she had no idea where she was. Or what had happened in the last hours. Mary struggled to keep her breathing even, lest she make the men aware she was awake. She needed time. Time to understand what was happening and time to decide upon her next course of action.

She wasn't at the asylum. Of that she was sure. There were no kind voices in that prison.

"I don't know her family name."

This last voice. It was familiar. She'd heard it before. Sensual and strong. Genuine. Now it was hard and strained with tension. She waited. Waited for any indication that she might be in danger, and if so she should bolt.

She strained to hear what these disembodied men would say next.

If she was lucky, the voices were a figment of her tortured imagination. They would disappear, leaving her to heal in solitude.

The length and breadth of her body burned. An ember crashed to the cruel, hard ground.

Everything hurt.

From the tense muscles at her neck to the throbbing pulse screaming inside her head, she was a mass of punishing sensation. She didn't even like to think of her belly and the roiling agony pulsing within.

"This laudanum was very poorly mixed," the older voice said. The tones were firm, yet reedy with the effects of a long life. " 'Tis almost entirely opium."

There was the rustle of fabric, a drawn-out silence. The other voice, slightly shaking now, asked, "You don't think she tried to—to end it all?"

The acidic pain humming through her flesh indicated this was all too real. But who had tried to destroy herself? It was foolishness to toss aside so carelessly the only gift one had. Life.

Mary struggled to think who could have attempted such an unforgivable thing. At the asylum, only one girl in the three years she had been there had triumphed against the keepers' watching eyes. The girl had died, hanging at the end of her twisted bedsheet, a pathetic figure dangling in her icy room. That was the last night they'd had coverings for their hard sleeping pallets. Henceforth, they had been stripped of anything that might have given them escape from their wretched existence. Even spoons had been deemed contraband, reducing them to animals, scooping their gruel into their mouths with blackened fingers.

"No, I don't think she did," the softer voice finally replied. "We will have to ask her, of course, but the doctor who prepared this tincture should be hanged and quartered."

Mary winced as faint light pierced her aching eyes. Despite her attempt to suppress it, a low groan escaped her throat. She'd taken laudanum, too.

It couldn't be *her* laudanum they were speaking of?

"Mary?" one of the men called urgently through her haze.

She longed to roll away from him, but she could barely flutter her lids. As she fought to keep them open, she caught sight of the ivory ceiling painted with gold leaf.

Gold leaf and plasterwork?

Where was she? She somehow knew the elaborate decor. Even if she did know one of the voices, she couldn't recall who the people in the room were or what they might do to her. "Wh-who?"

A weight pressed down on the bed. Fighting the agony in her limbs, she grabbed the sheets and struggled to pull away.

She had to leave before anyone tried to hurt her. She had to get free—

A warm hand circled her fingers. "It's Edward."

Instinct commanded she fling the hand away, but she stilled, a warm sort of unfamiliar hope giving life to her heart. *Edward?*

She slowly turned toward the man sitting beside her on the wide bed. Jet-black hair fell over his hard brow. Black eyes stared down at her, intense with a hint of wildness that verged on the frightening. A faint shadow of black beard dusted his square jaw and the V of skin, bared by his unlaced linen shirt, exposed taut muscles.

Every bit of him looked imperious and entitled, even in dishevelment. Yet a haunted air played at the planes of his face.

The duke.

A fresh wave of horror crashed through her. This man was meant to protect her and she'd—

She couldn't even recall what she'd done. One moment she'd been standing by the fire waiting for him, terrified of how she'd respond to being alone with him and the advances men always made, and in the next the world had rattled out of her control.

"Forgive me," she begged, then felt the rock of self-loathing spasm in her stomach. Once she had been petted and loved, and had had everything she could ever want, before she even knew she wanted it. Now she had no power at all. And had to beg forgiveness for every moment of her weakness.

Why did she have to keep doing things to be forgiven for? Hate laced through her heart. Hate for the man who had done this to her. Her father had longed for her to be broken. How happy he would be if he could see her now. He would merely say it was in her blood, that she had fulfilled her mother's mad strain.

"There's no need for forgiveness, my darling, and you must never ask for it again." There wasn't an ounce of sympathy in Edward's statement, just a sort of sadness deepening his tones. That factualness was far more comforting than all the soothing platitudes in the world.

Nothing to be forgiven. Yvonne had said it, too. But they couldn't possibly mean it. She was a disgusting creature not meant for society. Her father had made sure of that.

How she wished hot tears would sting her eyes, but none would come. She stared up at Edward, unflinching. "You don't deserve this."

"You have no idea what I deserve." His big hand clasped hers softly.

To her shock, she didn't pull away. Instead, she savored the touch, stunned by how right it felt.

His lips pressed into a tight line before he drew in a long, careful breath. "I must ask . . . Did you—?" He looked away, clearly unable to go on as his face darkened with some emotion she couldn't quite identify.

She shook her head slightly. What could shake this powerful man so? "Did I what?"

Another face came into view, one that had doubtless been in the room the whole time but had stayed hidden. He was an older man whose white hair shone silver in the candlelight. Heavy lines had turned his face into a beaten yet kind map of emotion. "I'm Dr. Carrington, my dear, and . . . what the duke wishes to ask is; did you mean to destroy yourself?"

Stunned, she looked from the doctor to Edward. *They think* . . . She opened her mouth to shout a torrent of fierce and offended denial. Before she could, she thought of the laudanum she had taken, and the wine . . . Of course they thought the worst. What else would one think?

She pulled her hand from Edward's and looked toward the damask-curtained windows. "No. I would never give up the only thing that is mine."

Edward let out an audible breath. Of relief? She turned back to face him. His eyes had lost their haunted look and whatever demon had been holding him these last minutes seemed to let go.

"That is what I had concluded," Dr. Carrington said. "The laudanum you drank was well over three quarters opium. Who gave it to you?"

Mary closed her eyes, a wave of nausea rolling over her. "It doesn't matter." She doubted she could keep talking about this. Or anything for that matter. She felt so ill.

"It matters," Edward gritted out. "You almost died. And someone else could die if they take something of its like."

Humiliation claimed her, a thick weight on her already worn heart. He was going to think so little of her—not that he already thought much. But she wasn't sure she could bear to see disappointment in his eyes. She didn't know why, but it was important that he not see her how she truly was.

No, she did know why.

For one brief, illusive time, he'd seen her as more than a wounded animal who needed saving. He'd seen her as a beautiful creature. A fascinating woman to keep. Now he would cast her out like the sick, used-up woman that she was. Carefully, she pressed her hands into the silken-smooth sheets and shoved herself into a sitting position. She swallowed back the rising sickness at her throat. "I think I should go."

Edward leaned toward her. "I beg your pardon?"

"I have nothing you could desire." Her own surety was surprising, given how paper-thin she felt. "I have neither mind, nor strength, nor a body that could make me of use to anyone, let alone you."

She could feel his eyes burning her, intense yet cold with calculation, the kind of calculation that only the most intelligent and hard humans could produce.

"Dr. Carrington," Edward clipped. "Leave us."

"Of course, Your Grace." Footsteps shuffled quickly out of the room, then disappeared as the door shut quietly.

Mary took in her body, small and draped in a coverlet. Her bare shoulders peeked from the linen, nearly exposing a small breast. Where was her gown?

She looked to the floor. The purple fabric lay drunkenly amid a cracked hoop skirt and a twisted corset. Of course. He'd had to remove them.

Slowly, it came back to her. She stared at the shimmering fabric and tortured undergarments. She'd almost died. The power of it was worse than the humiliation she had been feeling. Her near death hadn't been at the hands of the madhouse keepers, or the frigid cold of the black, icy nights of York. It had been here, in a duke's home, safe, warm, and beautifully clothed. It was her own hand that had nearly driven her from the world that she so longed to take her place in. She forced her eyes up to his face. "You . . . saved me."

His dark eyes widened, startled. "I . . ."

It was fascinating, the struggle working across his strong face. His brows drew together and he pressed his lips into a knife blade of a line. Vulnerability hovered in his eyes. The vulnerability of a little boy who knew the world was not the fairy tale he'd been told by his nanny, but rather an ugly, unkind place bent on crushing those who could not stand on their own.

She contemplated comforting him with her hand, a foreign, shocking desire. She allowed herself a moment to fortify herself before she reached out and, for the first time she could recall in years, willingly took a man's hand in hers. His hand. "Thank you."

He looked to her pale fingers entwined with his stronger ones. "Get well and that will be all the gratitude I ever require."

The world slowed as his words came down upon her. Was he indeed so foolish? Under that harsh exterior lay the heart of a true idealist? While it was beautiful and unbearable to behold, she found herself struggling to give his sentiment credence. "Edward. Sad though it may be, I don't know if I shall ever be entirely well. Not after—"

His face tensed and those onyx eyes sparked with anger. "You shall. You *must*. I will restore you."

The sudden passion on his austere features gave her pause. "Why?"

A muscle flexed in his cheek before he said darkly, "Because I wish it."

Suddenly, her heart ached for this good man who wished for something that would most likely never occur. "And your wishes are always realized?"

"*Always*." He declared it with ease but there was something . . . *unknowable* in his eyes that revealed that his true wishes, the wishes of his soul, were all dead.

She slipped her fingers from his surprisingly callused hand. A brew of ill portent and anticipation spun her insides. "I know men like you."

"Men like me?" he echoed, staring at her hand now a safe distance from his own, which rested lightly on her abdomen.

"You're a good man, Edward, but all the same you must have what you want when you want it, and if you don't get it . . ." Mary inwardly shuddered, the rage in her father's eyes coming to her mind. He had always been so kind, so generous, until one denied him. Then his generosity froze into a glacial cruelty that didn't stop at unkind words. She hadn't realized that when she was small. Not when she was his little pearl. The diamond and the pearl. That's what he had called her mother and herself. Two jewels to be kept and owned and, when rebellious, beaten into submission. Made to fit their settings as her father determined.

"I've known men like that, too, Calypso, and I am not one of them."

It would be the height of foolishness to believe in him and allow herself the naïveté she'd once basked in. "You're not ruthless, then?"

"I can be," he admitted without shame. "A man of my standing must be."

She let out a long sigh. This conversation alone made her a fool. She should keep her mouth firmly shut and simply allow him to do and think whatever he wished. What did it matter as long as she kept him pleased? Yet it did matter. She wanted to speak the truth with this man, even if she had also seen how hard her mother had worked to please her father. How frequently she had failed.

"You cannot force me to be better, Edward."

He contemplated her, those black eyes sharpening. "Mary, I will not force you into anything. I will, however, treat you with kindness, with politeness, so that you see that you deserve so much more than you have known."

She smiled, a glib, humorless twist of lips and teeth. "I have little experience in politeness and will not likely recognize it."

"Why is that?"

"We were discussing your circumstances, not mine," she redirected.

"So we were," he drawled. "To be clear, I do not derive pleasure from the suffering of others."

How she longed to believe him, to trust him, but she saw it in his eyes. He was holding back, hiding something as he tried to convince her he was nothing like the men she knew. But he had made people suffer. He would make people suffer still.

She would never tell him which girl at Yvonne's had given her the laudanum. Anger simmered in him, just under his calm surface. Anyone who attempted to hurt her would see that fury unleashed . . . In that, he was just like her father. No one was to blemish his diamond or his pearl. No one but himself.

"Let me try to help you," he insisted softly.

Mary inhaled slowly as she realized it wasn't for her that he desired her happiness. A force deep inside his ailing heart was driving him. "If I allow you to try, will you admit you may not succeed?"

"No, Calypso." Ever so slowly, he lifted his beautiful hand, a hand that any sculptor would sell his soul to set in immortal stone, and carefully cupped her hollowed cheek. "In this, I will not admit defeat. Nor should you."

Emotions dueled within her soul. One urged her to rest her cheek in his strong palm, giving over to a moment of safety and care, no matter how false. For, surely, it would prove false. She could not forget her father's lesson that all men wore masks hiding their true natures beneath. The other emotion, the one beating loudest through her blood, pushed her to run. Despite his seemingly pure wish, she longed to run from the inevitable destruction that came from men like him.

Despite her fear, she let the heat and strength of his touch hold her. It was a luxury she could ill afford, but perhaps this man's touch was worth the risk?

His soft breath of appreciation at her trust punctured the room and for a brief instant she felt safe.

Closing her eyes, she forced herself back to another time. A time when she had offered herself up to joy. Happiness was something she had once been immersed in from the first moment of morning to the last breath she took before sleep. Even in sleep her dreams had been full of a glittering future as a duke's privileged and well-loved daughter.

Yet she'd discovered every precious moment of it had been a treacherous lie, waiting to unravel under her father's carefully woven spell.

Mary opened her eyes and strained to take in the blindingly austere, creased white linen covering her body. He was going to continue to insist he could make her happy. She knew it from the many times her mother had attempted to reason with her father. No matter how she tried, or what point she made, it would end in fruitless defeat. It was a lesson she'd learned well. She carefully withdrew from him and said, "I need rest, Edward."

"Of course." He rose from the bed, the sudden relief of his weight causing the bed to shift. "One of the chambermaids will be available for whatever you require. I shall return to make sure you are . . . well."

She plastered a grateful smile upon her lips. After all, she was grateful to this powerful man. "Thank you."

He headed for the door, his strong legs easily cutting across the large room. Good heavens, his back was broad and strong. As if one could hammer him a hundred years and nothing would crack that proud carriage. If only she could lean upon it. If only she could allow herself to give herself unto that protection.

"Edward?" she called impulsively, pulling the sheet tight about her frame. "You insist on helping me to become better?"

He let his fingers rest upon the gold-plated door handle, his broad shoulders tensing under his linen shirt before he turned back. His profile appeared cut from stone as the light from the hall bathed him in a holy glow. With his black hair, cold eyes, and defined body, one might have said it was an *un*holy fire that encompassed him. He smiled, an unnatural expression on his daunting, chiseled face. "Yes."

"And you?" Dear god. Each word that dropped from her tongue dripped with foolishness. Still, that desire to be truthful with him compelled her to speak. "Do you need no help?" Her hands dug into the sheet, knowing the answer already, but needing to hear him admit the truth. "Do you allow anyone to help *you*?"

Edward stared back at her, the spark in his eyes dimming until they were two flat black pools. "Good night, Calypso."

Chapter 8

The instant of waking was one of unerring recrimination. Mary knew it well. That moment when her eyes snapped open from a black, mindless sleep only to realize she couldn't recall significant amounts of time. The wish echoed in her hopeless soul then. That long ago she had had the strength to spit her laudanum in her keepers' faces or not swallow when they forced it into her mouth and plugged her nose.

If only death were truly preferable to this poisonous feeling, she would have allowed herself to be beaten into oblivion rather than take the laudanum. But every time she *had* taken it instead of choosing to die. Now she needed it. In fact, she'd come to welcome it down her throat with great greedy swallows and the anticipation of a child desperately longing to wake from a nightmare. Only, her waking was the hell of visions and regret.

That unforgiving need for laudanum was what held her here, terrified and awake in a baroque bed of beautifully carved wood, where she stared up at the intricately swirled gold in the plaster ceiling.

Her fingers brushed over the silken sheets. The fabric felt so perfect against her tainted skin. Was there nothing she could do to free herself from this jagged path?

Gingerly, she rolled onto her side, testing how badly

battered her body was. Her insides still ached with a dull, throbbing wave, but at least her stomach no longer felt as if it might suddenly hurtle out of her skin.

She pushed back the heavy goose down covers and swung her shaking legs over the bedside. Cold air swallowed her, prickling her skin, and her bare feet dangled six inches above the floor.

It was an immense bed, meant for the great old lords. There had been several in her father's ducal mansion in Kent. Once, she'd skipped from room to room, playing on the towering beds, pretending she was Queen Elizabeth sending Sir Walter Raleigh off to claim as much treasure for her queenly estates as possible.

The only thing she was queen of now was of the mad.

Blinking down at her pale skin, she frowned. Carefully, she lifted the blanket higher, revealing more white skin. Naked. She was completely naked. Mary sucked in a slow breath and her gaze darted toward the door as if she might see him now even through the mahogany wood.

The beat of her heart thumped fast and loud to her own ears. Her fingers tightened about the sheet, drawing it closer to her naked body, as if she could turn the silk to armor.

Had he seen her?

Of course he had. He'd been the one to strip her bare. She turned her attention to the floor. Her corset and gown had been removed; she could still recall seeing them scattered on the woven wool carpet the night before.

She should have been filled with mortification and resentment. After all, she'd hated the men who had stripped her, dumping buckets of cold water on her

during her monthly bath. They'd forced her into na-
kedness. They'd jeered and taunted and pinched.

But she somehow knew he must have brought an
odd gentleness to it, as he had with everything. The
strangest, most traitorous question whispered through
her mind. *Did he like what he saw?*

Even more confusing, she hoped that he had. That
minuscule hope defied all reason and certainly all
sense, given her previous experience with men. It was
the first time she could recall longing, even if in secret,
to be desired.

A dry smile twisted her lips at the wondrous, dangerous realization. How could he have seen beauty in
the creature he now knew her to be? She was physical
and emotional wreckage. Hardly the type of woman
someone like His Grace should find appealing.

She dragged the top sheet from the bed and lowered
her feet to the floor. Tucking the folds of the luxurious
fabric about her frame, Mary walked to the curtained
windows, her bare toes pressing into the plush rug. She
pulled back the heavy champagne brocade and stared
out through the tall, rain-speckled windowpanes.

Gray light illuminated the gated park that sprawled
in front of the mansion. The morning light was so dim,
the scattered evergreens appeared oily instead of bright
green.

Another heavy gray day of winter pressed in on her
from the other side of that glass, but she didn't mind.
The clouds and their pinpricks of rain could do nothing
to her. There were more oppressive forces in the world.
She knew that well now.

The creak of steps in the hallway sent a shiver down
her back, an instinct of anticipatory fear that had taken
root in the asylum and would never let go. Not now.
Not ever. She whipped toward the door.

The heavy panel swung open and the duke peered in.

She wrapped the sheet more firmly about her frame and lifted her chin, determined not to let him know just how full of fear and self-recrimination she was. He had to see her as still worthy of his help. He must, if she was ever to be free of hell. "I am awake, Your Grace."

He opened the door wider and stepped in, a perfect black silhouette. Lord, he was devilish male perfection. His black morning coat clung to his broad shoulders and muscled arms in tailored excellence. The lines emphasized his strong waist and long legs. Even the black cravat tied above a black brocade waistcoat seemed to emphasize the edge of danger that exuded from his large frame.

As soon as he discerned her at the window, he stopped. In one slow, unending glance, his eyes traced from her bare feet to the folds of the sheet skimming over her hips to her breasts, then over her naked shoulders. It was a caress, with no direct hint of sex. It was simply there. The heat of his gaze and the appreciation of her form was a simple fact shown in the way his face tightened and the almost imperceptible widening of his eyes.

Her own heartbeat increased, pulsing at her throat, making her body seem suddenly alive in a way she had never known nor now understood.

He raised a black brow. "Are you better in body?"

She blinked. "In body?"

Sympathy warmed his hard features. "I assume your spirits are still significantly bruised."

She opened her mouth to deny it, but couldn't. The lie wouldn't form. "How do you know what I may or may not feel?"

He gave the barest shrug, a movement that stretched the fine English tailoring of his coat. "I have had my fair share of mornings bathed in shame. It is not a pleasant feeling, but one survives."

Survive? How much more did she need to survive? "You no longer experience shame?"

"I do not."

She eyed him, wondering whether indeed such a thing could be achieved. And if she could achieve it, would she choose to live so? "How fortunate for you."

"It makes things simpler." He took one slow step forward, testing the ground between them. "Society's instruction in morality is what makes you feel as you do now."

"You have unlearned such instruction?"

"After much practice, I have shed most societal strictures and limitations." Another slow step forward, his long, hard legs stretching against the superfine wool of his black trousers. "I urge you to do the same."

She couldn't tear her eyes from his muscled thigh. How had he become so fiercely strong when so many other lords were so incredibly weak? "Why?"

"You will never feel as you do again."

Her eyes snapped up to his. The very idea that she might never feel . . . this drenching self-hate again was almost too much to contemplate. An impossible and forbidden happiness. "Never?"

"Shame is a wasted emotion. Learn from your mistakes and take pride in the fact that you shan't make the same mistakes again."

A dry laugh rattled from her throat before she could stop it. "I assume you mean I should avoid a bottle of wine and a large dose of laudanum in the same sitting?"

He let out a small, deep sound of amusement. "I think there was more than one bottle of wine and it would seem wise to abstain from such volumes of opiates, though not for moral reasons. You care about your self-preservation, do you not?"

Along with the crackling tension of his simply being in the chamber, she sensed something else. Something she couldn't trust. "I do."

"Good." He closed the distance quietly until the closeness of him seemed to steal the air out of the room. "Then you will tell me who gave you the laudanum that nearly killed you."

She fought the urge to step back. She couldn't run. Not anymore. There was nowhere to go. Instead, she raised her chin, challenging him. "Why would I do that?"

He towered over her, a good six inches' height in his favor. "Because you wish to please me."

She cocked her head to the side, meeting those obsidian eyes, wondering what it would be to please such a man, and perhaps . . . to be pleased in turn. "I suppose the protection you offer me leads you to suppose you are entitled to such information."

"Yes," he stated.

She inhaled sharply, anger spiking through her. She had escaped a madhouse and run for her life, scratching and fighting across the country only to be standing before this man, entirely beholden to him and almost under his control.

Being controlled was something she would never accept again. If she did, she might as well waltz back to the asylum.

Carefully, he lifted a hand and stroked her too short hair back from her cheek, tucking it behind her ear. The very touch sent shivers over her skin. Surely, they were shivers of revulsion. But for the first time, she wasn't sure. There was something soothing and provocative to him and his touch. Tender and hot, meant to assure rather than command. Even in her anger, she couldn't stop the sudden wish for him to stroke her again.

He did. His fingers danced over her cheek, so softly it was barely tangible. "As your protector—"

"As my protector you are entitled to my body and my fidelity. Nothing more."

His brows drew together slightly and his touch stilled on her cheek. "A sentiment that does not presently apply."

"It *does* apply," she countered.

"You seem to understand a courtesan's creed quite well." His black eyes deepened to pitch. "Did your last lover do this to you?" His breathing remained slow and even, but tension ruled his body. "I could have him butchered into a plethora of pieces. Should you like that?"

Mary pressed her lips together, wishing she had held her tongue. How could she tell him she'd been a whore? A whore unpaid and free for the use of any man the keepers wished to give her to? She couldn't bear thinking of it. *Speaking* of it? She closed her eyes as the room swayed.

"You needn't fear my judgment, darling."

He was so strange in his relentless kindness. Hard, calculating, determined to save her and care for her, even if she'd been another man's. None of the forces in hell or heaven could bring her to confess the truth. He would cast her out in revulsion. Nor was she about to reveal that her mother had once been a famous courtesan. Such details would only lead him to the truth of her birth. For if he knew who her father was, perhaps he wouldn't be so ready to do battle with such a powerful man.

He would certainly learn she'd been put away. This fact might repulse him. That thought alone—that he would turn from her in disgust—struck a chord of dismay within her.

"Come," he coaxed, his strong, gentle fingers cupping her cheek and tilting her face up as if to ready her for a kiss. "Tell me who you are. Yvonne told me only that you were in need of a protector."

"How would it benefit you to know?"

His thumb stroked softly against her cheek, featherlight. "I could shelter you. I desire nothing more than to keep you safe."

"And well," she corrected.

A gentle sound that might have been mistaken for a laugh passed his lips. "And well."

"If you knew more, you would, in fact, desire me less, Your Grace." She shifted on her feet, tempted to pull away from him, yet unwilling to lose the growing connection between them. She had to recall why she was here. Her position was as his mistress and, terrifying as that might be, she had to start acting the part. "A general lack of knowledge about one another is essential to the intrigues of an affair, would you not agree?"

His sensual eyes scanned her face, searching as if he could see deep inside her and find the answer himself. "You will not tell me?"

Pointedly, she trailed her gaze over his full mouth, then leaned slightly toward him. "No."

He slid his hand to the nape of her neck, trailing his fingers into her short jetty curls. "Why?"

At the caress, her heart slammed against her ribs. To her shock, she felt no fear . . . only curiosity, and a sudden anticipation. "Because there is no reason for you to know."

Her breath came in short, shallow intakes as she slowly lifted her hand and shakily placed it on his hard chest. He tensed beneath her, his muscles impossibly hardening. The linen couldn't disguise the heat of his body nor the sculpted contours of his muscular shape. She couldn't identify what emotions she felt, only that her traitorous hand liked the feeling of touching him. "We shall be happier this way."

"But what if I truly wish to know you?"

She could find a way to please him and then be safe with him. But she wouldn't tell him about her past. Not ever. He couldn't know just how used she had been and what she had finally done to stop it. No one could ever know about the blood that still occasionally stained her hands, dripping along her skin in a constant reminder of her escape.

No one could ever care for someone so low. Adjusting her hand to his waist, Mary stepped forward, closing the gap between them until her sheet brushed his legs and boots. "Then you shall find yourself vastly disappointed."

His eyes flared with shock and the unmistakable heat of desire. "Calypso, you shall never disappoint me. No matter what you do, no matter what you say, I shall always be in awe of your perfect vulnerability, your perfectly imperfect soul."

She tilted her face toward his. Perfectly imperfect? Such a thing had never occurred to her. Suddenly, as if her body was responding to the hypnotic lure of his words, she angled her curves into his hard contours.

"Let me know the depths of your heart," he whispered. "Let me be its guardian."

Every bit of her skin was alive, desperately wishing she could let him in. But three years of terror had closed the drawbridge of her heart to all who dared traverse it. So, unable to say what he wished to hear, she let her eyelids flutter half shut as she murmured, "My heart is unknowable, even to me, but you can know me in other ways."

Please, heaven, let him take the offer, she prayed. Let him take it and leave her secrets hidden in the diseased recesses of her memory.

His gaze slipped to her lips and then his mouth was on hers. A brush of hot skin and gentle pressure. His hand held the back of her head carefully in place and his other arm came around to cradle her against him.

She remained absolutely still, trying to allow her mind to go blank. But she couldn't. The sudden warmth and gentleness of his kiss stole her instincts away and she eased into his embrace. Ever so slowly, she lifted her hands to his shoulders and held with a feather grip.

He played his mouth over hers, giving and giving with the softest of touches. Teasing her with chaste kisses and the promise of something more.

Mary let out a shocked breath of pleasure.

He took the sound as encouragement and eased her tighter against him. His mouth parted and he licked lightly at her lips. Opening to him in small degrees, Mary took his tongue into her mouth. The taste of tea was on him, spicy and aromatic as he stroked her.

It seemed unbelievable that this could be pleasing, but she couldn't deny the urging pressure to let him kiss her deeper. Carefully, she caressed her tongue against his.

His groan filled her mouth and he grasped her tight to his wide chest, his hands hard and suddenly full of demand.

Fear shot through her and she shoved at his chest. Hard. As she tore her lips away, his mouth smeared down her cheek. "Stop—" She panted. "Please."

His embrace suddenly stilled, empty of the pleasure that had been there a moment earlier. "What is amiss?"

Panic shuddered through her and she saw the image of a bloated face with bloodshot eyes above her where Edward's should have been. "No no no. I cannot!" She pushed blindly against the man holding her.

The arms abruptly let go and cold air stole across her skin where she had been warm a moment before. She stood swaying, her eyes blind to the room. She shook her head wildly. "No. Please, no." She could feel the keeper's callused hands, rough with dirt and cracked fingernails.

"Stop—" She choked, her throat tightening like a crushed reed.

"Mary," a voice called, desperate and hollow.

She could feel those rough, stubby fingers upon her cold flesh.

"Mary!"

She shook her head again, her hands coming up and clawing at her naked shoulders, trying to push the invisible hands away. Staggering, she scratched at her skin. She couldn't get it off. The hands. The filthy, hard hands pinching her skin. Any moment. Any moment those hands would shove her to the ground, lift her, and—

A scream tore from her throat. She brought her hands to her face, forgetting the sheet covering her body, and hid her eyes.

It had to stop. It had to.

The keeper. His muddy eyes, alight with hunger, loomed before her. She gagged on the smell of filthy flesh and its accompanying shame. As she attempted to flee from her own thoughts, she couldn't stop one thought from repeating over and over again. *This pain would never stop.* She knew that now. It would never leave her. She would never be well.

Chapter 9

"**M**ary!" Edward's muscles locked and he stood helpless, afraid that if he did reach out to her, she would fly apart. She stumbled a few feet away from him, her bare feet sliding over the carpet. Her short hair fluttered about her strained face as she shook her head wildly.

A sob ripped from her throat as she continued to swipe her hands over her shoulders. "Stop—" She gasped. "Stop!"

His insides twisted so hard he nearly choked. He longed to grab her and soothe her, but feared it might frighten her all the more.

"Mary," he called again, hoping to break through whatever had seized her mind.

She wailed into her frail hands, covering her face. Her shoulders trembled and she dropped to her knees with a soft thud. "Please," she whimpered. "I'll be good." She lowered her hands from her face and cradled herself. "I promise."

Whatever was left of his twisted heart shattered at the sight of her. She rocked slowly back and forth, her skin shivering as it prickled from the cold.

Holy Christ. What had happened to his Calypso? Her mind had been ruined, dismantled. Rage pummeled him. A blind, aimless rage at whatever bastard had done this to her. How was a man, even a man driven as he, supposed to change *that*?

Dry sobs shook her whole body as she continued to rock herself.

Edward ground his teeth, his hands flexing and unflexing with pent-up frustration. He couldn't just stand here. But what? What could he do? At last, he crossed to her and very slowly knelt before her.

Her eyes were wide, staring up toward the ceiling.

His heart demanded he reach out and pull her to him, but he resisted. "Who hurt you?"

She didn't answer, her body moving back and forth in a steady motion.

"You're safe, Mary." His own limbs shook with fury as he willed her to hear him. "You're safe. You're here with me."

She hesitated in her rocking and her brows drew together as confusion spread across her face.

Seizing on the change, he murmured, "It's Edward. Your friend. Your protector." It was true. He was. And it was more certain than anything ever had been in his life. She had been destroyed by another man, just like the girl his father had so brutally murdered. Just like that girl he had not saved. Now his very blood depended on protecting this woman. It was what he had been waiting for his whole life.

Blinking slowly, she lowered her eyes to his. Her body slowed its rocking. "Edward," she repeated carefully, her voice barely audible.

"Yes. Edward." He lifted his hand slowly, trying to draw her attention. "Look at me," he said softly, yet firmly.

Still shaking, she slowly turned her face to his. Her eyes widened in horror and recognition. "Oh—" She swallowed back her tears. "Edward."

Relief hit him as hard as a pugilist's blow. She'd come back to herself, away from whatever nightmare had stolen her away. It was a sweeter feeling than he had ever known.

"I—" The slender muscles in her throat worked as she swallowed again. "Forgive me."

"Cease asking for forgiveness. You're not at fault for any of this." How he longed to explain she never need ask for his forgiveness. It was she who needed the apologies. Apologies for a world that had taken her innocence and brutalized it until she was this broken woman.

But she wasn't broken. Damaged, certainly, but not undone. He knew it. Even now, blessed awareness and intelligence shone brightly in her violet eyes. And strength. Who else was as strong as she, who had survived so much?

Mary looked down and her fingertips traced over her thighs. "I don't know what to do."

He smiled, a gesture meant to assure. The very effort to turn his lips felt foreign, but it was important to set her at ease. "For now, all that matters is that you are here with me."

Edward started to reach out to her. She flinched and hugged herself tightly. He pulled back, holding his hands out to show he meant no harm. "I only wish to comfort you."

She lifted her fingers to her brow, worrying her forehead before nodding.

His muscles ached as inch by carefully bought inch, he reached out his hand and gently took hers in his. "Will you tell me what happened just now?"

Her fingers were still for a moment, then returned his grasp. "No."

His heart grew heavy, though he couldn't help but feel a small measure of relief that she'd accepted his touch. "I wish to help you."

Her face contorted into a map of pain. "Perhaps—" She sucked in a sharp breath. "Perhaps you can't." She stared firmly into his eyes. A sad knowledge filled her young eyes with shadows. "Perhaps no one c-can."

Her lips trembled and her face twisted with the effort of speech. "Not even God," she said.

"I refuse to believe that."

A dry smile curved her mouth into a mockery of a grin. "Ever the optimist?"

"I will not abandon you in this, Mary. I've made up my mind."

The smile faded, replaced by dead acceptance. "I won't bring you happiness, Edward."

"I don't seek happiness."

"Then what is it you do seek?"

"Freedom," he said, feeling the need for it so deep in his gut his body burned. "From the past. From memory."

And as he looked down upon her white, exhausted face, he saw recognition . . . and realized that that was what she was seeking, too.

Her Grace Clare Darrel née Ederly exited St. Paul's to the peals of glorious, booming silver bells. A crowd of onlookers as large as that at any royal wedding surrounded the flower-bedecked ducal coach that would escort her to her wedding breakfast.

An elated smile tugged at her lips, accompanied by a large dose of pride that sent her heart swelling. She had brought her family back from the brink of ruin by marrying a man almost three times her age. But such considerations were nothing when the man was a duke, especially one of such standing and distinguished demeanor.

She beamed at the large crowd of eclectic Londoners

that had come to see the new duchess, glorying at how many stood upon the steps. It had been some time since she had known such delight. For years, she had lived under the fierce commands of her father, and now she was free. Finally, she was going to be a powerful woman in her own right. Nothing was going to stop her from being the most popular or influential duchess since Georgiana, Duchess of Devonshire.

"Why didn't you wear the diamonds, my love?"

Clare tore her gaze away from the adoring crowd and gazed up at her handsome husband. "My mother requested that I wear her pearls. She was wed in them."

He smiled. "That was most devoted of you."

She bowed her head in acknowledgement. Indeed, there had been no more obedient daughter than she.

"But now you are my wife and as such you shall devote yourself to me and my wishes."

His words were warm, but she couldn't help feeling the censure in them. "Of course, Your Grace. Do forgive me."

"Forgiveness granted." His fingers tightened about her arm, pressing into her soft flesh just a degree more than possessive doting. "Always do as I ask, and you shall know only the greatest happiness in the world."

"Of course, my husband." She smiled up at him as sweetly as she knew how, certain it would be simple to please the old man with her smiles and pleasant nature. Surely. Her mother had assured that the duke had lavished his last wife with untold treasures. He would doubtless do the same with her. She could hardly keep her excitement at bay.

"Now to the wedding breakfast," he said, his eyes shining down on her with all the love any girl could ever hope to see in a husband's eyes. "We mustn't keep the royal family waiting."

Clare nearly laughed aloud with delight. She barely could believe the Prince and Princess of Wales had attended her wedding! All of Clare's friends were filled with envy. Happiness was finally hers for the having. At last, she would be the woman she had always dreamed of becoming.

Chapter 10

The books towered all around her. Hundreds of them. Mary stared in awe at the beautifully leather-bound copies of more novels than she could ever have imagined, stacked carefully on the mahogany shelves. This must have been twice the size of her father's library.

Several titles jumped out at her. *Pride and Prejudice*, *Les Misérables*, *Tom Jones*, *Wuthering Heights*, *Villette* . . .

How long had it been since she had slipped a book into her hands and vanished into a story? Years. So many years and stories lost. Hesitating, her fingers curled into her palms, aching to touch them, but unsure whether she should.

She'd almost stayed in her room, but after being locked away for so long, she couldn't ignore her new relative freedom. Slipping down Edward's wide stairs had been thrilling, and the first room she'd found was this one.

A sanctuary.

She took a step forward, her slippers sliding over the deep red and cream Turkish carpet. The long hem of Edward's dark navy dressing gown trailed behind her.

Wearing his clothing hadn't bothered her the way she thought it would. Surprisingly, the lustrous feel of the velvet and silk traced over her skin easily, as carefully as his own touch. She hugged the gown a little closer and glanced to the tall windows.

Though the drapes were pulled back, exposing London's dark night, lantern light spilled in over the carpets, dancing with the candles that flickered from the many candelabras throughout the library. The lights surrounded her in a soft glow, giving the room an ethereal feel of magic and hope.

In this room she felt so warm, so at ease . . . Well, *more* at ease. She was still unsure of her position and what Edward truly thought of her and what he might think if he found out the truth.

"Do you enjoy reading?"

She jumped, then whipped toward that deep voice.

Edward stood in the door, his shoulder pressed against the frame. His white linen shirt was open slightly at the neck, a careless posture.

It was all so strange. Being free and being here with him. She should have been terrified. But she wasn't. Not at all. "I do." She folded her hands tightly before her. "If the book is good."

He pushed away from the door and took two steps forward, close, but still far enough away to allow her space. She appreciated his effort. She imagined everything he did was calculated, even the decision to take only two steps.

He tilted his head to the side, his dark eyes molten in the firelight. "And what makes a book good?"

She opened her mouth, then closed it abruptly. No one had cared what she thought. It had been years since she'd had any sort of casual conversation. Eva, her friend in the asylum, had sometimes talked about normal things they had done in their lives, but it was always laced with bitterness, since both of them had been so sure they'd never be able to do those things again.

She scarcely knew where to begin. She glanced up at

the books, studying their golden titles. "I suppose a book is good if it can pull you into its world, so our world disappears. That the characters become as real as you or I."

He nodded. "And it must somehow touch our hearts."

She gaped at him. *Touch our hearts?* Could such a man as he care for such a thing from a book? "You like to be moved?"

"Of course. I often find it is far easier to be moved by a book than life."

"I find that difficult to believe."

His brows lifted. "How so?"

"Well, you seem moved by me." The moment she said those words, she wished she could take them back. As she understood, some men were truly averse to speaking of their feelings.

"Ah. Yes. But you are special."

"That is certainly one word for what I am."

He let out a gentle sigh. "You are far too self-disparaging."

"I don't see how."

He held her gaze. "There is something within you that shines with strength and beauty."

She looked away, unable to bear the admiration in his eyes. She'd nearly killed herself in his house. An accident, granted, but that hardly made her something wonderful. Quite the opposite.

"Mary?"

She didn't reply. Her throat was tight.

"You don't see it now, but you will. How marvelous you are."

Footsteps echoed down the hall. Mary tensed.

"Be easy," Edward said. "It's simply a repast. I had it ordered for here when I saw you slip in."

A footman entered the library, his hands laden with a large silver tray.

Mary took a step back toward the fire, creating more distance.

The young man in green livery silently walked to the large walnut table near the windows and carefully set the tray down. "Will that be all, Your Grace?"

Edward nodded.

As quickly as he'd entered, the footman vanished.

Mary pressed her lips together, avoiding the plates but unable to ignore the scent of rosemary wafting toward her. "I'm not hungry."

"I'm sure you're not," he said easily. "But won't you join me?"

Finally, she turned toward the tray. Two cream and gold porcelain plates waited. Salmon, asparagus, and small potatoes in parsley sauce stared back at her. "I suppose it would be the height of rudeness to deny you something so simple."

"Exactly." Though the sudden lightening of his eyes suggested he didn't find this moment simple at all.

She couldn't quite fight the smile that pulled her lips. He was trying so hard. The least she could do was reward his efforts. Tucking his large robe tighter about her frame, she crossed to the table and sat in one of the massive, ornately carved walnut chairs. "I should hate to be rude."

Edward smiled, a sudden, full smile that only added to the shocking lightness in his dark eyes.

She paused. "You're smiling."

He blinked. "I beg your pardon?"

"You. Your smiles—from the few I've seen, they're usually a bit forced. They don't reach your eyes." She stroked her hands over her robe, then forced herself to enjoy his own moment of vulnerability. "This smile did."

A soft laugh rumbled from him. "How strange, but I think you're right." That smile still played at his lips, warming his usually harsh face. "It must be you."

"Don't tease," she said. But she wondered. There was an affinity between them already, as if their souls understood each other's pain. It was the only reason she could fathom for how easily she seemed to trust him.

"I'm not, Mary. I do—I think it's your presence."

Unable to form any sort of weighty reply, she nodded and said simply, "Then I am glad."

Edward strode up to the table and sat beside her. Quietly, he passed her one of the plates. Then, from the crystal carafe, he poured two glasses of water.

His air of relief that she had joined him, that she hadn't run from the room, was so palpable she might have laughed, but that earnestness touched her. He truly was determined to see her well.

He lifted a silver fork, then lifted his brows as he gazed from her hand to her fork. A dare.

She narrowed her eyes at him, but took up the heavy fork. It was odd, but she suddenly felt overwhelmed by the beautifully prepared food before her. She'd eaten gruel, porridge, horrible soups made from lord knew what. Now the perfectly cooked salmon and delicately arranged vegetables seemed to represent a life she'd lost.

"The salmon is from one of my estates in Scotland."

She slowly lowered her fork to the fish and carefully chose a small bite. The scent of butter and that rosemary filled her senses and suddenly she felt a great wave of hunger. With more eagerness than she thought capable, she placed the fork in her mouth.

Flavors exploded on her long-neglected palate. A

groan of pleasure came unbidden and her eyes widened.

Edward laughed. A deep, delighted sound. "You like it?"

She met his gaze as she chewed and then she was smiling again. "I do."

"Then I am pleased."

Next she chose potato. Butter dripped delicately and her mouth watered. "You are easy to please, it would seem."

"Oh, I don't think so," he countered. "But whatever gives you pleasure? That pleases me greatly."

She took her time, savoring the mouthful of delicious food, astounded that anything could taste so absolutely wonderful.

"I was glad to find you in the library," he said abruptly.

She took another bite, having the sudden bizarre desire to ask if there would be dessert. Feeling lighthearted, she asked, "Were you afraid I'd run off?"

His lingering silence surprised her.

She set her fork down. "You were."

He studied his plate, taking a large piece of salmon. "Frankly, at first, when I found your room empty, I was afraid."

How impossible that seemed. Edward Barrons, afraid? Surely not. "Why?"

"You seem to be running from something or someone."

She was about to take another bite, but a moment of dread killed her appetite. "Edward, can't we simply just be here together for the moment?"

He leaned forward. "Yes, Mary. But you did ask."

"I did," she admitted, kicking herself.

"I still would like to know who you truly are."

She looked away. Here it was again. How could she

make him understand she had no wish to discuss it? "Please, Edward."

His lips pressed into a line for a moment. Then he nodded, but there was a determination in his gaze.

He wasn't going to let it go, she realized. She had to say something to stop him. "It's difficult when everything seems to be ruled by my past. When I think about it, I feel imprisoned. So I have no wish to share it."

"And you like to live in the present?"

She gave that a moment's thought. She'd been forced to live in memories for so long, what else could she say now? "Yes. I prefer it."

He gave her a most serious look. "Then perhaps you'd like some apple tart?"

A stunned laugh bubbled out of her. Was he truly teasing her? And was she enjoying it? To her shock, she was. "How did you know?"

"What?"

She shook her head at his purposeful obtuseness. "That I longed for dessert."

He widened his eyes. "Magic."

"Oh, Edward, you are such a contradiction."

He shrugged easily. "I'd hate to be boring."

"I don't think anyone could ever accuse you of that."

He placed his arm on the edge of the table and angled his body toward her. "Now, what makes you say such a thing?"

"You've taken in a woman like me. How many men would do that?"

"Not many, I grant you." He took a bite of asparagus. "But most people aren't worth knowing, wouldn't you say?"

"I really don't know." And she didn't. Her recent experience with people was limited to the cruelest of the cruel, except for Yvonne and Edward. "Perhaps we've simply been speaking to the wrong people."

He gave her a surprised look. "You're right. There must be whole groups of interesting people hiding about somewhere."

"Edward," she moaned, exasperated. "You're not nearly as jaded as you pretend."

His teasing expression faded. "I'm not jaded."

"Then what are you?"

"Disappointed."

"Oh." That had to be worse. "I'm sorry."

"Don't be. I feel as if things are about to change."

"Why . . . ?" She widened her eyes and laughed. This time, it wasn't exactly warm. "Because of me?"

"Because of you."

He stood and, much to her shock, bent forward and placed a soft kiss on her temple.

Instead of recoiling, she leaned into it. The gentle pressure, the care of it—it nearly undid her.

A look of longing softened his features, and her heart felt a pang. She wanted to tell him not to put hope in her. That she wouldn't be able to fulfill whatever it was he needed. But for now, that hope in his eyes was enough to give her hope, too. It had to be.

"Shall we read after dinner?"

She gaped at him. "I beg your pardon?"

"I vote for *Pride and Prejudice*. I shall read to you and do all the voices."

The idea of this man reading all the voices of the Bennet sisters, Caroline, and Lady Catherine seemed too absurd. "Even Mrs. Bennet?"

He gave her a mock scathing look. "Especially Mrs. Bennet."

She nodded happily, unable to reply, unsure why.

And then it hit her. In this moment, she was enjoying herself. For the first time in years.

"Now, dessert," he declared as he strode to the bell-pull.

This was only the beginning of their time together, she realized. She'd never imagined that she might like any man again. But she did. Oh, how she did.

Punishing wind whipped down the empty road, blowing the last of the winter leaves along the edges of the well-traversed path. The narrow dirt footpath was lined with grass, waving, silvery gray under the relentlessly cold wind. The only things unyielding, unmoving were the headstones standing upright and the angel-flanked family crypts that reached over the hill and wound under the old, bent, skeletal oaks.

The folds of Mary's heavy velvet cloak beat against her frame, battering her like angry wings. Water stung her eyes. Not tears of grief, as perhaps they should have been, just a natural reaction to the stinging chill. She had spent the better part of the week recovering. Edward had always been at her side, plying her with good food, reading, caring for her in a silent yet determined way.

After all the pleasant time they had spent together, she had not expected him to betray her by investigating her without her consent. She should have known better. She should have remembered that he was a man who always got what he wanted. And if she wouldn't tell him what he wished to know, he'd find it out some other way.

Though she hadn't acknowledged it, she'd seen it in his eyes that night in the library.

She lifted her chin, clinging to defiance. "Yvonne told you?"

"She gave me the name of this place, yes, but that is all she would reveal."

"Why are we here?" Her words flew upon the air, stolen from her lips before they'd even left her mouth.

"You know why, don't you?"

She did. It was to see something she had no desire to see. The world was so much clearer now that she'd significantly reduced her laudanum intake. The doctor's orders had been plain. Little by little, she'd weaned herself off . . . And the reality was, without the blunting effect of her drug, she'd begun to feel her circumstance with a glaring intensity.

As comfortable as she had been with Edward, she couldn't escape the fact that she was ruined and her father wished her dead. At any moment, someone might come to try to force her back to that place. "I want you to take me from here," she said through clenched teeth.

Edward didn't look at her. Instead, he looked out to the sea of cold stone monuments. "Not yet."

"Why?" But she knew why. And he had to know, too. It would be so much easier if they could simply talk things over. If she could feel *relief* by telling him about her past. But the trust in her soul had long since scattered like the lifeless brown leaves caught in the grass.

And Edward was testing that trust by forcing her to come here. The contradiction in him was impossible. Over the last days, he'd made her feel as if she might be leaving the past behind, but clearly his motivation for keeping her—for learning about her past—was why they were here.

It unnerved her to not understand what he truly wanted from their alliance.

"Come." He held out his hand, the perfect gentleman.

She shook her head, unwilling to take his offered arm. Unwilling to have that close intimacy again when she was so frustrated at him. At the moment, she couldn't accept the care of a man determined to thrust her into the pains of her past against her wishes.

It was horrifyingly laughable, really.

Falteringly, Edward lowered his hand back to his side.

When she looked into his beautiful black eyes, she knew it wasn't she he truly desired. How could it have been? She'd been wrong to think he'd ever taken interest in her secret self, locked up in such a hidden and far-off place, longing to be saved and loved.

Indeed, the more she reflected, the more laughable it became. She would have laughed, too, if she'd had the strength. For a time, she had thought she was truly beautiful in his eyes. But as they began the slow walk down the path through the cemetery of bone and rotting flesh, she knew with utter certainty that what she had seen in his gaze was hope that she could save *him*.

What a fool she'd been.

Her heart should have been immune to it, but as her fingers ached to slip into his strong grip once again, she found her heart cracking ever so slightly. A crack to add to a thousand others. Another one to ensure she kept her distance from the world.

Her soft, new kid slippers glided with ease over the rocky soil. She glanced at Edward from the corner of her eye. Anticipation gleamed in his black stare. And hope. More hope. It was surprising in some twisted way to give him that. "Do you know what you are doing?" she demanded.

"I know *exactly* what I am doing," he said evenly.

But he couldn't. He only thought he did. A man of

such natural arrogance, no doubt, was always certain his feet were upon the right path. She, on the other hand, had learned how easy it was for the path to slip away and to find one's self stolen away to unknown places and unknown routes filled with danger.

He stopped in front of a large crypt of Connemara marble, swirling green and white stone married to granite angels. It rested under a tall oak, the knobby branches reaching out to shelter it from summer sun. In winter, its long, outstretched limbs hung ominously bare over the crypt.

Mary stood quietly. She couldn't bring herself to move forward and trace her gloved fingertips over the smooth marble or the words carved into it.

Esme Genevieve Darrel
Duchess of Duncliffe
Beloved wife and mother
A diamond seized from this world too soon.
1830–1862
With her mother lays the pearl of the world
Mary Elizabeth Darrel
1847–1862

She'd never been to the grave. Now, standing only feet from her mother's remains, she once again wished tears would come or some rending pain would finally pull her apart. But nothing happened. There was no overpowering, soul-searing moment, only the sound of the wind whistling through the trees.

Edward stared at the crypt for several moments. Then his piercing gaze turned toward her. "I don't understand."

"Don't you?" She had known he wouldn't find what he was looking for. There was so much more.

He let his attention wander from her to the crypt. "No."

"Read the names," she said tightly.

He scanned the words. There was a single beat of silence before he said, "Mary."

"Lady Mary Elizabeth. Yes." Her eyes locked on the crypt until they burned.

Only the slightest exhale revealed his shock. "You're the Duke of Duncliffe's daughter."

"I am," she confirmed flatly.

"I . . . went to your funeral."

"Did you? How kind."

He turned to her, his shoulders squared and his gaze snapping with a hundred unspoken questions. "I don't—I don't know what to say."

A mocking smile forced her mouth wide. Even though she knew it was a grimace, the way her lips pulled against her teeth, she couldn't help herself. How she wished they could go back to his town house and sit and read. But Edward seemed consumed by the need to know what had nearly destroyed her. As if that might help her. "Imagine my position, then . . . if you don't know where to begin."

He shook his dark head, disbelief turning his sun-kissed skin pale. "What happened?"

"I died." It was so easy to push him. She realized it was cruel of her to find it almost enjoyable. But she'd been punished for so long. Even he was pushing her now, though he didn't realize it. "Yet, somehow, I stand before you."

"A miraculous incarnation, then, for you appear to have restored your fleshy envelope."

"I am reborn, you see." Her fingers curled as the slickness of the keeper's blood seemed to slither beneath her gloves, drenching her palms. "Out of blood."

"Make yourself plain, Mary. You didn't die—"

"I did worse."

"Worse?" he echoed blankly.

She turned to look at him, her skirts rustling over the dead leaves. It was finally here. She could no longer avoid the truth. Then what? Would he turn from her? She swallowed, gathering her courage.

"I went mad." She shrugged, desperate not to appear broken. "I still am."

"I beg your pardon?" It was amusing to see realization dawn on him in stages. At first, complete confusion, twisting his brows and opening his mouth in consternation. But as he stared at her, his face began to ease into understanding, then anger.

"He— Papa claimed I was mad. He kept saying I had to be sent away because I would become like my mother. That I would become a whore." Her voice tapered until it was a choking pain in her throat. "A defiant whore."

This time, as she looked at the incredulous man who had brought her to her own grave, a laugh did ripple from her throat. It was high and loud, piercing her ears with its sharpness. She clapped a hand over her mouth and swallowed the sound. She drew in a slow breath and lifted her gaze to his before she lowered her hand. "And we all know where lunatics go, don't we?"

"An asylum?" The word dropped from his mouth like a stone. "Is that where you've been?"

"It's not what you imagined, is it?" She took a step toward the crypt, the hem of her cloak skimming along the wintery ground. She lifted her hand and placed it over her mother's name. The eternal cold of the stone seeped through her glove, penetrating her fingers, chilling her with the harsh finality of death.

She'd known for a very long time that her mother

was dead. Esme Darrel had breathed her last at the bottom of her own stairs. Now she was moldering all alone, with not even her daughter's body to keep her company.

His voice cut strong through her reverie. "Mary, you're not mad."

"No?" Sometimes she wondered. Between the opiates and the months upon never-ending months locked away, she'd *felt* insane. Felt herself slip away until all she'd longed to do was scream. Scream until she had no voice left. Scream until she did indeed go mad with no reason left to comprehend her wretched situation. Her own mother had been murdered. And her own life? It was but a bleak span of nothingness. "How can you be so certain?"

Creaking branches and the mournful wind spun around them as she faced Edward.

He stood helpless before her. The Duke of Fairleigh, the man who'd been at turns so kind and so unyielding in his desire to help her. The sight was miraculous and tragic. She didn't know what to make of it. "I assume you are unaccustomed to being speechless?"

He drew in a long breath, his gaze askance as if he couldn't bear to meet her eyes. "I haven't felt quite this jarred since the day they hanged my father. If you must know."

Mary's stomach clenched. She must have been a little girl when it happened, or else she would have known. Such a thing would have been cried to every corner of the empire. "I apologize. I had no idea."

He swung his gaze back to hers, a twisted amusement sparking in his black orbs. "It is refreshing to meet someone who might possibly understand my own history. Only you, Mary, could understand the horror . . . the need to forget."

Her thoughts shifted from her mother to his ghosts.

Ghosts buried so deep they were but a specter in his eyes. "I do understand," she said simply. "This world . . . its only constant is in the unreliability of people."

"I was certain my father could never die, powerful, larger-than-life man that he was. I never dreamed he could be taken at all, let alone in such a manner. And you? I envisioned you trapped with an abusive husband. It never occurred to me that—"

She cocked her head. "I had been locked up with the bumble-brained?"

The muscles in his jaw flexed with anger. "How can you make light of it?"

"I don't usually, but what would you have me do?" She gestured to the lonely stone crypt. "Throw myself on my mother's grave and weep? Hardly necessary or helpful."

He inclined his head. "In that we are the same, then."

She lowered her arm and lifted her chin, clinging to her defiance now that he knew a part of her secret. "So now you know what you wanted to know."

"How are you here now?" he asked.

She clenched her teeth, a dose of terror rolling over her.

"Mary?"

She closed her eyes for a moment, seeing the blood, feeling flesh give to iron. "I escaped."

"My god. How?"

She opened her eyes, determined to make him understand that there was no going back. That she'd done unspeakable things. It was too late to hide those things from Edward now. He already knew too much. "I attacked a keeper. I may have killed him. And I escaped."

She waited, standing rigid for his judgment, for his eyes to shutter.

Instead, Edward took a step forward and oh so carefully cupped her chin. He tilted her face up toward him. "You saved yourself. You took your own fate into your hands and you chose life. Nothing could be more admirable or powerful than that."

Tears stung her eyes. "You're not going to send me away, then?"

"Why would I do that?" he asked, shock tightening his features.

"B-because of what I have done. Where I have been."

"I want you all the more because of what you have done, where you have been, and your will to survive."

With the affection she now felt, she couldn't help but forgive him for speaking to Yvonne about her. Far from rejecting her, he seemed to be accepting her completely. She wasn't sure whether anyone else ever had.

There was no regret in his voice.

At last she asked, "What are we going to do?"

"It is not what I shall do. It is what you are going to do, Calypso."

"And what is that?"

As one might swear a weighty vow, he looked full into her eyes. The anticipation in his own gaze was back, along with something strangely . . . deadly. She shivered even before his voice crawled low and worn like the gravel path, cold as ice along her skin. "You're going to destroy the man who did this to you."

Chapter 11

The pistol's shot cracked through the fog. Its butt kicked against Mary's kid-gloved hand. In the far distance, through the swirling dawn air and across the dew-covered, crocus-dotted field, a puff of flour wafted into the mist. A grim dose of satisfaction welled up in her. It had taken less than twenty-four hours for Edward to begin to make good on his promise.

And she'd taken it on with a thirst-filled passion that shocked her. She'd only ever thought of hiding, of running, but never of fighting back. And in one moment Edward had changed all that.

Here in the frigid morning, under the first breath of spring, in a pair of deep blue breeches and a linen shirt lent from one of Edward's smaller male servants, she felt oddly composed and alive. She loved the feel of loose male clothing, the small gray jacket buttoned just to her chin and the black boots that swallowed up her feet and covered her calves.

No wonder men kept their women in feminine clothes. What better way to imprison a woman than in corsets cinched with metal grommets that bent the ribs and gowns so drowning with fabric they left one entirely helpless.

"You're a fine shot, Mary," Edward announced proudly.

She turned to him, arm still outstretched, her body humming with exhilaration. "Indeed?"

Alarm burst past Edward's lips. He jerked to the side. Keeping his eyes trained on the weapon, he lifted his black-gloved hand to her wrist, diverting the pistol. "I do. Just don't use your skills on me."

Mary pursed her lips, nodding. " 'Twould be a shame to shoot such a fine teacher."

Those long, strong fingers of his lingered upon her wrist, the leather of the gloves the only barrier between them. "It feels good, does it not?" he inquired. "Life or death in one definitive shot."

Her heart shifted from its triumphant beat to a slower, stronger, more insistent one. She looked to his hand barely touching her, then up into his hard, dangerous face, and let her eyes drink him in. "Yes," she replied. "But I don't understand exactly why we're doing this. I'm not going to kill anyone."

His own gaze was unreadable, like twin depths of an opaque lake. He didn't look away. Rather, he held her gaze until the chill of the morning evaporated under the heat of his stare. "You are doing this because you will never be at the mercy of another person again. You will always be able to defend yourself."

It wasn't gratitude she felt. It was something different. Something far more powerful. Something like seeing her eternal soul in his eyes.

She so longed to believe he didn't care for her. That he was doing this purely for his own personal motives. If she believed that, her heart would be safe. But as his touch lingered upon her arm and his gaze deepened—alive with hot and tender emotions—she couldn't stop hoping.

Could it be that he truly wanted her? Her life had been so full of sadness that it was hard to imagine.

And, god help her, her heart longed to open to *him*. Despite the risks. Despite the fear. Despite it all, she saw he had within him the potential to be her other half. If they could just take the chance. "Edward, I—"

He shook his head gently. "No words, Mary. Not yet." Still holding her wrist in a gallant clasp, he knelt to the damp grass and plucked up a purple-throated flower, barely unfurled in its newness. He offered it up to her. A hypnotic symbol of her own life, and the trust between them, just beginning to open. "Just understanding."

Understanding. A thing far more powerful than empty whispered nothings. He didn't need to say what she knew. That the flower reminded him of her, bursting up from the icy landscape to embrace the sun. It was there on his face, the thoughts of his heart.

She took the bloom from his fingers, rolling the fragile stem carefully between her fingers, careful not to crush the fragile shoot, just as he was being careful not to hurt her.

Gently, he relinquished his grasp upon her arm, stood, and took the pistol from her. Then he withdrew a small silver and black powder horn from his pocket, focusing his attention on it. Methodically, he twisted the corker free. "There is an odd satisfaction in knowing that skill can shatter a man's skull."

As she twirled the little flower between her fingertips, she couldn't deny the truth of it. Though she imagined it was only a truth to a person who had had everything taken away. She studied his precise yet sensual movements as he poured the small black grains into the mouth of the smooth black muzzle. "And if you miss?" she asked.

He slid the tamp from its place beneath the barrel and pressed down a small lead ball and the powder. "With skill, you miss by choice."

She couldn't help but wonder how many he had killed, for one who could speak so confidently on the subject clearly had experience. Yet the thought didn't frighten her. It assured her. Edward didn't just take life; he restored it.

He stood with perfect stillness as he lifted his arm in a smooth sweep, and without even seeming to aim stroked the trigger. Black powder burst around him as the pistol flashed. She didn't need to look at the target to know he had hit it. Nor could she have looked—her gaze was locked upon him, upon his surety and knowledge that no one could harm him.

That was what she wanted, too.

She tucked the crocus into her belt, safe from the blows of battle, and held out her own gloved hand. "Again."

He laughed, a rich, gorgeous sound. Lowering the pistol, he bowed his head to accommodate the difference in their heights. For one brief instant she was sure he was going to kiss her. Far from recoiling, her body rushed to life at the promise.

Tendrils of jetty hair brushed his forehead, softening his hard features as he said, "I have something new in mind."

Her fingers ached to stroke back that rich black hair. "Do you?"

"Mmm." He shoved the pistol into the waistband of his black trousers and bent to retrieve his coat from the damp grass. "It's time to try something different."

Mary frowned. He was not going to kiss her. Not now, at any rate. "I want to practice."

"And you shall. Simply not this instant." He snapped his coat out, shaking the damp grass from it, then swung it high and slid his arms into the black wool. A fascinating process of muscles and effortless

movement. "Now I have something altogether different for you to turn your hand to." Edward lifted his
fingers to his lips and let out a sharp whistle.

Mary flinched at the punctured solitude of the quiet
dawn. "What—?"

Out of the fog swirling through the oak trees on the
edge of the field, a figure emerged. The transparent
haze clung to the man, emphasizing his towering
height and the darkness of his apparel. Even from
across the field, she could feel his presence. It was as
foreboding as Edward's looks.

Mary took a step back, her foot sinking into the soft
earth. "What are you doing?"

"Making you a woman to be reckoned with," Edward stated calmly.

The elation she'd felt slipped away, replaced by her
old fear. Fear of any man who might seize what little
power she had. Why would Edward throw her into the
company of someone else? She wasn't ready to be among
others. Especially other men. She held her ground. "I
want the pistol," she whispered.

"I'm sure you do, but I'll not have you shooting a
viscount."

Viscount? What was he playing at? "Did you tell him
who I am?" she hissed, her blood pounding in her ears.
She'd worked so hard to conceal herself. Now he was
casting her into the dubious presence of others. And
not just any others, but a noble.

She might be recognized—she looked just like her
mother.

"She's perfection with a pistol," the tall man drawled
as he neared them. His long stride ate up the earth as if
it were no distance at all until he towered but a few feet
before them.

Mary blinked at the sight of this contradictory figure. He was not at all demonic as she'd first suspected; in fact she was dazed by his angelic appearance. He was monstrously tall, taller even than Edward. His white-blond hair hung over his shoulders, the top half tied back from his face with a piece of black leather. A long black outrider's coat clung to his frame, emphasizing his overshadowing build.

His icy, almost white-blue eyes stared down at her from a regal face. High cheekbones, a strong nose, and a jaw so sharp it might cut gave him the air of an unfeeling and otherworldly being. She quickly corrected her opinion. He looked exactly as she imagined the archangel Michael would appear.

As his eyes narrowed with interest, Mary caught sight of his abnormally small pupils. Was she mistaken, or was the man foolish enough to walk about after taking to his opium pipe?

His narrowed gaze trailed over her in a critical trace. "Good god, woman, don't you eat? You're rag and bone."

The words, true but abrasive, hit her hard. She was eating—Edward had ensured that—but it was taking time to regain her strength. What a bastard this man was for pointing it out! An astounded breath escaped her lips before she drew herself up and replied, "'Tis a trifle early to be chasing dragons, my lord, don't you think?"

The frigid man's brows barely rose and his nostrils flared. Emotions seemed to unleash from his cold control for the barest moment, but then the edges of his lips tilted in dry amusement. "One must assume you, too, have gone after a dragon or two, madam, to recognize the signs."

She tensed at being caught out, then glared up at him. What strange god had a hold over this man? And why was Edward merely standing there? She wanted to dart behind him, but he was not offering his body as protection. She would have to brave it out.

Mary clung to the defiance and strength Edward had rekindled within her. "I own to it."

The man smirked, his blond brow arching. "Not surprising for a whore's daughter."

The accusation, true though it might be, rang shrilly in her ears. It also meant he knew *exactly* who she was. "I beg your pardon?"

"That is what you are," he said slowly, pointedly, explaining as one to a small child. "A whore's daughter."

She sputtered, anger bursting alive inside her. No one but her father had dared say such a thing to her face. "You— How dare you—"

"Can you deny it?" He leaned down toward her, his long blond hair hanging about his face like a silver curtain. His icy eyes held hers mercilessly. "Can you deny she spread her legs to any man willing to pay the price? Before she became a duchess, of course." His mouth quirked into a knowing smile. "And if I were to pay you, you'd no doubt forget His Grace and come dancing to my tune."

A shriek of anger tore from her lips and she threw herself at him. She collided against him and the air ripped from her lungs. She growled and reached up to claw at his face, but his hands grabbed her wrists in a fierce grip. Fury drove her in mindless determination. She brought her teeth down and sank them into the fleshy part of his chest, biting through fabric. She clung on, biting down harder and harder, relishing the feel of his yielding flesh.

He howled in shock, dropping her hands and grabbing her waist. "You devil!" he snarled, and in one move he yanked her from him.

Unbelievable satisfaction bolted through Mary as she spotted his ripped black shirt.

"She's mad." The viscount stared at her, his eyes wide with wonder and . . . something else. Approval.

"Yes," she hissed back. "Mad enough to rip the flesh from your bones if you ever speak to me thus again."

The soft sound of muted applause cut through the cold air.

She whipped toward Edward. "And you just stood there while he—" She swallowed, realizing she was not afraid. Not afraid of the biggest man she had ever met.

Edward cocked a black brow and lowered his hands to his sides. "I am not here to soften the world's blows, darling. I am here to lead you past them and teach you to give more than a few of your own. Do you still wish my help?"

She looked from one man to the next. The deal she was making was a dangerous one. Both these men were dangerous. It had always been there in Edward's eyes, the promise of a life lived on a knife's edge, but here now, in this quiet field with his deadly companion, she fully understood the extent to which he had gone to get what he wanted or to take his revenge out upon those he hated.

"Yes," she said. Finally. At long last, she had found herself again. Only this Mary was a Mary she had not ever known existed. "It is what I want."

"Good." Edward nodded, perhaps to himself. He gestured to the blond man. "Meet Viscount Powers."

Years of training compelled her to say, "How do you do?"

Powers eyed her slowly, his stare penetrating as he studied her. With a single lift of his blond brow, he seemed to find her wanting. "Clearly, better than you."

"Powers." A low note of warning entered Edward's voice.

"Yes?"

"Do not intimidate her . . . overmuch."

"Intimidate?" the viscount echoed. He took a step forward and looked down at Mary. "You're not intimidated, are you, little dragon?"

She straightened her spine, eliciting as much height as she could muster, and lifted her chin until her neck craned at the effort. "By you, my lord? I daresay you could not deign to touch my mother or my toes . . . let alone induce the spreading of legs."

Viscount Powers's eyes traveled over her face and then he threw back his head and laughed. "A born liar, Fairleigh. You've found a born liar." The laugh died and he held out his hand for her to take.

She marveled at his bizarre mockery, but she knew the insult he'd take if she slighted his gesture. With a boldness she did not feel, she reached out and took his massive hand. Something unruly jumped within her as he grasped her palm. In truth, his powerful hand reminded her of Adam reaching out to his Creator for enlightenment in Michelangelo's Sistine Chapel. She had no idea why. Not when he seemed to be recklessness personified.

He bowed. "And I do love a challenge." His voice was honeyed silk laced with a tempting drug.

How many women had been pulled in by this coil? She yanked her hand back. "A remarkable thing that you believe in love at all, my lord."

As if she hadn't just rebuffed him, he smoothed his gloved hand along his coat, wiping her touch away. "Of the physicality of love? What fool does not?"

"This man is your friend, Your Grace?" Mary didn't even bother hiding her disgust. And her fate was in these men's hands. What a trap. How she wished she did not need Powers's assistance, but apparently Edward thought she did.

"Friend?" Edward looked to the viscount. "Accomplice, perhaps."

"Spiritual brother," rejoined Powers.

Edward nodded. "Yes." Then he turned from them and began to stride across the field back toward the coach waiting along the dirt road. "Come."

Viscount Powers lingered, then lifted his hand to her cheek.

She froze.

His palm enveloped the better half of her face, tilting it back until her throat was exposed. "And like good brothers . . ." His gaze traveled to her lips.

Mary's breath locked in her chest. "Yes?" she forced herself to say clearly, refusing to let him see the effect he had upon her. Realizing she wasn't going to shatter. Not anymore. Never again.

He bit his lower lip for a second, then leaned down, his mouth but a breath above hers. "We share."

Then he let go, his gloved hand gone as quickly as it had fallen upon her. Striding after the retreating form of Edward, his shoulders were as square as any chivalrous knight's.

Mary stood alone in the field, her eyes blinded now by the rising sun burning the fog away. As the mists faded, she began to see clearly. Her knights were not chivalrous and had no desire to save her honor.

But save her they would, by whatever means necessary. They would wrench her from her hell. She sensed she could learn from them the hardness one needed to survive and take back what was rightfully hers. She would take it back. Nothing mattered more.

Chapter 12

"**M**adam, your resistance is most distressing." Candlelight danced over the bull-like bronze-haired man standing in Yvonne's sitting room. Despite his chocolate wool suit, one would have expected to find this man outside a dockside pub watching his bangtails take any comer, adhering to the dictates of his profiteering mind. She was closely acquainted with his type. Hadn't she once worked for such a man?

Yvonne painted her most seductive smile on her rouged lips and shook her red curls in as clear astonishment as she could muster. "Mr. Hardgrave, surely you are aware I am not a woman known for resistance but rather for pleasure and compliance?"

Mr. Hardgrave smiled graciously, his broad lips pulling at yellowed but otherwise unmarred teeth. "I am aware of your reputation." He inclined his head in mock appreciation. "A much deserved reputation, no doubt."

He lifted his head and his gaze probed her with the sort of sharpness one might expect from one of the street's most brutal toughs. "But in this case, you have reason to protect the young woman in question."

A rather unfortunate realization twisted Yvonne's stomach. This man would not buy her lies with ease. Burgeoning hints of a disgusting wish that Mary had never come to her snaked through her. It was weak and selfish, but . . . She had not been in the presence of such a man since she'd sold herself in back alleys for a bastard who'd sworn he'd loved her.

Despite her secret wish, she had to protect Mary. Esme had trusted her and had always been there for her. She and Esme had once worked closely together, courtesans to the highest bidders. She'd never forget the way her friend had cared for her, nursed her, bathed her bruises when a customer had become too rough.

Yes, she'd save Mary from this man.

God knew what such a villain would do to her. So Yvonne would convince him. Convince him as she had never convinced anyone before. She lifted her brows in confusion. "I have many young women under my roof, sir, and do not recognize the one you seek. Perhaps if you so kindly described her again, I might be of more assistance."

Mr. Hardgrave shook his own red head, anticipation warming his honeyed eyes. "Your scullery maid seems acquainted with the young woman, madam. She also seemed fairly confident that you are as well. *Intimately* acquainted."

Yvonne's mouth dried. The side panel in her wall meant for moments of quick escape beckoned. But she would never outrun him. "I beg your pardon?" she demurred, desperate to buy a few moments to compose any viable sort of ruse.

Mr. Hardgrave slowly pulled off his gloves, finger by finger, revealing blunt hands. The knuckles were roughened from frequent use. "Allow me to refresh your recollection. According to your scullery maid, a woman answering to the description I have supplied entered your establishment and was taken up to this very room."

A high, strained laugh pealed from her throat. "My goodness, what fantasies the child suffers." She wagged her finger at the inquisitive bastard who had forced his way into her hard-earned house with an authority that had inspired immediate surrender from her staff . . . Even from the men she employed to keep the worst sort out.

Mr. Hardgrave was not only the worst sort. He was the most dangerous sort, and she had little doubt he was the Duke of Duncliffe's implement. Somewhere along the greased and putrid slums of Seven Dials, someone of rank had taken interest in his skills, elevating him from filth to attempt the image of a gentleman.

It was the gentleman of taste and refinement in him she must now appeal to.

Taking care to swipe her full, green silk dressing gown back to expose a bit of pale leg and soft pink-ribboned garter, she headed toward her evening wine tray and lifted the crystal decanter. She poured two glasses of the tinted liquid. "Did you pay her?"

At his silence, she forced herself to *tsk* lightheartedly. "If you did, you wasted your coin. She would have said she saw a wild Cossack if you gave her a ha'penny."

"Undoubtedly, but in this instance I have reason to believe her. And I have other means than coin to induce information."

Yvonne's throat tightened, but she managed an admiring glance over her shoulder. "Of course you do. A fine, important man such as yourself."

He inclined his head, acknowledging the compliment as truth and not as a caress meant to soften his resolve. "Luckily for her, I was not required to do much more than glare at the child before she babbled the story out."

Yvonne cupped both cut-crystal glasses, a gift she'd bought herself after finally turning a profit at her hellish trade. Careful to keep each move without calculation and seemingly spontaneous, she cocked her head so that her red curls danced upon her neck. "As you say, a story." Blessedly, to her own ears her tone was carefree. "And why would such a man as you believe a silly little nit of a maid?"

She sauntered slowly toward him, the folds of verdant silk sliding over her body, molding to her tightly corseted waist, making her appear far more delicate than she was. She swept the train behind her with her slippered foot and let it slide slowly along the ivory rug. With a smile, she held out his wine.

He hesitated, then took the goblet in his hand. He smiled back at her. Amusement danced in his eyes. There was something else, too.

"Do taste the wine," she urged. "This claret is particularly fine, if I do say so."

He lifted the glass slowly toward his mouth, drawing the bouquet in through his nose. "Do not think me a fool, madam," he said easily over the wine.

Yvonne took a sip, letting the rich liquid linger in her mouth, coating her tongue with its oaky, spicy fruit notes before she swallowed. She licked the drops from her lips. "I would never do such a thing."

She took a step forward and trailed her hand along his bronze-striped waistcoat. "Consider my cooperation assured."

In one abrupt gesture, he threw his wine in her face.

Yvonne sputtered and jerked away. Shock and the stinging pain of alcohol in her eyes left her momentarily stunned. She couldn't see. The thick wine weighed down her lashes, even as it slid down her face and to her breasts in rivulets. Panic gripped her as she gasped for air.

Blind to him, she tried to take a step back. Her foot caught in the train of her gown and she tumbled back.

His hand darted out, catching her arm in a punishing fist. Each of his fingers dug into her flesh through the thin silk gown so hard he could have ripped her arm from the socket or broken the fragile bone. He yanked her toward his chest. With his free hand he ripped open her gown. "I suppose I should look at what you're selling."

Yvonne blinked desperately as cold air hit her breasts and exposed her pink brocade corset. The dressing gown hung in shreds about her waist. "If that is what you wish," she offered, her voice shaking.

"You'd do anything." His eyes worked over her face as if he could pull apart her features and search the inner workings of her mind. "Wouldn't you? To set me off my task?"

"Yes." She stared up at him, her own lids stretched wide with her determination not to cry. "Anything."

"I should pity you," he said tightly. "But I have no pity. Not for a creature such as you."

Yvonne struggled to pull back from his harsh hold, but his grip dug in farther, his nails piercing her flesh. She began to shake, almost naked now except for her corset and her stockings. "I don't understand."

"Then let me make myself plain." He gripped her harder, his fingers bruising. "I do not work for the Queen. I am not a constable. I do not care what laws I must break to achieve my ends."

Yvonne shuddered and attempted to curve in toward herself, desperate to escape him but unwilling to fight back until the moment was right. "I—I don't— I can't help you."

Mr. Hardgrave let her go abruptly.

She staggered, her heart slamming against her ribs. She whipped on her heel and ran for the poker by the fire.

His footsteps banged in heavy thuds against the

thick carpet. She'd not escaped him for more than a moment before he grabbed the nape of her neck. Pain shot across her scalp as he yanked hard at the thick coil of her hair. With one hand, he knocked the forgotten glass of wine from her grasp. It bounced on the carpet, its contents spilling in bloody trails over the snowy fabric.

Twisting her locks, he forced her to bend, her naked body exposed to him, her face toward the carpet. "Do you see that? Your face will soon be as bloody if you do not speak."

Yvonne gulped back vomit. It would be so easy to tell him where Mary was. She'd secure her own safety and be free of this monster. She would not have to face the long moments that were about to follow before she fell into oblivion. "I—" She swallowed, saliva filling her mouth fast. "I—"

He twisted her back toward him, holding her imprisoned. While keeping her skull firmly placed with one hand, he hauled the other hand back and slapped it against her face.

The crack reverberated through the room.

A gasp of pain ripped from her lips. For an instant, the room went dark. When she blinked he was still there, his body dominating her vision. Blood filled her mouth and slid down her chin.

"You have something to say?" His voice held the oddest degree of ragged excitement.

Tears slipped down her cheeks. "No."

"Fine, then." He hauled back his hand again, drawing his fingers into a fist.

Yvonne closed her eyes. She'd endured enough pain in her life to know she would endure this. She would. For Esme. For all the women who had thought they'd found love and found hell instead, she would endure.

Chapter 13

"**M**adam, you are so young, so beautiful. Surely a coral silk?"

Mary stroked the sapphire skirt billowing around her and smiled. It was sheer heaven against the skin. "Thank you, but no."

"Perhaps then a flowered—"

Mary lifted her eyes to the modiste. "No."

The woman's hands fluttered about her as she tutted. Ringlets bounced against her gentle face in her clear distress. No doubt it seemed odd, a young woman desiring to dress in dark colors. But Mary wasn't a debutante. She would never be that girl again and she had no intention of going back.

"Madame Solange," Edward said from the red velvet chaise longue across the room. "She knows her mind."

"But, Your Grace, it is highly irregular," Madame Solange protested.

"She is highly irregular in the best sense and shouldn't be dressed like all the silly young things of the season."

Mary's smile widened. Her sentiments exactly. "Now, a trim?"

Madame Solange gave a shrug and hurried over to the table decked with fringe, lace, and beading.

"You have exquisite taste, Mary," Edward said.

"So did my mother." She paused. It was so difficult

talking about her beautiful mama. But at the same time, she longed to remember her at her best.

"Tell me about her," Edward suggested.

Mary gave a careful glance at Madame Solange bustling over the trimming. Perhaps they shouldn't speak of such things here. But . . .

"She was very beautiful. My mother always picked the most beautiful gowns." Mary turned, catching an image of herself in the full-length mirror. She caught her breath.

At that moment, but for her hair she might have been her mother, picking a host of gowns for the season. And it wasn't a horrifying image. Not like in Yvonne's long hall.

Under Edward's care she'd already begun to fill out, to have curves to her, and to look like her mother, who had held London captivated despite her licentious past.

"You loved her very much?" Edward prompted.

"Oh, yes. Very much. She wasn't just beautiful in person. Her heart was more stunning than any face could be." Her own heart ached at the memories of her mother dancing with her in the parlor, declaring her to be the most wonderful of all little girls.

"You're very lucky." A hint of sadness filled Edward's voice.

Mary turned in the mirror, admiring the swish of the skirts. "I'm not sure I can agree."

"At least your mother clearly loved you," he whispered, the words barely audible.

That stopped her. She lifted her hands to her collar, smoothing it. Then, not wanting the modiste to overhear, she crossed to him. "And yours didn't?"

He shifted on the chaise longue. "No."

"I'm sorry."

"Don't be."

She blinked.

Madame Solange bustled over. "I do not think I have a proper trim here. I will return in a moment."

Mary nodded.

As the woman swept from the room, Mary took another step toward Edward. "Has no one ever loved you?"

His strong face paled. "That is a strange question."

"It is a bold question, certainly. But between us, don't you think we can speak of such things?"

His hands tightened on the red velvet. "Yes, I suppose we can."

She longed to take another step forward, until her skirts brushed his legs, but she couldn't. Not just yet. But how lovely it would be to throw herself down beside him and hold him in her arms and comfort him as likely no one had ever done. "So, then, will you answer?"

He met her eyes, unflinching. "I don't think anyone has ever loved me. Not the way you speak of it."

She pressed her lips together, suddenly seeing Edward in a new light. He seemed so strong, as if nothing could truly hurt him. But now she saw that wasn't true. He was hurting now. Perhaps he had hurt all his life.

"Don't pity me," he said tightly.

"I don't pity you, but now I see you're right. Despite everything that has happened to me, I am lucky to have been loved. Even if my mother is gone now, I was the most important person in the world to her."

"I'm glad." A muscle tightened along his jaw. "Every child should have that."

She knelt down before him and dared to place her hand on his knee. She gazed up at his face, wishing she could erase all the pain of that little boy. What kind of man would Edward have been if his parents had loved him? "Yes, Edward, every child should have that."

The door swung open and Madame Solange swept in carrying a large bolt of lace. "Now, I think you shall like this very much."

Showing no shock to see Mary positioned at Edward's feet, Madame simply began unwinding the bolt as if all were perfectly normal.

Perhaps it was. Edward had told her Madame Solange was incredibly discreet and her shop was the only place in London he could take her for ready-made clothes without the gossips spreading news of the sudden presence of a young woman with shorn hair all over the city.

Mary pressed her hand against Edward's leg, trying to convey how much his confession meant to her and how she wished it had all been different for them both.

She stood slowly and held out her hands for the lace.

Madame Solange draped the delicate fabric over her fingers.

It was dark blue and slightly beaded. Mary let out a soft breath of appreciation at the beauty of it. "This will be perfect."

"As you will be, my dear," the older woman said.

"Madame Solange is correct." Edward leaned forward, his dark eyes heating. "You are beautiful."

Mary fought a blush. Suddenly, it struck her how very much she was enjoying this. Out there, her father would soon be searching. Mrs. Palmer surely already was, and god knew what other dangers she might face. But here, in this moment, in a beautiful gown and with Edward approving her, she saw the world was a very pleasant place indeed.

*   *   *

Her Grace the Duchess of Duncliffe had begun to think she had made a grave error. She stared at the nascent purpling on her upper arm, wondering whether powder would be sufficient to mask it. The gown she'd commissioned for Lady Castor's ball had fashionable cap sleeves edged with Venetian lace. In the future, she'd have to be more careful about the styles she chose.

She didn't allow herself to examine the mark for long. His Grace sat in the corner, his body surprisingly languid for one who had just unleashed such violence. Tears still clung to her lashes, threatening to break free. She held them back. He hated tears.

Her husband hated many things.

But how was she to have known he hated flowers in a woman's hair? It was the height of fashion, after all, and she knew he had said to wear the diamond stars, but she'd thought just one white rose tucked into her tresses amid the diamonds . . .

"Call your maid."

His voice, rich and humming with authority, prickled her skin with revulsion. She'd learned to block that voice out when it called another woman's name as he rutted over her in bed. *Esme*. His last wife, who'd fallen down the stairs.

Clare swallowed.

Fallen.

How many knew the true Duke of Duncliffe? None. That was how many. For if they did, they, like she, would know that his wife had not fallen. She must have been shoved in one of His Grace's violent rages.

"Call her," he repeated, just the hint of warning in that deep voice.

She reached across her dressing table and pulled on the soft gold brocade bellpull. Any moment now, he would get up to leave and she'd have a few moments' peace. Any moment now.

Only he did not.

He sat in silence, staring at her with piercing eyes, his strong hands resting on the arms of the ivory silk chair. After several painful moments, he said, "I see you are curious."

She started, her fingers trembling as she absently reached for her silver-backed brush. "Curious, Your Grace?"

"As to why I have not left you to your own devices. But you see, my dear, it becomes clear to me that you cannot be trusted to dress yourself without my careful eye. You will thank me for my care and tutelage eventually."

"I—I'm already grateful."

He smiled, a kind, indulgent smile. "Is that true?"

She gagged on the words in her throat but managed to force them out. "Of course. You know so much more than I. I would be lost without your guidance."

His entire demeanor relaxed and he eased back against his chair, as benevolent as any husband could be. "Then perhaps we should discuss your plans for tomorrow." He frowned slightly, concern worrying his brow. "I do not wish you to involve yourself with your former friends. They are a poor influence and hardly befitting a woman of your stature."

Those tears that she'd kept under such control burned anew at her lids. She glanced away from him, staring at her own blanched face in the mirror. Her cheeks were sunken now from the little food she'd been eating. He'd told her that she had too much flesh, beautiful though she was, and that he would monitor her consumption of food and wine. Just to the right of her hand was the little diary he'd given her to write everything she put into her mouth—everything except for his member, that was.

Her life was disintegrating at a pace she couldn't quite fathom. None of it seemed possible. "But I've promised Lady Hertford I would attend her charity foundation for some time."

Her husband rose to his full height, a good several inches over six feet, and crossed the room in slow, even strides until he stood directly behind her. Lifting his hands, he placed them on her bare shoulders. His hands were smooth yet warm and firm, the hands of one who fenced, boxed, and beat his wife. They stroked her neck with the softest caress. "I will have my man give her a sizable donation and you will be done with it. Now, hand me your brush. I do so love your hair."

Clare lifted her brush. The heavy object stopped her hand from shaking. He took it with surprising gentleness and tenderly stroked it through her locks.

"You are so beautiful and in time you shall make me so proud," he said gently, as if in apology for his earlier unkindness. As if he'd merely snapped at her instead of laying his fists upon her yet again. "You'd like that? For me to be proud."

She nodded quickly. "Nothing could give me more pleasure."

He smiled at her in the mirror, then leaned down and pressed the softest of kisses to the top of her head. "Thank you."

Desperately, she twisted her hands together in her lap. She bit down on the inside of her cheek, suppressing a sob and praying she could keep the tears from spilling over her lids. Praying he would not see her revulsion for every touch he bestowed on her.

Who could she tell? Her parents? They had done

everything within their power to ensure her marriage to the duke took place.

There was no one.

She was alone. Utterly alone. She drew in a calming breath and decided to be very foolish, for if not now—if she did not try—her life would be a misery. "Do you not think it at all strange how little control I have over my life now? I—I am a wife and a duchess," she rushed. "A woman grown."

He continued to stroke the brush through her hair, but his piercing eyes met hers in the mirror. Smiling his soft, seductive smile, the smile that had won her heart, he asked, "How do you mean?"

"W-well. I have no choice over my gowns, my jewels, my friends, servants, what I eat . . ." She tried to offer him a conciliatory smile, but her lips trembled. "Anything, in truth."

"Why should you wish to? At this time, my judgment is far superior to yours. Perhaps in time, after you have learned to have more discerning tastes."

"But I long for my friends."

He continued to run that brush through her hair, reasoning with her as if she were a troublesome child. "The only person you should long for is your husband."

For the love of heaven, could she not say anything without him insulting her intelligence? "You are my husband and lord, and I wish to please you, but I also wish to have some semblance of—"

His arm raised in a flash of white linen. Her silver brush flickered in the candlelight; then its hard surface cracked against her cheek. Pain burst across her face and she fell out of the chair, tumbling to the floor. Her hands slammed into the soft surface, but her elbow caught on her dressing table and a streak of pain tore up her arm.

Her hoop skirt billowed up and she frantically tried to press it down so she might scramble away. But his fingers wove into her hair and began to yank upward. A thousand stinging needles pierced her scalp as he yanked her to her feet. He wrenched her head back as he stared down into her face, his lips pulled back in a ferocious scowl. "You will learn. You are my wife and you will please me. I tolerate nothing less."

"Forgive me," she sobbed, hating herself. Never in her life had she felt such black loathing for her own weak soul. She closed her eyes, knowing what was to come, understanding she had married an evil man. And so she prayed that soon she would forget.

Edward could not bring himself to speak as he and Mary rode back to his home in his ducal coach. He couldn't allow himself to open his mouth lest he speak the thoughts racing around in his head. He was using Mary. He was putting her in an untenable position. He'd taken her into his protection. But in this society that was no simple thing. Simply by being in his house, she was now his whore.

He thanked God it was his house and not some other man's, but he couldn't help wondering whether Mary would have sold herself to someone else.

Grinding his teeth, he stared out the window. She would have had to. For protection. God, how he hated the injustices of this world.

He felt sick at the idea that Mary or any other woman in such circumstances should have to sell herself out of sheer necessity.

After all, Mary wasn't with him for love or attraction. She needed him and had come to him as a mistress in exchange for help. He didn't blame her. He never would. Life had used her ill. But when one danced the tangled dance of selling, one's soul degraded in degrees.

Edward focused his gaze upon the figure that was at the center of his torment. In the shadowy night, her face was a pale oval as captivating as a crisp October moon. And just as hypnotizing. He couldn't deny the call he felt in her presence. A part of him longed to seize her up and never let her go.

He'd never been so compelled by anyone in his life. No matter what the past told him, Mary was different from the other women he'd known. She had to be. Somehow, he'd make her want him for more than just the protection he could provide. She would want *him*. He needed that now, just as much as he needed justice.

"Edward?" She reached toward him and gently placed her hand on his. "Are you . . . are you well?"

He savored the touch, wishing for so much more, knowing he couldn't have it. Not yet. Perhaps he shouldn't even try. Not when she might give herself to him only out of a sense of obligation. He let out a ragged sigh. "Yes, Mary."

"You seem most distracted."

"We all have pasts that haunt us." That was as much as he was willing to say. It had shaken him, discussing his mother, his childhood. He'd never once admitted to anyone that his lack of love might have affected him in some way. Yet Mary had managed to make him feel at ease enough to speak of it.

Now he was battling regret for having spoken out. That door needed to remain firmly shut. It had been closed for half his life and he was not willing to discover what would happen if it opened.

"How very true." A hint of amusement played across her face. She stroked her small hand down the enveloping sapphire skirts of her new gown. "Thank you. Again. It is good to be in gowns again, and not in castoffs."

"I'm glad." This was much safer ground. "And it is part of our agreement."

She nodded.

"It was wonderful to see you so confident, choosing your clothes." And it was. The strange feeling at the center of his chest did not come from a pleasure taken at dressing a new doll but rather at seeing that doll come to life and make her own choices. Mary had chosen every last bit of fabric and detail of her new costumes. From those choices, it was clear a remarkable taste for individuality and style had been ingrained in her long before. Had it come from her mother, perhaps? A famous courtesan would have such artistry within her very soul.

The amusement upon her face teased into a smile. A smile without any motivation, but pleasure. The first of such he'd ever seen upon her beautiful face. It was enough to steal his reason and enflame his frigid heart.

He'd never noticed it before, but there was a mischievous turn to those lips, as if she were perpetually contemplating some bit of trouble. When had that returned to her countenance . . . and when had it been beaten out of her?

"I do love it, you know," she said, her voice warm. "The gowns. They make me feel lovely."

For a moment he could barely breathe. She had no idea how stunning she was. "You are lovely, gowns or no. But I am happy they bring you such pleasure."

The coach rolled to a slow stop before his freestanding town home. Within a matter of moments, the footman jumped down from his perch, the well-sprung vehicle barely registering the movement, then unfolded the black steps.

The door opened and the servant's waiting hand appeared. Mary didn't even look at Edward for confirmation. She took the offered hand in her own, in new pearl-buttoned kid gloves, and swept down.

He could only imagine how glorious she would have been if her father had not so brutally cut her from the world and condemned her to isolation and pain. Even now, she was glorious in her slow-growing self-possession. Nobility had never entirely left her veins.

Grabbing hold of the doorframe, he followed her down, his boots crunching on the imported soft gray gravel.

Only a small glow of light circled them. Many lights were on within his home, but the gas lamp always glowing above his door was out. The entire portico was a thick, impenetrable shadow.

Mary took a step forward. He grabbed her arm quickly and she jerked at the touch, her head whipping back at him in distress. "Please don't grab—"

"Wait—" Edward narrowed his eyes, letting his vision adjust to the darkness. There was something on the steps. "Mary, in the carriage. Now."

"Wh—" She froze under his grip, her own gaze locked ahead. "Oh, my god!" she exclaimed before bolting forward.

"Mary!" he shouted.

But she wasn't listening. Her body propelled up the walk. Without thought to her own safety, she flung herself up the steps and then down beside the large bundle left like an unwanted piece of rubbish.

A strangled cry echoed through the air, followed by a low moan.

A woman's moan, and it wasn't Mary's.

Edward turned to his footman. "Send for a doctor!"

The footman's blue eyes flared and his wind-chapped

face whitened. He nodded his bewigged head, then twisted on his heel and rushed off into the night.

Edward swallowed and strode up behind the figures before him. Even now, he had a growing feeling as to whom he was about to find. Carefully, he knelt down beside Mary, wishing he could tear her away from this brutal scene, protecting her from the cruelties of life in a way she never had been.

Instead of wailing, she slowly stripped her gloves from her hands and stroked a tendril of crimson hair away from the woman's battered face.

That face was virtually unrecognizable. Swelling purple-green bruises marred its beauty.

He didn't need to see the flowing red-gold hair streaked with blood to tell him who lay upon his steps or what it meant.

Someone was indeed looking for Mary. And now they had found her.

Chapter 14

Mary couldn't look away from Yvonne's face. *I did this. No one else.* The flesh was torn on both of Yvonne's cheeks. Her lower lip was horribly split, like some overripe berry that had burst under the sun. Blood caked in blackish trails at her chin and temple. A piece of black linen had been wrapped around her slender body. One naked arm lay protruding from the shroud. In the bare light of gas lamps flickering from the diamond-pane windows at the front of the house, Mary could just make out the finger marks embedded in Yvonne's upper arm.

Mary ground her teeth together, desperate not to give full feeling to this. She couldn't. For if she did, she would never outlive the guilt.

"Yvonne?" Edward demanded with a heated urgency, though he did not touch her.

Yvonne didn't respond, her body still, the only proof of life the slight rise and fall of her chest beneath the black linen.

Mary forced her shoulders to relax, easing the muscles bunching in her neck. This was her fault. She might as well have come to Yvonne, a cudgel in her hand, and beaten the woman half to death. For though it had not been her hand that delivered these blows, it had been done in her name.

Edward remained surprisingly distant, his body

several inches from hers. "The doctor should be here in moments."

Mary nodded absently. They couldn't just sit here. She'd already experienced the demoralizing helplessness of doing nothing in the face of disaster. "Help me," she ordered as she leaned forward and slid her hands under Yvonne's shoulders.

Edward settled a staying palm upon Mary's shoulder. "She will be well."

Mary nodded, even as her voice shook. "How could I have let this happen?"

"Mary," he said, his voice deep and full of a surety that she had not known since she was a child. "This is not your fault."

How she longed to believe him, but now was not the time to debate her responsibility in what happened. There was a broken woman before them. "Yvonne?" Mary bent over the older woman's prone body. The courtesan was the only person she'd been able to trust when all the world had abandoned her. Mary brushed her fingertips against Yvonne's brow. "We're going to move you."

A slight groan slipped past Yvonne's lips. "No."

"Thank goodness." Mary breathed. At least she hadn't been beaten into a mental abyss.

Carefully, Mary rolled Yvonne into a sitting position, cradling her head. The red-gold curls rasped against her fingers, stiff with blood.

A cry of agony rumbled from Yvonne before she sobbed, "Just—just leave me."

"Never," Mary bit out fiercely. "I will never."

"Nor will I," Edward added. The dim light could not hide the grimness from his hard face.

Admiration for Edward lessened Mary's despair. He was so full of goodness, even if he refused to accept it.

There was utter truth in his declaration. He wouldn't leave Yvonne to perish. Nor would he leave her. It was written upon his very soul.

Edward crawled forward, his black trousers sliding roughly along the granite steps. He gently bundled Yvonne in his arms, her body seeming as small as a child's against his largeness. A final cry whimpered out of Yvonne before her body went slack in a merciful faint.

Edward kicked his boot against the tall double doors. "Grieves!"

Across the small square, candlelights flickered in the neighbors' imposing windows. Mary glared up at the curious onlookers, wishing she could curse them for having done nothing to help Yvonne. Yet the blame could not be placed at their feet. They likely had not noticed anything amiss when a carriage had rolled up earlier in the black London night and deposited a bundle upon His Grace's steps. Mary's lip curled in aggravation. Even if they had known, she doubted they would have stooped to help a whore.

Footsteps clattered on the marble on the other side of the door, bringing Mary's attention back to the matter at hand. Yvonne rested limply in Edward's arms, the bruises at her eyes beginning to swell the lids shut.

"Open up, Grieves!" Edward bellowed.

Almost upon Edward's command, the doors swung open and amber light poured out onto the steps. Grieves stood, his silver hair white in the evening light. His mouth opened and closed. "Y-Your Grace?"

"Don't just stand there, man. Let me pass."

Grieves backed up so fast his boots scuffed against the marble, sending up a screeching sound. "Can I— can I assist, Your Grace?"

"Let the doctor in as soon as he has come. Send him up to the red room."

Mary observed this all in a flurry of amazement. This must have seemed to the old butler like some bizarre reflection of her own brush with death. No doubt he'd never experienced such hideous experiences with women of ill repute, and in such quick succession.

"Of course, Your Grace," Grieves said distractedly as he stared at Yvonne's beaten face. "Will she be well?"

Mary stepped forward, wishing she could place her hand on the old man's arm. "Yes," she said firmly. "She will."

Grieves's eyes widened and then he nodded as if to assure himself. "Good. Good."

Mary turned back to Edward, but he was halfway up the wide, sprawling staircase. She couldn't help the sudden pride she felt that this man had chosen her. Edward Barrons was more than a duke. He was strong, capable, and he cared about the fate of women.

He would not leave them to twist in the wind till their lives were but a silent cry of despair. No. Not Edward. He was the champion of the damned.

And she was his lady.

Mary stood, a mess of emotions as she glared into Edward's fireplace. She should be with Yvonne right now, but there was too much to discuss. Too much to plan . . . And so, instead of holding Yvonne's hand, she was in Edward's private sitting room, attempting to organize her rioting thoughts and decide where and how she should run, lest her father destroy anyone else within her small circle.

The hunger for laudanum again coiled within her like a caged beast. For the last days, she'd held on, ignoring the continuous ache of her body as she decreased her consumption. But now, the pain of it throttled forward and she longed to lash out.

She closed her eyes, squeezing the lids shut till she saw red stars.

Oh, how she hated her powerful papa. In truth, "hate" didn't begin to describe her violent feelings toward him. "Hate" was too small a word, given the evils he had perpetrated upon herself, her mother, and anyone close to them.

"He will be coming soon."

Mary clenched her fingers into twin fists upon her silk skirts. If only Edward were referring to the physician . . . But the doctor had long since arrived, treating Yvonne and giving her enough laudanum to keep her safe from the horrors of the past hours.

It was her papa who was coming. One day, somehow, he would reclaim her and send her back.

She said nothing. It was unnecessary to acknowledge what they both already knew. The Duke of Duncliffe had sent her this message. And in the cruelest way possible, using her mother's dearest friend as the courier.

No one was safe. Any friend of hers was in jeopardy by mere association. It was only a matter of time before he caught her, and, when he did, she was as marked for death as a horse thief bound for the hangman's noose.

Mary bit back a strangled scream of brutal frustration. Would she never escape her father?

There had to be some way she could stop him. She refused to spend the remainder of her life waiting for death or imprisonment in hell.

Perhaps . . . perhaps she could kill him. She'd spilled blood before. Her mind rioted at the recollection of the keeper and the rough piece of iron that she had shoved into his fleshy body. What was more blood if it meant the Duke of Duncliffe would be cut from this world?

"Mary?"

Mary lifted a hand to her throbbing neck and rubbed

it against the tense cords of muscle, not quite prepared to face whatever Edward wished to discuss. She opened her eyes wide and stared unseeing into the molten gold flames of the fire. They licked at the coal, sending sparks up into the cavernous chimney. "What is to be done?"

"You cannot linger here."

Mary leaned forward and braced her hands against the marble mantel carved with birds and berries and swirling leaves. Her fingers fit smoothly to the warmed, sleek stone. "Am I to run again?"

It was so strange, for she wasn't asking Edward. She was asking herself. What course was she to take? Though she longed to, she could not leave this decision to anyone but herself.

A loud sigh rushed through the room. Edward's sigh. "I see no other choice. He knows where you are. What he's had done to Yvonne? That is merely a sample of what he must plan for you."

It was so tempting to lift her hands to her face and scream, but she was done with screaming. She was done with madness. She had to be if she was to survive. She so longed to be worthy of Edward's admirable strength, yet here she was, cowering again. Bitter regret crept into her plaintive demand. "And where would I *run*?"

"We," he corrected. "Where would *we* run?"

Mary blinked, then whipped toward him, her skirts whooshing against her legs. "I don't understand."

He stood, strong and noble, in the center of the room surrounded by his beautiful things. Somewhere along the course of the evening, he had slipped out of his coat and freed himself of his cravat. Now his starched white linen shirt hung open at the neck, exposing a hint of bronzed skin. The sleeves were rolled up to just below his elbows, baring strong muscles and the feathering dark hairs along his forearms. "Mary, you know I cannot let you go."

How she wanted to believe it. Wanted to believe it so bad, her heart thudded audibly. What would she give for this beautiful man to truly need her? She drank him in slowly, savoring the pure awe his simple pronouncement had lit within her breast. There was nothing but strength to him, unless she allowed herself to look past the picture he presented with such skill.

For the first time, she truly looked at this fierce man who had saved her. And she saw it, there in the slight vulnerable expression on his strained features and the way his hands were clenched in rigid fists as he waited breathlessly for her response.

She had no idea what to make of it. Her heart tightened to a terrified fist of its own, scared to open lest it be ripped to shreds. What did she mean to him? Did he desire her for herself? Or had he become as needful of whatever he felt she could give him as she had been for her laudanum? The questions wouldn't cease but reeled again and again through her mind.

Edward stepped toward her, speaking urgently. "This is only a temporary measure, to prepare you further to destroy your father. I've sent a note to Powers. We'll find a safe place." He paused in his litany. "We will not let your father escape his deeds."

"No," she declared. "I will not stand by while he brutalizes so many women."

"So we will disappear for a little while and plan."

She broke his hypnotic gaze. Barely able to believe he was not abandoning her when faced with such danger, she studied the fireplace mantel and its intricately carved birds. She felt like those birds, locked in stone, unable to break free. "I will never be able to thank you enough."

His footfalls behind her sent a shiver of anticipation over her skin. "You already know I don't wish your thanks."

She frowned into the fire. The heat shimmied through the thick folds of her frock and up her bodice to warm her sensitive flesh. "I'm still not quite certain what it is you do wish."

"I've told you," he said firmly. "For you to become well and free from your father."

She bit her lip. His words were so simple, but she knew there was a complexity beneath them that he wouldn't admit. At present, it was impossible to press him for the truth. She needed him. "You truly won't abandon me?"

"Never."

Mary lifted her head. There was no relief for her in his reply. Words meant so little. Words could be gainsaid by action. From all that she had learned, she should demand to know why he was so insistent on helping her. It was not love. No one could love a woman such as she. She would never be worthy of Edward.

She highly doubted Edward wished to expose his own weaknesses to her. And then there was her own dangerous secret, her knowledge of her mother's end.

"When we go," he added, "we will take Yvonne."

Mary's hands slid away from the mantel as he faced him. "You would do that?"

He leaned in to her, his body a towering cliff of strength and tenderness. "She can't be left here."

With those simple words, it was as if he'd linked a chain between them. Something stronger and more unrecognizable than usual gratitude heated her body, enveloping her in its foreign warmth.

"I was so afraid for her, Edward." Mary buried her

sudden trepidation. She was being foolish, fanciful, and if she didn't know better she would have sworn it was the faint traces of laudanum having its way with her. But it was imperative that she show him how much his thoughtfulness meant to her.

She took a slow step toward him, an incomprehensible feeling of anticipation springing alive in her breast. She'd known so many ruthless and selfish people that she could hardly believe she had found someone like him. "I thought . . . I thought perhaps you would forget her or send her off—"

"I could never hurt you in such a way, Mary." Edward held still, allowing her to come to him.

She stopped in her path. Her fingers itched to reach out and stroke his sleek hair back from his face. Instead, she fanned them out over her skirt, focusing on the weave of the fabric. "Hurt me?"

"I saw you," he said gently. "I saw the guilt and pain upon your face when we found her."

Mary sucked in a shaking breath. Her entire body seemed to rattle with that breath as if all the pain that had been stored inside her was clawing forth. "It *is* my fault." Another gasping breath shook her chest and a ridiculously useless whimper escaped her lips. "*I* did that to her."

"No," he gritted.

Grief and anger crushed any sort of self-pity she might have felt. "I never should have gone to Yvonne for help." She shook her head wildly. "I shouldn't have led him to her. I knew what he was capable of. What he has done—"

"Mary." His voice penetrated her pain like hardened steel. "If you hadn't gone to Yvonne, what would have happened to you?"

With every fiber of her soul, she focused on his

strong, avenging face. Desperately, she searched her thoughts for any reasonable answer. All she could find were memories of herself, curled up in a ditch, half dead, hugging herself for warmth and starving for lack of food.

"Where would you have gone?" he demanded again, unflinchingly.

"Somewhere." She couldn't think of anything but the memory of laudanum racking her bones and the icy rain trickling down her spine. "Anywhere to keep her safe. I risked her life. I risked—"

"Cease, Mary," he commanded roughly. "Would you have yourself dead in the street, or worse?"

It was on her lips to say yes, but it wasn't true. She still longed to live, no matter that God had forsaken her. "No."

"Why is that?" he asked. His eyes probed hers, searching into the torturous memories that still held her prisoner.

"Because . . ." A tear slid down her cheek, unbidden and unwanted. The power of that single tear nearly undid her. Surely, now that one had slipped free she would be lost on a tide of tears. She gasped. "I don't wish to die."

His handsome face struggled with emotion. "Because you are worth something. You are valuable to this world. And you shouldn't die for other people's sins."

Mary drew herself up, throwing her shoulders back so she wouldn't curve in on herself like a battered child. So that she wouldn't give in to a storm of tears. "I have so much anger, Edward." Her voice rasped against her throat, cutting at the air like rusty razor blades.

"You have a right to be angry. The suffering you

have known is greater than most know in their entire lifetime."

She grabbed fistfuls of her gown and twisted the fabric, needing to rip and tear and destroy what was inside her. "It's choking me. I—I can barely draw breath."

"Then spit it out." His large body tensed with the fullness of his own anger at her pain.

"I want to kill him so much," she hissed. "I want to destroy him, to take from him all his self-respect and power. I want him to grovel the way he made my mother do time and again. I want to beat him with a cudgel until he cannot move. I don't care if he ever understands what he has done—I want him to pay."

Edward did not back away from her shocking proclamation. Instead, he vowed, "I promise, one day he will. He will pay dearly for the pain he has caused."

"Will he?" She longed to believe justice would at long last be meted out. But everything in her past told her not to give a tendril of hope to that ridiculous dream. "Justice is not something that is consistent in this world," she said, her voice flat. "I want to rip out whole parts of my mind so that I never have to recall what happened to me. I want to tear it from my flesh so that I never feel self-loathing or pain again. But more than anything I wish to see my father dead."

Edward stretched out a hand to her, his face finally blanching. "Mary—"

"Do you know what it is like?" Hate laced her whole body as she gave voice to the despair that had lived in her so long. "To be taken against your will, to be used like a thing?"

Edward's jaw clenched, but he stood silent at her onslaught.

"Do you? To be held down and fucked no matter

how hard you scream? And when you've lost the will to protest, you simply consent because it is the easiest thing to do." It tumbled out of her so fast, she could barely draw breath. "Can you understand that, Edward? I want that for my father. Can you give me that?"

Edward stood before her, his bleak eyes helpless at her fury. He didn't offer false comfort. Nor did he pretend to understand. She admired him for it, for nothing he could say would appease the vengeful beast within her.

"I didn't think so." The fury slumped out of her and her shoulders bent. "I'm tired. I'm so tired of him. Of what he did to my mother, to me, and now to Yvonne." A terrifying thought shot through her. "What if he does it to you?"

Edward closed the small distance between them. He slipped his arms around her, careful, gentle. "You mustn't be afraid for me. Your father can't touch me. Nothing can. I am here for you, no matter that I can't understand what has happened in your past. I am here for you. Do *you* understand that?"

Mary half smiled. "I know."

She stood in his arms, her arms at her sides, loving how reassuring his hands felt pressed against her back. "It is why you took me in, is it not?"

He gazed down at her, his shoulders curving to allow for the difference in height. "Yes, but now it is more."

She raised her chin, tilting her head back. The frightening desire to lift her hands to his shoulders and return his embrace dawned upon her, but she held still lest she break this moment. "More?"

His brow creased as he struggled to speak. "You've come to mean something to me."

"Tell me," she murmured. *Make me believe.*

Whether he was aware or not, his hands pressed

ever so slightly against her corset and tucked her in just the smallest degree closer to his body. "I—I've made mistakes enough to ruin a host of lives, but you . . ." He rested his chin against the top of her head. "I don't know how to say it, but . . ."

Mary allowed him to hold her so close, though a nagging argument inside continued to command her to step back. But another part of her, a stronger part, wished to remain in his arms, hearing this captivating confession of his. She allowed herself to be guided into the hollow of his body as if she was his match, his pair.

"You've shown me that no matter how brutalized we are, we can rise again."

Slowly, she lifted her hands to his shoulders. Uncertainly, and without a thought for what might happen next, she rested her fingers against his crisp linen. "So not only am I Calypso, I am a phoenix?"

"You are." His voice deepened with passionate admiration.

"No, Edward." Her fingertips trailed up slowly to the curling hair at the nape of his neck. Oh, it was soft. Softer than she'd ever imagined it. It was intoxicating, the nearness of him. Much to her shock, she found herself pulling him, urging his face closer to hers. "I am still among the ashes. I have not yet flown."

He lowered his head toward her in careful, slow stages. "But you will."

The scent of leather and spice filled her senses and the sudden desire to taste his mouth and be one with this strong man burst within her.

"Yes," she murmured before lifting herself up onto her slippered toes and giving over to her blossoming passion. "I will."

Chapter 15

One could never fall if one felt such ecstasy. Mary slipped her hands into his hair, savoring the hot taste of his mouth and the careful touch of his lips. Was this the pleasure of freely giving oneself? With no condition or expectation?

She would never plummet to the hard earth with this feeling of wonder. She would glide free and alive in this kiss, in his glorious touch. Mary opened her mouth in a gasp of delight and immediately tasted crushed mint and the hint of red wine.

Without thinking, she pushed herself against him, as if she might climb inside his strong fortress of a body. The full bells of her skirt batted at her legs, the hoop dancing out, but she gave no notice. If anything, she longed to be divested of her garments and *feel* him.

Freedom was in his touch. The freedom of knowing that she was giving herself because she wished it, not because she had to or had anything to gain but the pleasure of the moment.

Carefully, she lowered a hand to his chest, just over his heart and its solid beat. Gently, she pushed.

He broke the kiss, his breath ragged. "Forgive me."

Her own breath came at a rapid pace as she let her hand hover over the thin linen covering his hot skin and hard muscle. "As you are always telling me, there is nothing to forgive."

A slight smile touched his lips and he began to step away, but she grabbed him, her fingers holding tight to his shirt. "There is something . . . I would like to do."

Stilling under her touch, his dark eyes flashed with desire as they searched carefully over her face. "Whatever you wish."

Every bit of her urged her to lower her gaze, but she would not be meek. She wanted this.

"Will you hold me?" She could hardly believe what she was about to say, but she said it anyway, "On the bed?"

His gaze gentled even as desire fired within it. "Are you certain?"

"Yes." She let her muscles relax and held on to him not with any sort of fear, but with the surety that Edward would never harm her. Not as so many had done before him. "I can't promise you any more than that."

Though his body hummed with need, he said, "My only wish is your happiness. It always has been."

Mary was certain Edward's motives were guided by some pain that was integral to his soul. He truly believed all he longed for was her happiness. She would not argue the point. Not when he was regarding her with such desire and tenderness. She nodded assent for both of them and said, "Come, then."

He took a step back, letting his muscular arms trail through her fingertips. He slipped his hand around hers, then started for the bed. Something, instigated by any other man, that would have driven fear into her wits.

She tugged against his hand. "Wait."

"Mary?"

"I wish . . . I wish . . ." It was impossible for her to give words to her need, so she reached to his waist and before she could stop herself grabbed fistfuls of his white shirt and slipped it free of his trousers.

He held absolutely still as she worked the fabric up his torso, his jetty eyes riveted to her face.

"Lift your arms," she said softly.

At her command, he slowly raised his arms above his head. The muscles of his waist and chest rippled into new valleys and peaks of living iron. It was a miracle of creation in a fluid series of movements. Mary's mouth opened slightly as she took in his beauty.

She'd never seen anything like him. Her own breasts, covered in verdant silk, caressed his stomach lightly as she stepped closer, reached up onto tiptoe, and tugged the shirt above his head.

Gallantly, he bent so she might whisk it from his body. The fabric hanging limply in her hands was heated from his skin. She was suddenly overcome by a desire to bury her face in it and drink in his scent, but then she let the shirt drop to the floor. After all, she needn't turn to his garments for his warmth. He was there for her to touch as she pleased.

With her eyes she devoured his muscles, sinuous planes, and dusky taut nipples, and she could just make out the faint tracing of veins in his strong arms. Arms that could crush or give succor to her, depending on his whim.

A slight trail of dark hair started at his navel and headed down into his black trousers. She couldn't help but think of the keepers for one moment. They had been foul and cruel with bodies given to indulgence and domination. There had been nothing beautiful about them.

Edward was a thing of beauty and she wanted to see all of him. To see the clear difference between him and the keepers.

Wordlessly, she reached for his buttons. Hands shaking, she slipped the ivory circles free. She unfolded the flap baring the soft skin stretched taut over his pelvis and the darker hair just above his sex.

With every touch, her heart thundered in her ears. She kept expecting him to grab her and tear her clothes off, but he stood silently under her ministrations, giving her complete and free rein over him.

Empowered, she felt herself slide her hands into the waistband of his trousers and work the molded fabric down his thighs. The black wool peeled from his powerful legs. She couldn't quite bring herself to look at his sex yet. That part of the male anatomy had been a tool of pain. Right now she only wished to contemplate the other, more appealing parts of his flesh.

The fabric caught about his knees and to move it any farther, she'd have to kneel . . . and . . . A laugh rippled from her throat.

"Are you laughing at me, sweetheart?" His voice was a whiskey rumble in the firelight.

She swallowed back another laugh but couldn't quite manage to conceal her mirth. "Of course not, but . . ." She leaned away from his glorious warmth and pointedly looked up into his bemused face. "I suppose it would have been more logical to remove your boots first."

"Oh, my sweet Mary, what does logic have to do with you and me?" He reached out and tucked a lock of hair behind her ear. "Would you like me to remove them?"

She savored his intimate touch. "No." She wished to keep going in her new sense of discovery, not stand by placidly and watch. "But I would be grateful if you sat upon the bed."

He considered his trousers bunched about his knees and then looked to the large four-poster bed across the wide room. A slight look of consternation creased his brow before he smiled wickedly. "Whatever my lady commands."

And he began to waddle.

It was the only word for his ridiculous movement. Edward Barrons, Duke of Fairleigh, waddled, half naked, to his bed. Only someone of his nature could have still appeared dignified while his bound boots shuffled across the burgundy rug.

Mary clapped a hand over her mouth, suppressing a giggle. Then she caught sight of his hard buttocks, the muscles shifting and tightening with each step, and her urge to laugh died away. There was something about the way his body moved that evoked the deepest need within her. How could it be so hard yet lithe?

He placed his hands atop his thick, snowy covers and hoisted his knees up onto the bed, giving her a quick view of his arse. She quickly averted her gaze so she would not bear witness to anything she wasn't quite ready for.

He shifted about on the bed, then called, "Is this what you wished?" Palms resting on the bed, he eyed her carefully, waiting for her will.

She eyed him, her hands clasped before her. "Yes. Now stay right there."

"Certainly."

Mary crossed the space quickly before her burning nerves could play false with her. Only, this time, she couldn't quite avoid looking at his sex as she neared his long, treelike legs. It wasn't completely erect, of that she was certain. The length was hard, but not pressed up against his belly. Rather, it bobbed in the most amusing manner. As she gazed on it, it seemed to be aware of her attention. It gained ever so slightly in size, swelling the head and stretching the girth.

Good lord, the way it moved . . . She had nothing

like it upon her own body, and there, just responding to her gaze—well, it seemed impossible that she had ever been afraid of such a thing. For as it moved, it seemed to be greeting her, asking in a hopeful manner for her attention.

"You don't have to do this," he said softly.

She jerked her attention away from his groin and up to his face. It was creased with an odd mixture of concern and desire. "You mistake me, Edward."

"I do?"

"It is interest, not fear, that has me so transfixed."

"I'm glad I don't frighten you."

"You see, I've never been able to look upon a man on my own terms. It has always been on his."

For a moment, Edward's face darkened, as if he would go out right then and kill the men who had harmed her. Instead of expressing fury, he said, "I promise, I shan't touch you. I won't do a damned thing you don't ask me to."

"And if I asked you to stand on your head?"

Edward began to scoot toward the edge of the bed so he might stand again. "It shall look rather ridiculous, but if it is what you require—"

She pressed her hands to his bare shoulders, urging him not to move. "No, no," she said, laughing. "But I am glad to know you would go to such lengths at my command."

"Any lengths, Mary, to see you happy."

"Oh, Edward." She focused on his soft lips, recalling their pleasure and longing for them again. "You say such foolish things."

"I say only what is true." He smiled a lopsided smile. "Not something I can always claim."

She'd never seen such a boyish expression on his face. And it was for her. Somehow in her presence he'd

found a part of himself he must have lost. The realization was difficult to take in. She'd long ago thought
she'd never be worthy of a man like him. Not after
what had happened to her. But when he looked at her
like that, she hoped. Oh, god, she hoped.

And for the first time in as long as she could recall,
her heart ached with longing to be loved. He could love
her. Couldn't he?

It was an absurd thing to wish.

"Yes, well . . ." She yanked her gaze from his face
and forced herself to look at his boots. "First things
first."

She leaned back a little and placed her hands together, eyeing him with the tenacity of a determined
schoolmistress. "Will you extend your legs, sir?"

Without a word, he stuck his long legs into the air.
"Are you sure you don't desire help? Boots are devilish
tricky."

She arched a brow at him. "I think I can manage a
pair of boots."

"As you say."

Mary approached his large foot, sizing up the piece
of ornately sewn leather with a mixture of determination and suspicion. She grasped the heel and toe of his
right boot, then tugged at the polished bit of handy
work. To no avail. She scowled down at the offending
item. It was all that stood in her way of beholding Edward entirely nude and she would not be defeated.

She readjusted her grip and yanked. The boot remained in place but *she* nearly fell upon her face, she'd
tugged so hard. "Good grief!"

His mouth twisted up in decided amusement. "Corsets are your curse. Boots are mine."

Mary wiped a hand over her forehead. Good lord,
no wonder gentlemen required manservants.

"May I?"

"No," she countered firmly.

He clamped his lips shut, though the corners were twitching.

She could do this. She'd gotten herself out of an asylum, crossed half of Britain companionless, and learned to fire a pistol with enough accuracy to blow a man's head off. She could certainly manage to slip off a pair of gentleman's boots.

She blew out a breath, then came to a less than dignified decision. Hoisting up her skirts, she swung one leg over his two extended ones. Her hoops bobbed and swayed in a most alarming manner, nearly sending her keeling over like a sail lost to a good wind. Still, she managed to plant her slippered feet onto the floor and grip the damnable boot. Gritting her teeth, she yanked forward with all her might. For one second, she was certain the leather piece of torture wouldn't yield, and then with a slight sucking sound it popped free and she wheeled forward, boot in hands.

She faced him with triumph. "You see!"

He beamed at her, white teeth flashing. "I do indeed. You have vanquished my boot with admirable aplomb."

She dropped the boot with a satisfying thunk to the floor. "One more."

He gave a nod, clearly wise enough not to offer any more assistance.

Mary quickly mounted his other leg and whisked the second boot off with a much surer motion. She smirked at the black object.

"May I lower my legs now?"

"Of course." She dropped the boot to the floor to join its mate. "And now you are free for me to look upon—"

"My trousers."

"Oh. Oh, yes." She'd forgotten his black trousers

were still about his knees and calves. An unpleasant sensation danced at the edges of her memory, threatening to ruin the whole moment. But this was Edward. Not *them*.

Mary drew in a slow breath. There was nothing for it. If she wished to draw the trousers off herself, the easiest way would be to kneel.

Her head floated strangely as she lowered herself to the soft rug. Tentatively, she gripped the wool about his knees, then tugged it down his calves and over his feet. His knees were at her eye level . . . and his groin. She couldn't quite fight the strange, exhilarating desire to trail her fingertips up his calves and thighs to that hard organ and investigate.

"Only what you want, Mary," he said, his voice rough but controlled.

Only what *she* wanted. She smiled to herself. "Lie back for me."

Edward swung his body horizontally onto the soft bedding and lay relaxed, one arm propped beneath his head and the other casually at his side, as if lying nude before a woman's gaze was the most natural thing in the world.

Perhaps to him it was.

Mary bit her inner cheek and worked it for a moment. What she wished to do warred hard within her as she recalled past experiences. "I'd like to touch you but I don't . . . I don't wish you to touch me in turn."

"Of course." He gazed up at her with half-closed eyes, those sooty depths hot under his hooded lids.

Mary took a step forward, the hem of her skirt brushing the bed. Then, inch by careful inch, she extended her hand. Slowly, she placed her palm over his heated thigh. She splayed her fingers, marveling at the strength beneath her touch. Smiling to herself, she tickled her fingers over the coarse black hairs on his leg. It felt so different, so much rougher than the silkiness of her own hair.

Methodically, she raised her hand up his thigh to his hip. The skin was much softer there and she felt the bizarre urge to press her lips to the spot. She shoved the notion aside and slid her hand to his carved belly.

Suddenly his sex tightened and seemed to bob toward her hand as if in need of her approval and affection. Her brows drew together in confusion. "Why does it do that?"

A low rumble of laughter shook his chest. "Don't ask me how, but it knows you are there and it hopes you will maneuver your fingers down and touch it."

The hard organ, stretching now toward his belly, reminded her of a pet longing for a caress. It was so odd, the way it swayed toward her outstretched hand.

"Do you wish to touch it?"

She eyed his cock, not sure whether to think it a dangerous thing or something worth investigation. "Yes and no."

"Why no?"

She couldn't explain to him. The degrading words simply wouldn't form, so she said simply, "Unpleasant associations."

"Just because one dog bites you doesn't mean they all will."

A twist of outrage shuddered through her. How dare he try to make light of her horrors. And yet, what he said was true. Edward had never given her any reason to fear him. "Fine, then." She reached out and grabbed him.

He yelped. "Gently," he wheezed.

Instantly she eased her grip and allowed herself to focus on the feel of him. It was the strangest contradiction of hot softness over steel. The flesh was pliable under hand, yet rigid. And, oh, was it hot.

The muscles in her stomach tightened and the world pulsed about her as she stroked her fingers over him toward the swollen head. At the tip a tiny jewel of liquid rested atop the small slit. Out of sheer instinct, she rubbed her finger over the little ball of moisture and rubbed it over the head.

He gasped and his relaxed form turned rigid, his hands digging into the sheets.

She yanked her hand away from his sex. "Does that hurt?"

She knew so little about the male anatomy except for that it could be used cruelly against the female sex.

"No, Mary. It feels wonderful. Bloody wonderful."

"Truly?" From such a small touch she could cause such pleasure? If this was the case, why were so many men driven by a need to fuck so harshly?

"Truly." He studied her closely while his breath came in hungry, shallow intakes. Pleasure ruled his body, urging his hips toward her gentle touch.

An unseemly dose of jealousy drove her pleasure away. She would never feel such pleasure at the hands of a man. Not even Edward. Her own body had been taught the opposite of enjoyment, and would never yield up to bliss. "I—I'm not sure if I wish to—"

Understanding conquered his own desire. "Would you like to just rest with me?"

Relief replaced the indecision in her heart. How was it he could so comprehend her? She slipped away from him, missing the warmth of his skin against hers, but eager to join him on the bed. "Yes. Yes, I would like that."

He gestured to her gown. "I think you will have to remove your hoops."

She glanced at the yards of material that draped out several feet over cane circles. It was true. She could hardly rest upon the bed with them on. In fast handfuls, she pulled up her thick sapphire skirts and petticoat. She reached for the tape at her waist and tugged. In one swish of motion, the hoops plummeted to the ground and landed with a clatter.

Approval warmed his eyes before he held out his hand. "Take your ease."

Without a second thought, she clasped his hand. Gathering the copious folds of petticoats and overskirt into her other hand, she climbed onto the bed.

Edward sat up and pulled the top blanket up over them. Gently, he tucked it about her. "I want you to feel safe with me."

Tears stung Mary's eyes and she eased toward his naked body, burrowing close. As he curved his arm about her shoulders, tucking her to his chest, she did feel safe. Safer than she had felt in a lifetime.

Chapter 16

"It's about bloody, sodding time."

Edward blinked furiously at the sudden light piercing his lids. Mary's once languid and trusting form tensed against him with alarm.

He didn't need to see to know the owner of that blasted voice. In fact, he much preferred his eyes closed, as if the disembodied voice was an invasion on his pleasant dreams, not an actuality.

Mary had given him such a gift last night. He barely believed he could be worthy of such trust. Oh, he'd worked for it. But until that moment when she stood proud and brave and yanked his boots off, determined to be close to him, he had not understood how important that gift was to her. To him.

The clunk of the curtains against the curtain rod eliminated the possibility that the invading voice was indeed an illusion. All he wanted was to hold Mary and revel in this new bond that they had forged.

Regretfully, he opened his eyes, his pupils adjusting to the bright light in slow degrees, making the man across the room by the windows appear a faceless shade.

"Powers, what the hell are you doing in my room?" Edward didn't sit up, lest Powers consider it an invitation to stay. It was best not to encourage the blighter in any way.

"I've been here a hundred times before," Powers replied brightly. "Why shouldn't I be here now?"

Edward scowled. "I have company."

Powers busied himself, tying back the curtains. "Once again, I've been here when you've had *company* a hund—"

Edward winced as Mary's form slid away from his. The feel of her body had been a balm on his withered soul. He was tempted to reach out and pull her against him, but instead he humphed and added, "Christ, are you an imbecile?"

"My father is," Powers virtually chirped, his mood seeming blithe. He turned to face the bed, his long duster coat swishing about his form. "I thank the fates that in this circumstance it was not hereditary."

"I'm not entirely certain of that, my lord." Mary's sharp reply filled the room with irony as she shuffled under the thick down blanket to the side of the bed, either for the purpose of murdering Powers or to flee. It was hard to surmise which she preferred, given the mortified irritation etched on her brow.

"Good." Powers clapped his hands together in faux enthusiasm. "She's awake."

"And not amused," she parried.

"Well, I am. Or at least full of bliss that you two have finally consummated your—"

Mary threw the covers back, baring her sapphire silk gown. The skirts were so voluminous that, even twisted about her limbs, they still entirely covered her lower extremities. "Contain your misplaced *bliss*."

Powers dragged his eyes over her fully clothed form. "Woe to the world, madam," he mocked. "You know not what you miss." He then diverted his attention to Edward, buried safely underneath the covers. A slight sniff precipitated Powers's march forward and abrupt seizure of the linens.

Edward kept a death grip about the bedding, sensing he was about to be bared. "What the devil—"

"Time to rise—" Powers yanked the covers from the bed in a determined snap. He froze, his eyes widening before a huge guffaw twisted his features into an amused grin. "I do apologize. You've already risen."

"Cease your demented prattle." Edward ripped the sheet from Powers's hands and tucked it about his waist.

"Failed, did you?" Powers gauged Mary appreciatively with a quick sweep of his gaze. "The lady must lead a merry dance."

"Go to hell," she hissed.

With her short hair mussed from sleep and her gown swallowing up her petite legs, she was more desirable than any woman Edward had ever known.

"Have done, little dragon." Powers swept a twirling little bow. "Learned a thing or two and was sent back to corrupt the world at large."

Mary curled her lip in disdain and then turned away from him, scrambling to make her way off the bed. "Sod off, then."

"Before you cast me out of your thoughts so entirely, you'll be pleased to learn that I know who has beaten our dear bawd to a pulp."

The residual irritation Edward had felt for being so rudely interrupted crumbled at this information. He vaulted from the bed, safely clothed in his sheet. "Who?"

Mary turned back toward them standing beside the bed, her back ramrod straight.

"A man named Hardgrave. A name never more

apt." Powers crossed to the mahogany table in the corner and lifted a crystal decanter full of whiskey. He poured himself out two inches worth and knocked back half in a single swallow.

Edward watched, detached, a part of him wondering how long Powers could keep using his body so harshly. Before he drove himself back to the hell he claimed to already know so well.

"Rather early for a drink, my lord," Mary said tightly.

"It's never too early, my dear," Powers intoned, swirling the whiskey carelessly in its glass. "You should know."

Mary's lips tightened into a white line.

"Or are you a model of sobriety these days?"

She said nothing.

Edward did not mention that Mary had begun to taper her laudanum intake these last several days. When she wished to reveal this advance she would. Through the gradual decrease of her intake, it would only be a day or so before she was free of it. Still, one never knew when the siren song of opium might call . . . and one who had been in its thrall almost always answered. He'd never understand the mind of one caught in the throes of addiction, but he knew the effects all too well. A gift from his dear mother.

Powers drank from his cup, almost defiantly. "I have not yet been abed . . . unlike yourselves. This"—he gestured with his glass—"is a nightcap."

Mary shifted uncomfortably. "In my service? 'Tis dangerous upon the streets at night."

Powers rolled his eyes. "No, m'dear. I don't do things for you." He thumbed at Edward. "I do things for him."

Mary heaved out an exasperated breath, her concern for Powers evaporating. "Yes, I understand. I am the plague, the apocalypse, the end of all manly accord. Now what did you find in your untold hours of toil?"

Powers's brows rose in feigned hurt. "My, we are verbose. The apocalypse? I quite like that. I shall start calling you Death and buy you a pale horse. Or perhaps you're Pestilence. Hmm. I don't recollect the good book suggesting a color for your equine companion. I shall—"

"Powers," Edward uttered tightly. It was tempting to shake the man when he prevaricated. But it would do no good. Powers shared what he wished to share only when he wished to share it.

Powers tsked. "Such temper . . ." He moved back to the window and fingered one of the heavy drapes. His eyes closed for a moment as if glorying in the sun filtering in through the glass. "And on such a splendid day."

"Perverse. That's what you are," Mary pointed out. "You keep us waiting for naught but your amusement."

"No, no." He tsked again. " 'Tis delayed gratification, madam." Powers snorted as he raked her with a mocking glance. "Something entirely different than perverse. I'm sure either Edward or I could educate you in the matter."

Mary froze on the spot, her face coloring with fury. Edward also saw in her face something . . . not quite identifiable. Curiosity?

Edward swallowed back the nasty taste of that last thought. But, yes, curiosity definitely lurked in her violet eyes. Christ, he should stop this here and now. He knew he should, but he couldn't quite bring himself to castigate Powers. His own sick curiosity drove him too hard. Powers was a master with women, just like himself.

How would Mary bear up under Powers's obvious

interest in her? No. What he and Mary had shared the night before—innocent and good—couldn't be shaken by any offer Powers might make.

Edward swallowed back a good dose of disgust and commanded, "Speak or leave. I have not the patience to dance with you."

Powers's lips parted in amusement. "But you know I love a good dance." He rubbed a gloved finger against the deep cleft in his chin with protracted contemplation. "I know," he said as if he'd just experienced the ecstasy of transcendental thought. "Mary, give Edward a damn good kiss and then I shall reveal my news."

"What?" She gasped.

Powers smirked. "You can have a sip of my whiskey if the thought is so appalling."

"Why?" she cried, her voice ripe with frustration.

"It amuses me," he purred as he lifted the glass to his lips and drank another deep swallow.

Mary's gaze skittered from Edward to Powers. A look of consternation creased her forehead. It was there. She sensed that there was something more dangerous than a kiss straying in these waters. But she could not make it out. Who could, without knowing the workings of the minds of men such as these two?

"You will cease this delay?" Mary asked warily.

Powers clasped a hand to his heart. "Certainly."

As she took a step toward Edward, anger fairly hummed from her, but then her discontent disappeared from her face, replaced by hard certainty. She stopped in her progress toward the bed.

She turned slowly toward Powers, her entire stance one of cold determination. She glared at him. "My life is not a game and you will treat me with respect."

Powers's eyes narrowed slightly. "Will I?"

"Yes," she said firmly. "Because you are not so en-

tirely uncaring as to use me thus. You know how I have
been treated. What danger I am in. Would you truly
dance about with me in this?"

Powers's lips tightened into a white line and he
glanced away.

Edward could hardly believe it. What was that expression? Anger . . . No, it was a sudden flash of shame.
Viscount Powers was ashamed of himself. It was a
sight Edward had never thought to see.

Mary placed her hand on Powers's forearm and
said, gently but firmly, "Now cease your games and
share your news."

Edward's breath stilled in his chest at her words.
Had she just made such a declaration?

How would Powers respond?

Edward waited, wondering if, for once, Powers
would drop his mocking guard.

"Very well," Powers said with a slightly too bright
air, as if he had not been affected by Mary's plea at all.

She removed her hand from his arm and stepped
away. "Thank you."

Powers closed his eyes for a brief moment, then
opened them, miraculously composed considering the
dressing-down she'd just given him. "Your father has
remarried, to the daughter of an earl. Clare Ederly." His
wicked smirk returned. "She's younger than you. Sev-
enteen."

"She is damned," Mary murmured.

"Mmm." Powers agreed, pouring himself another
whiskey.

"And what of Hardgrave?" Edward demanded,
cursing the world for condemning the poor Ederly girl
into such keeping. But right now he had only one care
in this world, and she was standing beside him, no longer the broken young woman he had met, but a fiery

creature of passion and courage . . . who still wasn't in the least bit safe.

"A bloke born in Seven Dials, he's a Mrs. Palmer's man. Mary, I believe you know Mrs. Palmer?"

She winced. "She runs the Palmer Asylum, where I spent too many years."

Powers nodded. "Hardgrave's reputation for discretion has ingratiated him to men of rank as a reliable villain." Powers plunked the decanter back down on its silver tray, but this time he didn't replace the stopper. "He has the constitution of a bulldog. Once he grabs on, he doesn't let go."

"He will not be easily stopped," Edward surmised wearily.

"Exactly, my brilliant friend. Last eve was just the beginning of what we should expect."

"Then we should go," Edward said, already calculating what needed to be done.

Powers merely toyed with his drink, his lips pursed in exaggerated consideration.

Edward crossed to the bellpull by his fire and tugged. "We can be away in a few hours."

"Edward—" Mary's shoulders straightened, matched by a determined slant to her eyes. One of realization. "I think—I think my father is mad."

"We're all mad, love," Powers cut in. "He's just . . ." Powers twirled his fingers about and whistled. "A bit cocked up."

"*A bit*?" she echoed.

"I grant you, he's done his nut better than most. But think, how many men beat the daylights out of their wives, then walk down the street, a bloody great grin on their faces? Nobody knows and nobody really cares."

"I care." Her words were a deadly swipe through the room, silencing both Edward and Powers.

After a prolonged moment, Powers whispered, "There. There you are."

She blinked. "I beg your pardon?"

Edward nodded, understanding exactly what Powers meant. "The woman you truly are, Mary."

"One who does not fight in fear or flail out of anger," Powers began.

"But one who believes in something. In herself and her own worth," Edward finished.

"I don't understand," she said softly.

Edward smiled at her, his heart alight. "You will."

Powers slammed down his snifter upon the mahogany sideboard with a degree of finality. "Now, as wonderful as this moment is, I shall not hie hence, until I state my intentions."

"You're bound for Australia?" Mary quipped.

"No, Mary dear. I am bundling you, our bruised bawd, and his lordship here to my estate."

Her eyes narrowed. "But if my father wishes to find me, he will pursue us. Besides, I don't trust you, for all your mysterious encouragement. I'd rather have my eyeballs yanked from my sockets and fed to dogs than go with you."

Powers leaned forward, diminishing a degree their height difference. "Knowing Hardgrave, that is an imminent possibility."

Mary paled. Still, she didn't back down. "You can't be serious?"

Powers didn't reply. His silence was enough.

Edward glanced from Mary to Powers. The nagging fact that these two had a great deal in common grated on his nerves. They both chased the dragon, they both were scarred, and they'd both sold themselves to get what they needed in this life. If he had believed in such things, he would have assumed fate had put them together for a reason. What that reason was, he had yet to surmise. "Powers is correct. It's the best place for us to go."

Mary whipped toward him. "What? Why?"

Shoving them even closer together was now the last thing he wished, but circumstances forced him to point out, "It takes us out of London and it will be some time before Hardgrave guesses that Powers would help you."

She lifted her chin. "I will not run away."

"You shan't," Edward assured. "The estate is fairly isolated and it will give us time to plan and ready you."

"For revenge?" she asked.

Powers strode for the door. "And more, my dear. Much, much more." As he opened the panel carefully, there was a dangerous glint in the viscount's eye. "Be ready in an hour to depart. And, Mary, Edward and I will see you have your desires fulfilled." He smiled slowly. "Oh, and, Edward—you look happy. It's most strange."

Powers slid out the door and left it open. His boot steps echoed down the hall.

Happy? It wasn't an emotion he was overly familiar with. But dared he believe it? Even with all that had happened, he realized that, yes, with Mary he was starting to know happiness. He couldn't lose that. It was far too precious.

Edward waited for the sound to dim entirely before venturing, "You'll go?"

"Yes." The passion and softness that had lit her features the night before had disappeared from her countenance, leaving in its place the face of the battle hardened. "I'll go, but I do not care for him."

"Not many do."

Mary pressed her lips together, weighing her next words. "He's dangerous."

"Yes . . ." Edward fought for words that would correctly convey how he felt about Powers. "But in this, he is necessary."

Chapter 17

"**A**re you certain you wish to ride him?" Edward fought to keep the concern out of his voice.

From her incredulous look, he must have failed.

She stroked her hand along Whip's russet flank. "Why shouldn't I?"

Edward shifted on his riding boots, standing amid Powers's massive stable yard, holding the reins of his own horse. "He's a bit of a brute."

Mary grinned at him. "I should hope so."

"But—"

Without reply, Mary swung up into the saddle, her breeches stretching over her legs. And she was off, dashing out of the yard.

"Bloody hell," Edward gritted. He mounted the gelding and urged him forward into a brisk canter.

By the time he reached the top of the hill, he spotted Mary halfway across the moor. Suddenly, she pulled up Whip and reared the stallion onto his hind legs.

Then she waved.

She bloody well waved.

Edward let out a groan of frustration, then laughed. Mary was always going to be full of surprises.

Tapping his heels against his own horse's barrel, he charged after her.

When he finally caught up, she'd slowed her stallion

to a walk. The cool air and excitement had pinkened her cheeks.

Any fear he'd felt dissipated. "You are a fine horse-woman."

She gripped the reins lightly, keeping the massive horse in check but at ease. "Oh, well. My father didn't have a son, and I supposed he wanted to teach some-one to ride. I was in the saddle when I was three."

"Ladies don't often learn to ride such temperamen-tal beasts."

"True." Mary reached forward and stroked her hand along Whip's sleek neck.

Edward felt a moment of ridiculous envy at the way she touched the stallion, so easily, so happily.

She sat straighter in the saddle, gazing far out to the horizon. Her features were relaxed, as if this was the best day in the whole of history. "You should have seen people's faces when I rode to hounds the first time."

Edward quirked his brows "A wild thing, were you?"

"Mmm." She let out a long breath. "It's the only time my father encouraged me to be reckless. Said a proper Englishwoman had to know horseflesh."

It shouldn't surprise him. The Duke of Duncliffe just seemed to be so controlling of his women that to give his daughter such a chance to be free seemed odd. But then, horsemanship was one of the true pedigrees of their class. If Mary was a great horsewoman, she'd be more of an asset. He pushed such thoughts aside, ad-justing the reins between his thumbs and palms. "I haven't ridden much. Not in some time."

She gave him a wicked smile. "Neither have I."

At first, he considered cursing himself for saying something so insensitive, but he stopped. She wasn't angry with him, but making light of her situation. "We shall have to change that," he said.

"I adore it. Thank you for suggesting it."

"I had no idea it would strike such a chord."

As they road over the green countryside, the sea suddenly rolled in the distance. The crash of the waves drifted toward them. Here in the fresh salt air, away from everyone, it was almost possible to believe that Mary wasn't in danger. That they were simply able to enjoy each other's company.

"Riding is such release." She lifted her face to the sun, closing her eyes for a moment. "Don't you think?"

The solid step of the horse, its rolling gait, the sheer power of the animal was invigorating and peaceful at once. He somehow felt totally present, unmarred by past or future. "I never really thought about it, but yes."

"You can be totally free riding. No pretense. Just you and the horse."

"And I suppose your companions."

She flashed him a smile. "I could leave you over the next dale and be off on my own in a moment."

He swallowed. "Is that what you'd prefer? If you wish to be alone—"

"No, Edward. I enjoy your company and I'm glad to share the day with you. Now, I'm racing to the sea—do try to keep up."

Mary gave Whip a slight kick and they were off, hooves tossing up the turf and Mary's delighted laugh echoing through the air.

Edward paused for only a moment, wondering who the blazes this woman was. Whoever she was, he was damn glad he'd found her. He urged his horse on and . . . he couldn't keep up.

He couldn't fight the feeling of awe in his chest. Mary was such a wonder.

As he came to the beach, she was already there, dismounted, her boots sinking into the sand. "Are you a snail?" she called.

He swung down and took the reins, striding toward her. "No, madam. You are an absolute fox. Dashing about like that."

She stroked Whip's neck and the stallion, usually so volatile, turned his face toward her and nosed her chest.

Mary laughed again, a free sound. "Aren't you beautiful," she whispered to Whip.

"Shall we tie them off?" Edward asked, once again slightly jealous of Whip.

"Yes, let's." She took Whip's reins and tied them to a large tree trunk that had washed up along the beach. The stallion whinnied, then began munching the tall grass around the log.

Edward followed suit, happy for her to be the leader in all this.

She gave him a cheeky grin. "Come on, then."

Something about the horses had changed her dark mood. The worry that had creased her face vanished as she skipped—yes, skipped—along the sand.

She stopped suddenly and stared out to the sea.

"What's wrong?" he asked as he strode forward.

She drew in a long breath. "I was thinking of someone."

"Who?"

"Another girl." She continued to stare out to sea, lost in some memory. "Someone who I hope has found happiness. I think she has."

For one moment, he let anger tear through him. How many years had her father stolen from her? And her friend? Who had ruined that girl's life? Fate seemed a brutal thing.

But then again, what if Mary had never been in the asylum. Would they ever have met?

Mary turned and headed farther down the beach, her head high.

As he watched her leave deep prints in the sand, her short hair tousling in the wind, he couldn't help but feel grateful that the fates had brought them together, no matter the path.

He ran after her until finally he kept pace beside her, silent for a moment. "You know, somehow, this will all be well."

She glanced up at him, her face surprisingly gentle. "Yes. I have to believe that."

He took her hand in his, twining their fingers. "I will make sure it is."

She bit her lower lip, then slipped her hand from his. "We are being far too serious," she said as she bent down and began tugging off her boots.

"What the bloody hell are you doing?"

"What does it look like?"

A mischievous look brightened her pensive face as she sat in the sand and stuck her foot up toward him. "Turnabout is fair play."

"I beg your pardon?"

"You take off my boots now."

"Aha." The muscles in his abdomen tightened. He loved touching her. In any way. And now he was going to be touching her ankles.

He didn't waste any time. Gently, he took her foot in his hands and lightly caressed the leather.

She grew silent as his fingers spread over her foot.

He tugged.

A peal of laughter escaped her as she slid forward along the sand. "Oh, dear. That didn't quite work as planned."

He grinned back at her. "Perhaps if you brace yourself?"

"Yes, sir." She dug her hands into the sand.

He tried again, and this time her boot slid off in one go, exposing her delicate foot encased in a functional wool stocking. It was one of the most beautiful sights he'd ever seen.

Mary was not only letting him touch her; she was encouraging it.

"Are you daydreaming?" she asked.

"I am admiring."

"My foot?" she asked skeptically.

"No, the weave of this rather superb wool," he said as he stroked his palm along the bottom of her arch.

She gasped. "You're a devil."

"Quite possibly. Now hold still." He repeated the process with her other boot, reluctant to let her go.

"Now the socks," she said.

"I beg your pardon?"

"I am hardly going to run about in the foam with my socks on."

Edward's heart thudded. She was letting him undress her. Not entirely, but from Mary this felt as if the mountains were moving and the sky was suddenly going to open up with a thundering crash of glorious light. "Whatever madam requires."

Meeting her still gaze, Edward slipped his fingers into the edge of her stocking, then oh so slowly peeled it down her calf. He allowed his fingers to trace her skin, skimming it lightly.

Her chest rose up and down in fast breaths. "Now the other," she whispered.

Carefully, he repeated his performance, watching her face for any signs of displeasure. Instead, her pink cheeks deepened with color and her lips slightly parted.

When he stripped her foot of the fabric, she held still for a moment, her ankle in his hand. The world expanded around them, only the crash of the waves breaking the silence.

"Thank you, Edward."

He knew she wasn't thanking him for removing her boots and stockings, but for so much more. And this time, her thanks resonated in him—it hadn't come from obligation, but because there was something between them now.

His throat closed as emotion filled him. She was so precious, so important. And, slowly, she was recovering. *This*. This was what she needed. Playfulness, and horses, and the beach. To be looked after and cared for, focusing on the beautiful things of life and ignoring the bitterness of the past.

No. That wasn't right. She'd never be able to rest as long as her father was still out there, waiting to send her back to the asylum. Would she? His sudden doubt shook him, but he cast it off as quickly as it had come.

He caressed his thumb over her calf. "You're welcome."

"Now let's see if on your feet you can catch me." Suddenly she jumped up and darted down the beach into the rushing surf.

Edward let out a groan as he yanked his own boots off, hopping about like an idiot.

"Don't fall over," she yelled above the crashing waves.

"You, madam, are going to pay for leaving me helpless with my boots."

She turned and ran backward for a few moments. "And whatever are you going to do?"

He charged after her, splashing into the cold water. For the first time, he dared. He clasped her into his arms, holding her.

She stilled for a moment, then relaxed into his embrace, raising her own hands to his shoulders. "Well?"

For answer, he lowered his mouth to hers and pressed the softest of kisses to her lips.

She angled her head back, then slid her hands up to the nape of his neck, urging him to kiss her deeper.

Almost lazily he kissed her, taking in her breath, teasing her.

She gasped against his mouth and parted her lips.

Taking the invitation, Edward tasted her tongue. In that moment, he felt lost. Utterly lost. He'd never cared so much about a woman in his life. And he had no idea what to make of the swell of emotion.

Tentatively, she tangled her tongue with his and then pulled back, her mouth slightly swollen, her eyes wide. "I never thought it could be like this."

As he held her close, he whispered, "Neither did I."

Chapter 18

Mary didn't stop running from the stables until her lungs burned and perspiration streaked down her cheeks from the exertion. When at last she slowed, Powers's manor towered across the manicured lawn. The Tudor facade lurked in the shadow of ancient oaks and cinder gray stones, cradled in gnarled mystery. It looked much like its master, with all its tempting glory and sinister secrets.

Yvonne's bright yellow skirts were a beacon on the lawn. She'd set herself up with table, chairs, and a magnificent tea. Mary considered heading for the back of the house and escaping Yvonne, but in truth she needed the older woman's company.

Sucking in slow breaths to ease her aching lungs, Mary lifted her head and walked calmly forward. The day's events had left her confused. And she had no idea what to make of the conflicting emotions stirring within her.

"Mary! My dear." Yvonne held up a pale hand and waved it in greeting. The horrid bruises upon her face had faded to mere shadows and the cuts were small, barely noticeable spots now. But the damage invisible to the eye was far more significant—two broken ribs, and Yvonne had yet to recover the full ability to walk without her ivory-headed cane, which was propped against her ornately carved cherrywood chair.

Even so, the woman held a sense of self-worth and self-respect that would rival any duchess as she sat upright, savoring one of the splendors from Powers's cellar.

Yvonne reached toward the silver bucket on the table. A bottle of French wine in its green bottle, half consumed and uncorked, sat nestled in ice. "Would you care for a glass?" she asked, lifting a crystal flute and pouring the bubbling liquid.

Mary smiled, wondering whether Yvonne had already consumed a bottle on her own, she was in such fine spirits. She glanced about the table legs.

"No, no," Yvonne said, reading her thoughts. "It is far too early to have imbibed so devotedly." She held out the champagne with her delicate fingers. "For you."

Mary took the glass by its stem and lowered herself onto the chair beside Yvonne's. They'd yet to discuss what had happened with Hardgrave. Edward had attempted to discuss that night with her, but Yvonne had broken down into inconsolable sobs. Neither Edward, Powers, nor even Mary had dared to bring the subject to light again.

"I cannot believe how fine it is!" Yvonne sighed. "I have lived in London so long that I had forgotten the beauty of the country."

Mary's previous experience with the country had been dragging her worn body along mud-soaked roads in search of laudanum and safety. Though it had now been several days since she had avoided the ever-present temptation of laudanum, thoughts of it, even in this lovely place, were never far from mind.

Yvonne tilted her head back, closing her eyes. "Doesn't the air smell delicious?"

Even in her agitated state, Mary could appreciate the

scent of peat on the air, the sweet fragrance of early-spring flowers giving weight to the air. "Yes."

Everything about the growing evening was delicious, except for the undercurrents of sadness that never quite let her be. But there was so much to be grateful for. The sun was setting slowly, casting its shadows on the sapphire rug draped over the perfectly cut grass. Silver trays of strawberries, salmon sandwiches, bread and butter, and caviar placed artistically across the table encouraged one to sit for hours in the waning evening.

Up above the perfectly groomed lawn and under the shadows of the house, a liveried servant stood waiting in attendance for any need they might have. Powers lived well. Very well. "I spent the afternoon with Edward," Mary said, unsure how to really begin.

"I saw you two galloping off into the distance." Yvonne sipped her champagne. "You know, I think you've made quite a conquest."

"I don't know what you mean."

Yvonne rolled her eyes. "My dear girl, to be direct, do you wish to bed the duke?"

Mary hesitated at the blunt question. She was still terrified of men. But Edward wasn't *men*. He was her caretaker, the man who had seen the beauty in her soul. When she thought of his touch upon her skin, she didn't shudder. This day had awakened an entirely new feeling. Curiosity . . . and desire.

The kiss on the beach had seemed to promise something. She hardly dared contemplate it, but it was there all the same.

Could she bed Edward? There was so much more to it than a kiss, and that was frightening.

Still, she smiled to herself. The answer was yes, because Edward would *never* touch her in any way that hurt her. "I do."

"I know you've been afraid," Yvonne said softly. "And I've seen your turmoil. I hope you take no offense at my asking, but I can see you wish to be close to him."

Mary nodded carefully.

"The only thing keeping you from that closeness is you."

Yvonne was right. Mary lifted her chin. She'd suffered enough in this life to deny her the pleasures of the present. Fear had ruled her too long. With Edward, there was nothing to be afraid of and it seemed wrong to deny the intimacy they both desired.

Yvonne laughed a delighted laugh. "There—I see it on your face. You've made your mind up and I promise you that you will not regret it."

Mary drew in a deep breath. Now that she'd made her mind up, as Yvonne had put it, she could hardly wait. If she could have, she would have gone to Edward right away.

Yet she couldn't leave Yvonne. Not yet. The woman was still struggling with her recovery. So Mary leaned forward and pushed the dish of strawberries forward. "You must eat. That is what Edward is always telling me in any case. We must eat."

She'd filled out considerably and had a physical strength now that she hadn't possessed in years.

Yvonne's mirth dimmed. She stared at the table covered in its beautiful repast. "I wish I felt some sort of hunger, but I do not."

Yvonne had lost weight. A great deal of it. The softness that had once given her a voluptuous air had faded into sharper angles in the last weeks.

"You see," Yvonne began shakily, "I can't stop thinking of what I did. And I feel ill. All the time. It consumes me and I cannot bring myself to eat for the feel of it."

Mary placed her hand over Yvonne's. "You did nothing."

A tear slipped down Yvonne's cheek as she gazed at Mary's hand on hers. That single drop trailed from her chin to her champagne. "Oh, my dear. The feel of your hand touches my heart, but I did the most terrible thing." A sob racked her frame and she pulled her fingers from Mary's and pressed them against her lips.

Mary didn't know what to do or say. She, too, had known the unpleasantness of isolated pain where the world seemed such a faraway and unattainable place. She had not wished to be hugged or consoled. All she could do now was sit and wait and not judge this woman who had helped her so much.

"Mary . . . I—I told him. I told him where you were. I couldn't stay strong. I was so sure that I could. With those first blows, I vowed to myself I wouldn't speak. But I . . . did."

"He brutalized you, Yvonne. I will never forget how badly you were marred. Anyone would have spoken."

Yvonne sobbed again. "I suppose I was a fool for thinking I would not be like everyone else."

"If anyone is a fool, it is I," Mary countered quickly, her own guilt grabbing hold of her in its cutting talons. "It was I who drew you into this. If anyone deserves blame, it is I."

Yvonne's eyes narrowed and her face grew hard. "It is your father," she hissed. "And men like him."

"I wish . . ." Mary gulped the words back with a swallow of champagne. She couldn't dare give life to the thought.

"What do you wish?" Yvonne coaxed as she assessed Mary.

She shook her head vehemently.

"Come. We have both bared ourselves."

Mary glared down at her bubbling wine, wishing for the power men had. Wishing she did not have to be a prisoner of her sex. "I wish I did not need Edward."

Yvonne regarded her with subtle concern. "But you wish to bed him? I thought you liked him."

"I—I like him very much." How could she ever admit she liked him far too much? With each encounter between them, she found her heart softening toward the hard man who had given her hope. "It is just that I wish I could live this life without needing the protection of a man for fear of other men."

Yvonne's look was wistful, tinged with the bitter note of acceptance. "What woman has not wished such a thing? Though you have more cause than most."

Mary worked the folds of her skirts with her fingers. "I want to be Edward's equal and I don't think I ever can be if he is my rescuer. I feel I am using him."

"But, my dear," Yvonne soothed, "he longs to be rescued in turn."

Mary dropped her gaze to her lap. "I know it, but how is it possible that I, a woman, can do for him what he cannot?"

Leaning back against the chair, Yvonne sighed tiredly. "You know what happened to his father, but he is inundated by his own feelings of guilt . . . He, too, longs to find peace. Perhaps you, a woman, can find a way to give it to him in a way no other could."

Mary gripped her champagne flute so hard its grooved pattern pressed into her fingers. How could she give anyone peace? She had only just barely reclaimed herself . . . Aside from that, she didn't deserve a man like Edward, not after what had happened to her. Society would not welcome her back into its fold. Finally, she gave voice to her greatest fear. "What if I can't? What if he can't? He cares for me. I know he does, but I am afraid he may never be able to do more than that."

"Does he need to?" Yvonne asked softly.

Mary looked away. Admitting that she wished Edward's love seemed a weakness. She should be grateful for his help and that should be enough. But he'd never had love. Never been taught how to love. Would he even know how?

Yvonne shrugged. "As long as he gives you what you desire, does it matter?"

Mary wished she could recoil at the harshness of such words, but the world was a harsh place.

Was it indeed that simple? Two people using each other for their own gain? What she had begun to feel for Edward didn't feel so cold. But it was dangerous to give one's self completely to a man.

Her own mother had understood the business of it well enough and it had not been until she'd given her heart that she had lost everything.

She'd give as much as she could to Edward to help him as he had helped her. But she wouldn't be the fool her mother had been.

Mary contemplated the small brown vial and considered that she had come for a small tincture of headache powder for Yvonne. It was not the powder she contemplated now. Her rational mind spoke to her with utter conviction. To pick up the slim bottle from the medical chest, to finger the faded brown paper labeling it laudanum was an exceedingly dangerous proposition. But it was not her rational voice that was speaking the most convincingly or with such strength.

Another voice slithered through her mind. A suggestive voice, offering a merciless pleasure, whispered, *Take it, Mary. Take it. You will only have a little. Just a little.*

And all your confusion and all your pain will disappear on a tide of blissful peace.

It was a powerful, almost undeniable call. Even though she had not had laudanum for days, seeing this bottle, feeling it in her hands, and smelling its scent . . . Her skin crackled with need. Some doppelganger creature, a ferociously insistent version of herself, had crawled inside her. It raked at her sinew with sharp, ragged nails, desperately attempting to consume what for years had simply been a medicine.

'Tis a prison, she hissed back at the creature. Even as she spat at the poisonous twin within, she found her fingers stretching out to the small medicine chest left conveniently open. Her fingers skimmed over the ipecac and headache powder, drawing toward the laudanum bottle and relief.

It was not her hand dancing over the colored containers. It seemed to be someone else's pale appendage that finally traced the rough cork stopper, then clasped at the bottle. Slowly, she lifted it from the chest, the weight surprisingly light in her palm. Desperately, she wished to rip the stopper out and tilt it to her lips. Oh, how she wished it. For, certainly, after so much time she could control her need now to just a few sips?

But last time I almost died, her rational voice countered feebly.

But this time will be different, soothed the other.

This time you will not drink so much of it nor drink wine with it. You will be safe from ill effects and will be awarded with the peace you have been without for far too long.

Mary fingered the small cork, her breath coming in odd little catches. If she drank it, in a few moments blessed oblivion would trace through her veins and she would be floating on a sea without concern or fear. She wouldn't have to worry about Edward or whether he could ever love her or how she had put Yvonne in such danger. And, yes—she could control herself. She could. She was no weakling to be lured into hell again.

Without allowing herself to reconsider, she popped the cork and lifted the bottle halfway to her lips.

You can learn to be as normal people. 'Twill be easy to learn to take but a sip of laudanum for a temporary ailment, the twin, so animalistic with its driving argument, reasoned. Many must learn to curtail their eating habits when they have overindulged. And so can you learn to take laudanum in moderation.

She smiled. How foolish she had been to be so cruel in denying herself a bit of relief. Of course she could learn to take it in small doses. Look at what she had endured over the last years. Surely, a person who had gone through so much could summon the power of will to stop before she had consumed too much. Her hand shook in anticipation as she lifted the bottle to her lips. Even before she drank, her entire body relaxed, so relieved that it was about to welcome its old friend.

"You won't, you know."

Mary jerked the bottle away from her mouth, twisting her arm so she could hide it behind her skirts.

Powers stood in the doorway of the small pantry, his shoulder pressed lazily against the frame. Daylight haloed him, basking his face in shadows.

"I beg your pardon?" she said quickly, her heart racing so harshly she could barely speak those few words.

"You won't drink just a little." He cocked his head, his face impassive. "You will drink most of the bottle. And someone—Edward, myself, though not Yvonne with her wounds, or a servant—" He shrugged lightly, not moving from his careless rest against the doorframe. "They will find you on the floor quite incapacitated. You may not be dead . . ." He trailed off and his brows rose ever so slightly. "But then again—"

Mary narrowed her eyes and pinned him with as much animosity as she could muster. "Don't be ridiculous."

"Am I?" he asked gently. "Being ridiculous?"

The immediate, burning fury at being caught fizzled, replaced by soul-breaking recrimination. Hot tears stung her eyes as she realized what she'd been about to do. How was it that she could now cry so easily? It didn't seem fair that after years of no tears, she was suddenly inundated.

It was like slowly coming out of an unyielding dream. She gasped for breath. Her body began to shake and she set the bottle down on the table, thrusting it far from her reach. "H-how do you know?"

He pushed away from the doorframe and crossed the short distance between them in slow, measured strides. "I have seen it many times. That moment in which a line is crossed from simple use of alcohol or opium to consuming the substance with such determination that one will die in the pursuit of getting it down one's gullet." Powers gazed down at her without accusation but with such kindness, his eyes seemed ablaze. "You've already crossed that line, Mary."

A dry cry racked her body and for the first time since she had left the asylum, she wished she were dead. She wished she could burn apart and collapse, never to face such an ugly truth about herself again.

"Shhh, now."

And much to her astonishment, cold, calculating Powers folded her up against his big chest. Even more astonishing, she allowed him to do so. His chest against her was like a great fortress of comfort, fending off the terror so wholly swallowing her up. "Wh-what am I to do?" She gasped.

As he rocked her gently, swaying with his arms completely bound about her, he said, "It is quite simple. You don't drink laudanum, love. I don't recommend the consumption of wine either for those such as us."

Mary pressed her fingers against his linen shirt and blinked. "Us?"

"Of course," he said against the top of her head. "Unlike you, I have chased my demons for many years. And I still fail in my battles with them. But I don't want that darkness for you."

"But you've never—" She swallowed, unsure whether she could force the words out. It was so hard to expose her own weakness to such a man as Powers. "Never accidentally tried to kill yourself, as I have done."

A soft rumble of laughter came from his chest, jostling her cheek against his sternum. He stroked his own cheek against her hair. "One night when I chased the dragon, sweetheart, I woke up in my own piss and vomit, shaking, terrified . . . I was utterly alone except for a few bastards who were picking my pockets in the filth of London's East End." His grip about her tightened as though he were anchoring himself in the present so he would not lose himself to that past. "I should have been dead."

"You?" She marveled. "But you're so strong. So . . . powerful."

"How flattering, but then again . . . so are you."

"No." She shook her head slightly. "If I were, I wouldn't wish to drink the laudanum."

A bark of a laugh came from him. "The drug overtakes us, Mary. It is our master and we owe it our allegiance. Do you think it will give us up so easily?"

"But I don't wish to . . . *worship* it."

"You must wish to stop. With all your heart, and then . . . you must talk to me whenever you wish to take it. As I must talk to you. Perhaps . . . together we can stop. I know I've tried many times, only to end up back in a den, smoking my brains away. Perhaps . . . we can save each other."

What he was proposing sounded so wonderful, a tendril of hope sprung in her soul. It also sounded terribly intimate. "And Edward?"

"Edward will never judge you, good man that he is. But he will also never understand the control the drug has over us. He has never felt that soul-rending voice demanding that you consume your drug until you've no mind or soul left. Edward is . . . not truly capable of understanding the likes of us."

"But he—"

"He is good, and strong, but his demon is of a very different sort. He doesn't let anyone in. He can't, you see. He's afraid of his own taint."

She frowned. His supposition sounded so like her own, it frightened her. If Powers, who had known Edward for years, doubted his ability to ever love . . . "Have you ever been loved?" she asked.

A sad smile turned his lips. "Oh, yes. I was married once, you know."

She gasped.

"Hard to imagine, isn't it?" he quipped, but there was a darkness now to his light eyes. "She died sometime ago. As did our daughter."

"You make it impossible for me to hate you." She breathed.

"Well, I am ever fractious."

"I never realized."

He shrugged. "We all are walking through fire, Mary, but I'm not sure you should expect Edward to put yours out. Or that you can put his out."

"Why are you saying this?" As quickly as she'd felt

for the man, she suddenly felt hollow, as if he'd stolen all her air.

"Because I don't wish to see either of you hurt. All his life, Edward has run from his pain, pretending he doesn't feel it. But he does. Until he stops, he will never let anyone close, because letting someone close means facing yourself."

He paused, as if considering how much he should say. "It's why Edward and I don't call each other *friends*. He's always there for me and I for him, but he never tells me about his inner life, his broken recollections. We don't share those kinds of things, because he can never let anyone see *him*. He's been trying to escape himself since his father died. Do you understand?"

"Oh, god," she whispered. She did understand. Edward had briefly told her things, but then he'd always grown silent, as if he'd regretted sharing anything about himself. Her fingers itched for the laudanum bottle and she realized that she, too, wished to run away from her pain. "Can't we stop? Running?"

"I can't answer that."

She squeezed her hands into fists and sucked in harsh breaths, desperately trying to quell her panic. "I'm helping Edward run from his pain, aren't I, instead of facing it?" She fought back a sob. "That's why he needs me. To run."

"Easy, easy," Powers soothed, stroking her back in small, repairing circles.

"I want that laudanum so badly now."

"It is only what is natural to you. For years now, you have had laudanum in you. For happiness, for sadness, for pain, for nothing, you have had laudanum. Why should you be different in this harsh moment? Or the moments that will follow? Rome was not built in a day, my darling."

A half laugh slipped past her lips, despite the apprehension thudding in her heart. "No. No, it wasn't."

"You are worthy of love, Mary. Never forget that."

She pressed her forehead against his shoulder.

"Do you hear me? Only you can give yourself that worth. No one else—not Yvonne, not I, not even Edward. Only you."

After a long, calming breath, she tilted her head back. "I hear you. And thank you."

"You feel better?"

She gazed at his face. What she saw was a hard man, brittle, near broken, who deserved to be free of his suffering as much as anyone she had ever known. "I don't feel quite so alone in my weakness."

He smiled, but there was an aching sadness in it. "You aren't alone, Mary. You will never be alone because I am just like you and you are just like me. No matter our external differences, we are driven by the same mad need."

To her own shock, she hugged him tightly, briefly, savoring the moment, savoring this first friendship since her imprisonment. "And together we shall triumph over it."

"Exactly," he confirmed, though his eyes had flared at her embrace.

"Thank you."

"There is no need for thanks. For you help me, you see."

She dropped her hand away from his face. "You are quite the puzzle."

"As are you, little dragon."

She looked askance, ashamed she had almost forgotten Yvonne. "I still need what I came for."

He arched a brow. "And that is?"

"Headache powder."

Powers nodded, turned, and went to the medicine chest. He rummaged through it, then slipped a bottle out, holding the brown glass aloft.

She slipped it from his fingertips, her heart pounding hard at her narrow escape.

Carefully, he stepped back from her. "Now go. Think not overlong on this small event and be kind to yourself. No one deserves it more."

She took a few steps to the door, but then she paused and looked back. He was returning the laudanum bottle to the medicine chest. "You deserve it, too, you know. Kindness." She worried her lower lip before adding, "I hope you allow yourself to have it."

He nodded, but there was more pain upon his features as she turned from him and went in search of Edward. Her heart lamented Powers's sorrow with every step. She wished she had known from the first moment of their acquaintance that Powers had not just been some indulgent lordling but one who had also been hurled through hell's barbed gates. But now she did . . . Now she had a friend.

It was the most remarkable thing in the world.

Chapter 19

Edward glanced up from his reading and his heart leapt against his ribs. He could scarcely believe his eyes and didn't dare blink lest the apparition vanish.

Mary stood in his doorway in a silk dressing gown, her short curls teasing her pale face. She'd slept beside him the last few nights, but virtually fully clothed and not under the covers.

The sight of her standing there, clearly naked under the light silk, claimed his reason and he immediately said the most ridiculous thing: "Where have you been?"

He nearly bashed himself for the possessive note in his voice. What the hell was happening to him?

Clearly, *she* had happened to him, awakening feelings he'd never had, nor had to contemplate. Something had occurred to him on the beach earlier. Before, he'd cared about her, needed to help her. But tonight? He felt the need to *own* her. And that was bloody terrifying. He'd seen where that emotion led by his parents' example.

Mary strode into his bedchamber like a goddess deigning to visit a mortal. She was indeed Calypso, *before* she'd been cursed. Everything about her was perfection. That jetty hair he so adored had taken on a luster that gave her a pixie air. Taken with her vivid amethyst eyes, still slightly too large in her slender face, he was nearly breathless. It didn't help that her only covering was a lush, sapphire robe dripping with black webbed lace. The rich fabric skimmed her form like a constant lover. The lover he so desperately longed to be.

"I might ask you the same," she returned throatily, a gamine grin on her face. "You were gone for most of the evening. You missed dinner."

Edward shifted uncomfortably in his chair by the fire. There was so little between them and yet so much keeping them apart. "I went for a very long walk. Besides, I couldn't find you after our ride."

God, he sounded like such a child. Why was he being such an ass after such a perfect day?

Fear, he immediately realized. Fear that, now that he cared, she might abandon him. As others had done.

"Did you look for me? Was I so difficult to find?" she teased.

He wished to accuse her with a vehement *yes*, but even he couldn't bring himself to play the complete fool. He'd had this conversation at least a hundred times, but in the past it was always he who had been the one to slip off. It was a deeply unpleasant sensation to realize he had become that thing he so loathed: a harpy. "I supposed you needed your own time," he acceded grudgingly.

She nodded absently, listening but not truly hearing as she took slower, more purposeful steps into the room. "But I wasn't really alone. I had a chat with Yvonne and then . . ."

Her pale leg emerging from the fold of the gown nearly consumed his brain and it was all he could do to recall that he was irrationally irritated.

He was half dressed. His shirt open. And though she'd seen him naked, this seemed far more intimate, with her in such deshabille.

He swallowed, trying to think of something to say. "And you saw Powers." It was the first thing to come to mind, and the most possessive.

He shut his mouth immediately and looked away. Christ. He sounded like a shrew. A male shrew. How perfect. But he couldn't help it. He knew Powers's talents and manipulations so well. Fool though he was, he couldn't quite dismiss the possibility that Mary might transfer her allegiance if she deemed it favorable to her cause. Such thoughts gave life to painful recollections. Recollections of his own tainted past.

After all, she was not with him for affection. He had to remember that or he'd be completely lost.

"Edward?"

"Hmm?" His focus slipped away from the memories that had been dormant so long, and he returned to the woman before him.

"I do believe you have a touch of Othello about you."

He folded his arms over his chest, wondering how she could make light of him at this moment. "I'm not going to strangle you, if that's what you are suggesting," he drawled.

She paled, her entire body drawing up.

"Forgive me," he quickly begged, desperate to go to her but unwilling to give her reason to fly. Horror washed over him at his own thoughtless cruelty. "You know I would never—"

"Do I?" She took a step back. Anger, not fear, blazed from her as her fingers came up, clasping her robe tighter about her petite form. "From what I have seen of men, they are capable of a great many things. My father never raised a hand to my mother until after they'd wed."

After such a perfect day, why did he and Mary suddenly feel like opposites? How could he have allowed his own personal fears to endanger the one thing he desired above all? He swallowed back that painful proposition, not allowing it to take root, for it felt like a mocking truth echoing within his skull. "Mary, sweetheart . . . You know me. You must be aware, I would never hurt you in any way."

The tension slipped out of her slowly and her hands fell back to her sides. "I am slowly awakening, Edward, and in truth I don't know you. Not truly. You must admit you keep a fair bit of yourself secret from the world, including me."

He ignored the veiled invitation to confide in her. He wouldn't open himself to perusal. Not to anyone. He'd tried it once with her, admitting his mother had never loved him. He'd immediately regretted it.

But that didn't mean she had not seen inside him for the man he was. Or maybe she did see. Maybe she saw that futile boy and then the even more futile man he had grown into. "I know this is difficult. I wish I could speak more, but I can't, Mary. I can't."

"I understand," she said wearily.

Frustrated anger at himself pummeled through him. Could he not give her what she so needed? Had this all been for naught and now he disappointed her? "I'm not sure you do."

"Oh, Edward." She sighed. "I am trying, but if I never know what you are truly feeling, how can I entirely understand? Perhaps you don't wish me to. Perhaps you would rather push me away."

Perhaps he was pushing her so that he would never have to speak of his experiences. He was meant to be helping her, not the other way around. "I am just a man, Mary, and right now a rather foolish one."

Mary groaned, half amused, half dismayed. "Oh,

Edward. You are not *just* anything. You are far more and I wish to know it all."

Suddenly, as he stood before her, a terrifying dose of vulnerability seeped into him. He forced himself to stand there under her gaze, wondering what she truly thought of him. Fearing it. Surely, she could see what he truly was?

A man who didn't deserve love, who could at best hope to atone for his family's past.

She moved toward him, her hands slowly tracing along the tasseled belt at her waist. "You are *more* man, *more* fighter, *more* lover than anyone I have ever known." With each phrase, she tugged at the belt, untying it. She lifted her eyes to his and deliberately opened her robe until the sharp contrast of deep velvet and white flesh was before him.

Desire rushed straight through his veins and his breath froze. The soft swells of her breasts were taut and inviting. Pink nipples brushed teasingly against the velvet, twin hard points offering themselves up to his kisses. And below, her slender belly curved down to the soft thatch of dark hair covering the secrets a man treasured above all.

Well, most men.

For it was her trust that he treasured most, and at last—at long last—she was giving it to him. "What are you doing?" he asked stupidly, his voice rough.

She raised her chin as she pulled the belt entirely free. "I am here to make love to you. After all, we deserve a chance to be together. To find something good in our trials."

To find something good.

His fingers ached to reach for her, but he wouldn't. Not yet. "You're certain?"

Hesitantly, she reached up and eased the robe from

her shoulders and let it drop to her feet. Standing entirely naked, with nothing but the light of the fire upon her body, she gave a small nod.

"Say it," he whispered, wondering how he had been so blessed when the entirety of his life had been a graveyard. Here she was, offering him salvation in her trust.

"I want you," she breathed.

A groan tore from his lips, and though he tried to slow his movements, he strode toward her, pulling her naked body up against his. Hot skin to skin, soft against roughness, rubbing and caressing—he couldn't think of anything but giving her everything.

Controlling his unruly passion, he tilted her head back and lowered his mouth to her neck. The pulse of her vein beat wildly against his lips. For all her bravado, she was afraid. Though he longed to make her his without delay, he would have to go slowly. Indeed, he wished to go slowly. There would be only one chance to show Mary that he was nothing like the men she had known.

He still cradled the brandy snifter in his left hand. Carefully, he lifted it to his lips and drew some of the burning liquid into his mouth. Then he kissed her passionately, slowly, allowing her to adapt and open to him. The brandy trickled like honey, a sweet burning desire between them.

She swallowed and licked at his tongue as if she wanted more. As if she would bind them.

Quietly, he took her hand and led her to the bed. He sat down upon it and looked up at her wary face. "Our bodies were made for pleasure, not pain, Mary."

She nodded sharply, clearly doubting, even if she had kissed him as though no other man in the world existed.

"It is only some who bastardize what is meant to happen in passion and pleasure." He took another full drink of brandy, then placed the snifter beside his bed. Drawing her to stand between his thighs, he slid his hands up her back and offered his mouth up for her kiss.

She rested her fingertips on his shoulders, then lowered her lips to his. The gentle touch of her tongue nearly undid him. He opened to her and let her taste the brandy again.

The kiss turned from gentle to hungry, a give-and-take of tongue and mouth and soft gasps of pleasure. He stroked his hands up and down her back, then eased her down to lie upon the bed beside him.

Gently, he stroked his palm along the side of her face. He had never felt this tenderness before, nor the longing to give all of himself so that she might have everything. Propping himself up on one arm, he allowed himself to take in her body. She no longer had the harsh edges and bones of a woman starved. Now she was soft, with the look of a well cared-for lady. He'd done that. Brought her back from the edge of pain to care. That was exactly as it should be. And that look upon her face, of wonder and determination? It was his—his to care for, and to ensure it was never replaced by fear again.

After all these years of shouldering his parents' scandal, of never believing himself deserving of intimacy with a woman like Mary, here she was, giving herself to him. And he was going to savor every moment.

Mary didn't understand the feelings racing through her. It was more than curiosity awakening every inch of her skin. Something was growing deep inside her.

Those hot brandy kisses breathed life into her and now it was flowing through her breasts, making them tighter, fuller.

He had yet to caress her body, but just the spicy glance of his eyes was enough to give her this feeling of desire. It was unfathomable. There was a strange power in it, even though she was doing nothing but offering herself. He wanted to please her. Even without words, she knew it. It was the only thing that mattered to him, shining like diamonds in his usually opaque eyes.

Mary lifted her hand to his hard face and stroked his brow. "Make love to me, Edward."

He said nothing in turn, but followed her request. Reaching back, he pulled his linen shirt over his head and let it drop to the floor. He placed his hand at the base of her neck, then stroked not down but up. His fingertips trailed over her chin, then teased her cheekbones. The featherlight touch traced her lips, then eyelids, each movement sure and full of tenderness.

It had never occurred to her that such touches could awaken her. The core of her body grew heavy with fire. Her own breath quickened and she wound her hands into the soft sheets, half of her afraid of what he would do next, the other half sliding into what he was offering to her.

He lingered, his mouth hovering above hers. "If I do anything you don't like, anything that makes you uncomfortable, tell me and I shall cease."

She couldn't bring herself to answer, so she merely nodded. His hooded lids were molten with desire. In the gentlest of caresses, he slid his fingers over her breasts. The faint touch sent shocking sensation through her. A thousand tingling points danced upon her skin and she arched under his touch.

"Mary," he murmured. "Open your eyes."

She snapped her lids open, not even realizing she had closed them. His black hair was right in her sight.

"I want you to see *me*. To think only of *me*." He traced his tongue over a taut nipple. "To know you are *here*."

A shuddering breath escaped her lips at his care and her hands shot up, winding into his jetty hair. He sucked and licked and kissed her breasts, teasing them to the point of worship. No one had ever touched her thusly. She didn't want to think of what *had* been done. But certainly there'd been no reverence of her body.

He slid down the bed and sat back onto his haunches. In the candle and fire glow, he was a maze of shadows. Hard planes and muscles worked beneath skin bronzed from the sun.

A thrilling anticipation tightened her chest as she gazed on him. On Edward.

He massaged his splayed palms over her stomach and down to her hips before he took her thighs in his careful grip and parted them. She pressed her lips into a firm line, keeping her gaze locked upon him. Here was the moment she dreaded. The moment when all the pleasure would turn to pain.

He eased his knees between her calves and then adjusted himself down so that his big body lay between her thighs. "I'm going to kiss you now."

How on earth could he kiss her from there? "Edward, I don't understand—" And then she did. His mouth traced feather light over her hot core and she cried out in alarm and sudden pleasure.

"Do you wish me to stop?" The heat of his breath against her folds teased her all the more.

She flicked her vision to the top of the canopied bed, her eyes taking in the intricately folded crimson fabric. Did she wish him to stop this shocking invasion of her most private place? She slipped her hands into his hair and pressed him closer to her burning center.

He needed no more encouragement. In hypnotic circles his tongue worked over a part of her body she'd never known existed. The smallest point at the apex of her center tightened into the most intense pool of pleasure. With gentle sucks of his mouth and flicks of his velvet tongue, he worked her into a fever.

She tossed her head, and her chest rose and fell in frantic breaths. It was almost terrifying, the way she responded to his suggestions.

Then a single finger teased her opening and she tensed.

"Do you trust me?"

She wished to say yes, but she didn't. "I'm afraid," she confessed.

Edward began to move away. "Let me hold you, then."

"No!"

"Mary, please."

"I don't wish you to stop," she protested, hating herself for being such a coward, wishing . . . she could give herself to him pure, not tainted.

"But—"

"Please, Edward," she whispered as tears stung her eyes. "I don't want to be afraid any longer. Show me I don't need to be afraid."

"Oh, Mary." His voice seemed to crack in his throat. "You break my heart."

How could she tell him that hers was already broken? That no matter what they did, she didn't think it would ever mend? Still, she could have this. Couldn't she?

He climbed back up the bed and pulled her close to his hard body.

She frowned. "I told you—"

"I want you to be in control of this." He lay beside her and pressed a soft kiss to her lips before he urged, "Take your hand and put it on top of mine."

She craned her neck back, her brow arching with confusion. "Why?"

He closed his eyes and smiled. "For this once, trust that my superior knowledge in these matters will work to your advantage."

She gave a small nod. "I suppose I can't begrudge you that."

He smiled, his eyes alight with something stronger than need. "Thank you."

Tentatively, she placed her hand over his strong one. Then he lifted his palm and rested it between her thighs, his fingers resting over her folds.

She was unable to blink at the stunning sensation of his caress.

"Now guide my hand to do as you desire."

She had no idea how to go about it. But she wasn't going to give up. She moved her fingers over his in a slow circle, mirroring how his tongue had touched her with such evocative sensation.

His fingers slid into her slick folds and teased the moisture all over her. In one stroke, he touched a part that was so pleasurable it was almost too much to bear. She gasped back a cry of amazement.

"Embrace the pleasure, sweetheart," he whispered, pressing kisses over her temple and cheeks, leaving her mouth free to draw in shocked breaths.

Understanding now what she could do, she moved her hand over his in circles and pressed down harder, then lighter. He followed her every command until she was lifting her hips from the bed.

"I need—" She panted. "I need."

He let his middle finger rest just over her opening and she pushed down so that it slid into her core. At the same time, he pressed down on the top of her folds with his thumb and her entire body contracted with a wave of pure, wild joy. It flowed over her again and again. Her voice rose to an unrestrained cry and he bent down and swallowed it up with a kiss.

After a moment, he eased his hand away. He brought that hand up to his mouth and sucked her moisture away, his eyes closing as if the taste were the only delicacy in the world. "Are you ready to try more?" he asked, his voice so rough it flamed her already wild emotions.

Dazed, she nodded. She'd entered a world she'd only ever heard mention of in whispers by other girls at the asylum. Some of them, in times past, had experienced the pleasures between man and woman, but Mary had never been quite able to believe them.

Once again he parted her thighs, only this time a bit farther before he carefully eased his body on top of hers.

She stilled. Though she was still riding the pleasure of a moment before, instinct told her this would be unpleasant. She pressed her palms down into the mattress and braced herself.

His face was creased in concentration above her. "I promise. Any moment you wish me to cease, I will."

She nodded, sure that she would indeed wish to stop, but even more sure she wouldn't deny him. Nor would she deny herself this chance.

He took his hard cock in hand and gently slid it through her slick folds.

Instead of terror, another feeling shimmied through her. It was the strange, instinctual need to move her body toward his, not away. The tip of him was soft and slick, sliding over her with marvelous seduction. Suddenly, her arms came up and wrapped around him and her hips tilted, inviting him in of their own volition.

With a soft groan, he rested the full head against her opening and rocked carefully against her. At first, she was certain that she was going to feel pain at his entry, but then her body opened to him and welcomed that hard shaft.

His cock entered her with ease, filling her completely. In long, slow thrusts, he stroked her. Again and again he thrust, his cock angling to brush her most sensitive spot, throwing her body to peak after peak of unbelievable need. Her hands pressed at his hard back as if somehow she could meld them into one being.

A moan tore from her throat and he bent and kissed her. His tongue tangled with hers. Abandoned, her body rose to meet his and she knew that, in moments, she would come apart with pleasure.

With his hot mouth over hers, he slid his hand between them and teased her just above her entry and she cried out. This time, the pleasure so complete, she could think of nothing but the bright stars erupting inside her.

As her muscles clenched around him, he let out a fierce groan, then pulled out of her body quickly. His fingers clamped around his hard cock and he worked his hand up and down in swift movements until he came, his seed spilling on the sheets.

As his entire body relaxed against hers, Mary stared up at the crimson canopy again. This time she felt relaxed with the pleasure he had just given her. Tears of sheer joy filled her vision. She blinked quickly. At last, she no longer need fear her body or that of a man's, but now . . . Now, what did she do with her heart?

*   *   *

An unholy, feral sound tore from Edward's throat. Just as he was sure his mind would sunder with fear, soft hands stroked his back and a voice called to him, "You're safe. You're safe, Edward."

He blinked in the moonlit room and gasped cold air into his lungs. The blankets were flung down about his waist. He sat bolt upright in a large bed, Mary's small body carefully curved next to his. Her delicate hands, small yet strong, moved over his shoulder blades and up to the nape of his neck in soothing swoops.

At first, his thoughts refused to do his bidding. Even now, he could see his father hanging from the frayed hemp rope. His hands shook with the memory of grabbing on to the old man's legs and yanking to break his neck. And then there was the chorus of his mother's gut-wrenching sobs pounding through his head. Her slim, dainty hands had been beside his, yanking at the duke's legs. They'd had to break his neck when the old man simply wouldn't strangle fast enough, lingering in misery.

It had been a hideous death. There hadn't been a hint of honor to it. Shame had ruled that day, accompanied by a full taunting crowd screaming what a murderous bastard the duke had been. Not many dukes had been hanged in all of England's history, but Edward had made sure that that would be the outcome.

The old man should have gotten away with it. He would have, had it not been for Edward. The jury had not been able to ignore Edward's cold, factual testimony. His father had raped, tortured, and bludgeoned to death a fourteen-year-old girl in their town house. A host of dignitaries had tried to convince him not to testify, but he'd adamantly insisted.

The alarming feeling that he would never escape those moments danced painfully through him like boiling water in his veins. His father's grunts as he died mixed so perfectly with the screams of that girl. As chilling a memory as his father standing above the body, his hand wrapped around the bloody candle-stick.

"Tell me," Mary urged with a surprising amount of firmness.

He jerked at the sound of her voice. He'd been so deep in his thoughts, he'd forgotten his salvation. His gaze bored into the night, unable to shake an ever-growing sense that everything he had gained in Mary's company was going to end. He couldn't confess to her. Not yet. Not until he had come up with some way of imparting the knowledge without . . . what?

She would despise him. She would never trust him. Sick blood ran through his sinew. Christ, he was cut from a far worse cloth than her father.

Both men were murderous. That should have made it easier for him to confide in her. Instead, it sent a cold chill over his skin and sunk into the pit of his stomach. If he did not bind her to him before he found a way to explain, she would leave him. If she ever knew the truth—how he had been defeated by his own coward-ice and not come to the aid of that girl until it was too late—that confidence in him shining from her would fade to loathing and fear.

How would he ever bear that? He wouldn't. He would fall apart and diminish to a husk of a man, drowning in sin and regret. No, he would wait to tell her. Somehow, he would find a way.

"Edward?" she said with a softer note, her fingers pressing insistently against his back.

"It was nothing." His voice trembled. He clamped his hands down on his thighs to hide their unruly twitch.

An exasperated sigh passed her lips. "I know night-mares, Edward—better than anyone else, I should think. That was not nothing."

"I—I simply dreamed your father had found you. I was powerless." At least the last part wasn't a lie. He'd *felt* damn powerless.

The penetrating nature of her stare forced him to turn to her.

Mary's skin was cool marble in the deep of night, matched by her violet eyes, two glistening stones. Slowly, she drew her hand up to his face. A sad smile touched her lips. "I hope one day you will trust me as you expect me to trust you."

Without another word, she gently eased her hand to his shoulder, urging him back to the downy mattress. Carefully, she tucked the covers around them and she nestled into the crook of his arm.

Terror laced through him and locked his body in a paralysis of thought. He'd never known anything like this moment. Her acceptance of him and her trust as she rested her body next to his.

Of all the women in the world, Mary was the least likely to trust anyone, and she trusted him. He stared up at the plasterwork ceiling, drawing in slow, steady breaths until he felt her body drift off into slumber. A thought struck him. What if she shouldn't trust him? What if he had been leading her astray in all this be-cause, after nearly twenty years, the justice that had been served to his father had not made Edward happy or whole. Instead, it had left him empty. He'd never known what happiness might be until Mary had awoken something in him long dead.

And it had nothing to do with revenge.

Chapter 20

"**N**o," Powers taunted. "Again."

Mary growled with frustration. The wooden knife in her hand refused to follow her commands. Or at least so she kept telling herself. In truth, it was her clumsiness and ineptitude that wouldn't allow her to beat her far superior opponent. Powers was larger—much, much larger—stronger, and faster, but that was no excuse. Anyone who hunted her, even her father, was likely to be all these things.

So instead of making a host of excuses, she focused on the blond bastard. He wasn't even mussed. Not in the slightest. Powers's hair—lush silver strands—brushed over his strong brow, emphasizing the coldness of his eyes and that wicked jaw.

His black silk shirt was open at the neck, revealing a distracting manly décolletage. The sun-kissed skin was smooth and hard and the light fabric clung to his tree-like torso.

It was alarming, her consideration of his person . . . and the fact that he was indeed very similar to herself. If Edward could read her thoughts, he would suffer apoplexy. But she could not help the contemplations that rustled through her brain. Edward was perfect. A saint compared to herself . . . and she would never deserve him. In the end, Edward would see that. After all, he never spoke of them in terms of a relationship that could carry on after she'd exacted her revenge.

Powers, on the other hand, was the devil himself, and, well, didn't she belong in hell?

The viscount strode toward her, his long legs stretching against his formfitting black trousers. Towering over her, he glared, no mercy in those eyes. With a dismissive snort, he grabbed her knife hand in a fierce grip. The rough pads of his fingers slid against her skin, biting with surprising demand. He yanked her back against his front. Now fixed behind her, he worked her arm in a large figure eight. "You must keep the blade out and to the side, and you must use your arm like a pendulum."

The heat of his body caressed her through her frock, sliding against her back. She could have sworn he'd lingered a moment longer than necessary before he jerked away.

Mary shoved a lock of hair back from her forehead and braced herself for the next bout. "Why can't Edward teach me?"

As if she'd summoned him, Edward strode through the stable yard gate, his boot steps firm and his black garb immaculate in the late-afternoon light. "Because Powers is the better knife man."

Powers waggled his brows, an irritating habit of his, and said brightly, "No one better to slit a man ear to ear or nose to nob, sweetheart."

"Your wit is astounding."

"Oh, come now. You adore it," Powers drawled as he shrugged his damp linen shirt back over his hard shoulders. Indeed, Powers's otherworldliness fairly shone from his gold-kissed skin. Mary had to take her earlier considerations back. The gods had nothing on Powers's perfection.

Edward, on the other hand, was grounded upon the earth and had a forbidden beauty that Powers would never attain. But would she ever be worthy of the man that walked the ground, who lived his life with honor despite his proclamations that he wasn't a good man? Would he ever be able to let her in?

She allowed herself to focus on the present moment. The deep scent of earth, horses, and hay surrounded them. There was no warmth to the setting sun's light, and yet a slight sheen of perspiration had broken out across her brow in her exertion. She wished she could enjoy the luxury of deshabille the way the men did, but her clothes were all firmly in place.

Wishing for some sort of gesture or confidence from Edward, she let her gaze skirt to him.

He stood about ten paces off, his coat slung over a stable door. He leaned up against a wooden beam, his arms folded over his wide chest. All she wished was to recall how splendid the previous night had been . . . and yet, even that thought only reminded her how unworthy she was of Edward's affections—even now he couldn't share his fears with her. Last night, he'd lied. She knew it. He hadn't dreamed of her father stealing her away.

She'd heard it in the tenseness of his voice. Perhaps he would never be able to tell her, to allow her more than just physical intimacy. Perhaps a more worthy woman could win his secrets from him.

It was one thing to be his mistress, but a man like Edward deserved an equal as his companion, not a used-up laudanum drinker like herself. A well of shadowy pain circled in around her as her mind wandered off to the keeper Matthew and his attentions.

"You're not focusing, love," Edward said.

She blinked, the image of Matthew melting away. "I

don't care for the blade," she declared defiantly. "Give me a pistol any day."

"Yes, we all know you can shoot a nail at twenty paces," said Powers, cocking his head side to side, examining her. "But that won't serve you if you wish to do the job quietly and not be sent up for a lifetime . . . or dropped to a quick stop."

Edward's mouth tensed. "A most unpleasant end. Sometimes the stop isn't so quick."

Powers's gaze shifted quickly to his friend.

Mary dug her booted toe into the dirt, wishing she could ask what undercurrent was taking place between the two men. She should just ask, but she had no wish to be told it was none of her affair.

"Come on, then," she said, palming the knife again.

Her skirts were heavy and swishing about her legs. Powers wouldn't let her practice in breeches. Said that she was likely to face an attacker in skirts, so she would fight in skirts. He was damn irritating with his pragmatism.

Powers walked back toward her, his body lithe and easy, balanced upon the balls of his feet. The man was pure grace when aiming to slice one open.

"Look for his weaknesses, Mary," Edward called from his place on the edge of the yard.

Mary fought a snort. Weakness? Only a low blow would find his weakness. "Where's a bottle, then?"

"I could still put you in your coffin six sheets to the wind, sweetheart."

Lord, she hated it when he called her pet names. He somehow managed to make them sound like such insults, even after the secrets they had shared. "Says a great deal about you, doesn't it?"

"Only that I'd have to be dead before you could strike me."

Mary scowled. She shifted on the balls of her feet, circling around, waiting, hoping for any opening. Before she could dart in, Powers stepped forward, feinted to the right, then swirled in and grabbed her about the throat. The wooden blade pressed into her jugular.

She winced and danced on the tips of her toes. "Yes, thank you for another display of your vast superiority," she rasped.

He grinned down at her. "Of course."

"Mary," Edward said, his voice worn. "You need to think differently. You can't outmatch him for size or speed. What can you use against him?"

Mary flinched as her back protested the arched angle. She didn't particularly care for the view, either. Powers's face was alight as it only could be when in the full fledge of gloating. What the hell could she use against the devil? "Release me," she ground out.

His fingers surreptitiously stroked against her collarbones before he pushed her away. That icy blue regard of his flared momentarily, then shifted to the hay-strewn ground.

He desired her.

Whether he wanted to admit it or not, Powers wanted her. Perhaps because he did see himself in her eyes.

And that was his weakness.

Mary tamped down her sudden anticipation. "Again."

"Love to, darling." Powers stalked back into fighting stance.

Mary matched suit but this time she allowed her gaze to grow heavy, thinking of Edward's touch upon her skin and imagining it was Edward she spoke to, not Powers. "Do we truly have to fight? Isn't there another way?"

Powers kept his stance, yet hesitated. "Are you in possession of some skill I am unaware of?"

She trailed her glance over his mouth, then very carefully licked her own lips. "I think you could improve my skill."

"Yes?" His voice roughened.

"Before we continue, could you show me . . . ?" She took slow steps forward until she could reach out to touch him.

Powers held still, watching her with curiosity. "Speak, then."

Finally, she gazed at his groin, shocked at her own ability to be so brazen when she felt nothing for the man. "You have another tool I think I could make use of. Would you . . . won't you . . . give it to me?"

Powers's jaw slackened, and as if her words were a suggestive stroke, the bulge in his breeches hardened. And just as he opened his mouth to speak, Mary darted forward, swinging the blade in a figure eight. On the downward slash, she struck his abdomen, causing him to stumble back.

She grinned up at his stunned face.

Powers shoved her away from him, his face flushing with anger.

"Enough," snapped Edward.

"I found his weakness," Mary said simply, lowering her arm and fingering the grooves of the practice knife.

"Yes." Edward's face was tight, his entire body as stiff as a cat thrown into a pond. "Yes, you did."

"And you proved where your mind lies." Powers threw his blade down, any of the kindness that had once been in him gone now. "In the gutter."

"Right along with yours," she countered, pinning him with her disdain.

Powers's eyes narrowed. "Don't push me."

"She's right." Edward shoved away from the wall

and strode forward, his usually graceful gait stiff, kicking up dirt and hay.

Nothing betrayed Powers's irritation except for a slight tightening of the muscle under his right eye. "Pardon?"

Edward placed a hand on Mary's shoulder, the fingers gripping possessively. "She wouldn't have succeeded if she wasn't right."

A muscle clenched in Powers's oh so perfect jaw. "Edward—"

"I think that is enough for today." Edward lifted his fingers to Mary's chin, then tilted her face up toward his. Deliberately, he lowered his mouth to hers and took her lips with a hot kiss.

Every bit of her commanded she melt under the kiss, but she knew what this kiss was for. It wasn't for her pleasure. It was a marking. It was unpleasant and, for the first time, Edward's kiss tasted bitter to her tongue. He saw her not as a woman but as a possession. And the knowledge burned her heart to a cinder.

Chapter 21

Edward strode back and forth before his banked fire. He'd made a terrible mistake. All this time, he'd been certain that to make Mary well, she needed justice. After all, he had sought justice years before and he'd thought it had helped him carry on.

He'd been so wrong. He'd limped through the last years. Alone.

Justice hadn't given him peace, or freedom. He was still tormented by memory, unable to heal. Unable to open his heart to Mary.

What good had justice done? None. It had left him cold.

There had been something on Mary's face today. A hardness completely unlike the joyous expression she'd had on the beach. It was one he recognized all too well, for he'd worn it for many years.

It was quite simple. He had gotten it entirely wrong. Mary didn't need to destroy her father. She simply needed to move on and build a new life. To celebrate the good and not dwell in the pain.

What a fool he'd been to give her revenge when he should have been giving her happiness. He winced. *Happiness.* He'd not had much of it. Perhaps he couldn't give what he didn't understand.

Once Mary had her revenge, she would no longer need him. She would go on with her life, but what kind of life would it be? Why hadn't he tried something else? Something that would have made her face shine as it had when they'd teased each other riding horses and splashing in the sea.

He didn't know what to do, of course. Nothing in his life had taught or prepared him to help another human being in such a way.

But he would never forget that look as she had gone back to Powers for more practice. A look that placed the destruction of her father above everything.

He slammed his fist against the fireplace mantel, welcoming the sharp pain. He let out a slow breath and forced himself to tame his fighting emotions.

He was bleeding. He scowled down at the broken skin on his hand and the seeping crimson.

"Whatever did the fireplace do to deserve such treatment?"

Edward stilled and quickly wiped the blood away on his black trousers. A traitorous smile teased the corners of his mouth. He couldn't hold back the sudden relief flooding through him that she was here. In *his* room. "Alas, it was giving forth a very poor heat."

The quiet rustle of her dressing gown mixed with the pops and crackles of the fire as she neared him. She knelt down before the hearth and her slender white hand stretched out, clasping the brass coal tongs.

Every part of him thundered to life at her presence. He loved her black hair, short though it might be, and her scent. The smell of delicate rose soap wafted up toward him and filled him with the strangest urge to treat her as if she were made of glass. But Mary was not made of glass—she was made of the eternal metal of the earth. For she was certainly strong enough to cut him from her life if she so chose. And move on to whoever else would give her more strength.

216   *Máire Claremont*

The surety that he couldn't do the same singed his soul with punishing fire. In the past, he'd always done so, but with this woman? He needed her now in a way he'd never thought possible.

She dropped a few pieces of coal onto the fire, then hung the tongs back on their stand. "Surely, this will accomplish a more cheerful heat, and bruise you less."

He offered his hand to her. "How right you are."

She slipped her fingers into his grip and allowed him to pull her up. Resignation lined her delicate features. "Edward, today—"

"I understand." He had no wish to hear her reasoning about the scene between her and Powers and the moment they had shared. Powers was capable of offering her more assistance. It was why he had involved the man. Wasn't it? Or was it because he knew the man would play at Mary's affections? To test her loyalty. The very realization made him sick. And yet . . .

Her fingers tightened around his slightly. "You do?"

"Yes." Carefully, he clasped her hand in both of his. He stared down at his hands enveloping her small one. If he could, he would never let it go. Her hand belonged in his. It fit his strong fingers and palm in a way no other woman's had or ever would. "Now *you* must understand."

Uncertainty shadowed her beautiful face. "Edward?"

"I think we should stop," he said evenly.

She blanched. "You wish me to leave?"

"No," he corrected, shocked she could think such a thing. "Not at all. I want you to stay with me, but differently."

"I don't understand."

"Mary, I don't think you should pursue revenge."

The words felt so right. At last, he'd said what had been eating him half alive. Gently, he reached up and teased his thumb along her jaw, wishing nothing more than to seal his declaration with the marriage of their lips.

Her brow furrowed. "But you said—"

"I know what I said. I was wrong."

"Does Powers agree?"

"Powers is a dangerous man and unhappy. I doubt he would know what was good for your welfare if it punched him in the face. And I don't like the way he looks at you."

Her fingers yanked at his, bidding for escape, and she pulled her head back from his touch. The earlier openness that had softened her face was replaced with confusion. "Edward, why are you trying to take this away from me? It's the only thing I have."

He wanted to deny it, to say she had *him*, that he would be her protector, but the unfamiliar words wouldn't pass his lips. "I want you to be happy."

"Your words are not making me happy," she said tightly. "I think I should go to Yvonne."

He couldn't let her go. He had to make her understand. "Can't you see the mistake we have made? Revenge will leave you hollow."

"You're the one who urged me to it," she protested.

His insides burned at his guilt. "Yes, because I know nothing different. But we must try another way. Couldn't you be happy as my mistress? Just you and I. Like when we read in the library, or the other day riding across the land?"

"Your mistress. I see."

But she didn't see. Some ugly emotion masked her features and his heart spasmed.

"Edward, I became your mistress weeks ago because I was running from my father. It is not the life I had envisioned for myself as a girl."

"I—"

She held up her hand. "I must say this. You know the common practice of mistresses," she said. "I will sell you my allegiance and in turn receive—" A strange sheen glossed her eyes and she seemed not to be looking at him at all, but staring off into some unseen perdition. "Protection and money."

He was botching this. Badly. How had he not realized the idea of being a mistress would be so abhorrent to her? Somewhere along the way, he had never learned how two people truly interacted, people who cared about each other. "Well, yes. But—"

She flicked her gaze back to his and in one quick jerk whipped her fingers from his. Pointedly, she folded her hands before her, creating a barrier between them. "If you wish me to simply be a mistress—no revenge, no chance to empower myself—what will I do when you grow tired of me? Will I simply pass from man to man? I have known that already, Edward. It was a much uglier prison, of course, but I have no desire to return to that way of life."

His hands hung suspended between them, ineffectual and empty, as his gut dropped to the floor. "You and I aren't like that. I would find a way to make you happy without vengeance."

"No, Edward," she whispered, her voice so low and rough his name was barely audible. She drew in a slow breath, which pressed her breasts against her dressing gown, before continuing coolly, "This is something I must do. And if you no longer approve of it, I think we should end our agreement."

He blinked. They'd never signed papers. At first, he'd intended it, but there had been no official position or conditions. He would never wish for that. Not with Mary. "Agreement?"

Her eyes shuttered him out, the pallor of her cheeks as icy as a body left out in the cold. Not even the heat of the fire could penetrate the frigid emptiness growing around them. "Yes, that you give me protection and I give you myself."

The words were so frigid, he could scarcely believe she was speaking them. Even if to some degree they were the truth.

Yet, with every word, she was slipping away. He was losing her. Somehow he had to make her see that he had set her on a path of loneliness, the path he'd walked most of his life. Revenge had never healed the hole in his own heart.

"Mary, we are more than that—"

"I owe you so much," she raced. "I know that. I give you my gratitude."

The intimacy between them was fading swiftly as their relationship was broken down to coin and a sense of obligation. Was that all it was? It couldn't be. "I don't wish gratitude," he gritted.

Her gaze snapped, afire with anger. "Yes. You do. Or you would not speak thusly to me. You would not try to sway me from my path and speak simply of being a mistress. I care for you, Edward, but once I wanted so much more. And while I may not deserve it, I'd like to think that I can have some semblance of my dreams."

She swallowed, pausing, it seemed, to steel herself. "And I do owe you my life. But I had dared to think that you might . . ."

"What, Mary?" He didn't understand. How had they descended to this place?

Shaking her head, she said softly, "I don't dare to think it now."

He didn't know what was happening, only that she

was slipping from him with each word that passed between them. "Mary, I care for you."

Her face twisted up for one moment, as if she might let the torrent of her emotions spring forth. Perhaps she would proclaim her affection, but instead fury poured from her. "Then how can you try to take my revenge away?" she exclaimed. "Do you know what you are asking? To forgive the man who locked me away, who forced me to live in misery and pain, and who killed my mother? You want to let him go free?"

Horror gripped him. He couldn't stop himself. He clasped her arms with his hands. "Mary, I didn't know about your mother. You never told me."

She looked away, her face white. "They were fighting and he pushed her. She crashed down the stairs." Her voice lowered, empty. "She never got up."

"Oh, Mary, my darling. But you must see that you can never bring your mother back by—"

"No more, Edward."

"I will do whatever it takes to help you recover," he whispered.

"Can you give my mother peace?" she whispered.

His heart wrenched. "No. And neither can you."

Her face creased with pain. "I can try."

"I won't let you destroy yourself."

"Let? Edward, you don't own me."

He felt as if he did. He did want to own her. To claim her entirely as his. "You are mine. Mine to protect."

She peered up at him. "Please, don't do this," she begged.

"I don't understand."

"Don't make me choose between my revenge and you."

He stilled, the world swinging harshly. "I would lose, wouldn't I?"

Her so-proud face lowered, her chin dipping, unable to face him. "You don't love me, Edward. I am not even worthy of your love. I am not worthy—" The slender muscles in her throat worked as she struggled to speak. "To be your wife."

Wife? It had never even occurred to him. Edward didn't know what to say. He had never contemplated marriage. He'd been content to keep things as they were between them. He'd never thought to marry *anyone*. Not with the blood that ran through his veins.

"You are more than worthy, Mary."

A spark of hope flared in her eyes and he hated himself for it.

"But it won't be me that you marry. I can't. I will never wed."

"I see." She breathed. "What are we to do, then?"

"Stay with me. Heal."

She lifted her gaze to his, her blue eyes heavy with the pain of years of struggle. "No, Edward, not if I can't have my revenge."

There it was and he had created it. The agony of it surprised him. He had always wondered if she would choose another man when she needed help that he couldn't give. Now it wasn't a man she was choosing; it was vengeance—a much colder companion. And he'd bloody well shoved her into its arms.

God, how he longed to pull her to him and settle this without words, but that was the worst thing he could do with her. "You sound as if you are saying good-bye."

The anger sifted out of her as she stood, tired yet determined. "I am not saying good-bye, but I will not have you treat me as if I have no choice but to be yours. I *chose* to come here. Did you not choose me, too?"

He dug his fingertips into his palms before admitting tightly, "I saw you. I had to have you. And that is what I can say."

"Tell me," she urged, "at long last tell me what it is that haunts you. Why you chose *me*."

He jerked his gaze away, already feeling racked with scouring pain as the memories threatened to cloud in on him. "It—it is not pleasant."

"You know about the asylum and my father. Perhaps it might help you to share some of your troubles."

Just speaking of it sent tremors of panic through his blood. All he wished to do was run. Run anywhere. Away from that which had ruined his life. "I don't speak of it, Mary. Not to anyone."

"Speak to me." There was an urgency in her voice as if his reply would determine the fate of her world.

Edward stared down at the face that had captivated him from the first moment he'd seen it and he considered the possible paths he might take. He could bare himself to her, bare himself as he had never done for anyone. The weight that had pressed upon his blackened heart could finally be lifted. But that wasn't why he had found her. It wasn't why he had taken her into his life. He was here to save her, and if he confessed what he wished, she would hate him. She would hate everything about him and his blood. But she had to know so she could understand why it was so important for her to give up her quest for revenge. So that she could heal, as he never had.

"Edward?" she said softly, taking a step toward him. A step back to how they had been.

Poison rose up in him as he opened the door to the past. Not too wide. Just enough that he could share a semblance of it. As the memories slipped out, he grimaced. It was always the same on the other side of that door. Images of his father, hanging. Neck breaking. Of the girl his father had raped and beaten to death sprawled on the drawing room floor. The sick horror of it strangled his throat. He shook his head and slammed that damned door shut. He couldn't tell her. Not Mary, not when she had been so brutalized.

Her hands came up to his face, the soft palms caressing his cheeks. "Edward. Say it. Whatever is causing you such pain, say it and you shall be free of it."

He rested his face against her palms for a moment, desperately wishing to give in, but if he did, he would lose her. He might even lose himself. Jerking away, Edward faced the fire.

"Why are you so afraid?" she whispered.

"I am afraid of nothing," he snapped, bracing his palms on the mantel.

"Fear and I are intimate acquaintances, Edward. You are in its bed."

Her words struck like knives. He dug his fingers into the carved marble, starting the trickle of blood again from the scratch on his hand. "Stop."

She came up behind him, her strong presence lingering only an arm's length away. "We cannot live our lives in fear. You taught me that."

"I am not afraid," he growled.

"You are afraid of what I will think or say," she countered.

"You are calling me a coward."

"You are only a coward if you live in fear. And that is not who you are."

Edward hung his head, the weight on his shoulders so heavy that at last he could not bear it. "What do you know of who I am?"

"I know you are strong, and powerful, and though you wish no one to know it, you are good."

At this, a harsh groan tore from his throat, one that

belied her supposition that he was good. Edward lifted his head and glared back at her, letting the full weight of his torment fill his eyes.

She blanched and took a small step back. And there it was: fear in her eyes. Fear of him. And she wanted to know the truth? For all her bravado, if he told her . . .

"Edward . . . Whatever has hurt you so badly—?"

Anger rippled through him so fast and hard he could not stop the eruption of words that burst from his throat. "What do you wish to hear? That my father was a monster? That my mother was a conniving and brutal whore? That I am the child of such a union? That I come from a long line of sadists? That I have fought all my life to ensure I didn't become like them?"

She did not step back but rather reached out toward him. "Edward—"

"You wished to hear," he mocked, throwing up a barrier between them, unwilling to let her touch him. "But let me tell you—it is not fear that stops me, but shame. Shame of who I am."

"You told me once that you no longer experienced shame."

He had. And he'd thought he meant it, but now, standing here, he knew it wasn't the truth. He'd simply buried it.

When he didn't reply, she let her fingers flutter to her side. The earnestness on her features was as powerful as any touch. "Who you are is beautiful."

He longed to sink into her care and not expose her to his darkness. "You might not think so when I tell you what you desperately long to know."

She remained silent, the only sound now the crackle of the fire and the howl of the wind at the window.

He'd come too far in his own stupid raging to stop.

Somehow, she'd caught him up in something. For all his resolve, she'd won. "My father raped a fourteen-year-old girl with such violence, she died. It was brutal and bloody."

That strong, shadowy gaze that had captivated him the moment he saw it widened, but she still said nothing . . . Nor did she retreat.

God, he longed to. To hide from this moment. But he'd gone too far now to stop. He squeezed his lids shut, evoking the horrors of the past, but the image of blood and ripped flesh flicked them back open.

"My mother procured the girl for him. She wanted to keep my father so intensely, to keep him hers, she was willing to pander to his every desire." That twisted need of his mother's had ruined her, left her a shell of a woman, and he wondered whether his father had ever truly given her the love she had been so determined to keep.

Edward bit the inside of his cheek until the iron of blood flowed over his tongue. The pain was the only way he could force himself to remember. "I'd only started at Eton and come home early for holidays. As far as I understood, my mother had promised the girl a place in our household. This, of course, was not the case."

"I wasn't supposed to be at home." He spoke the words, but it was as though someone else was uttering the phrases as he disappeared from the room and plunged into memory. "I heard the screaming. I ran toward the sound."

Edward closed his eyes again. The blond girl was on the floor, naked, her chemise cut away from her pale young body. There had been slashes along her thighs. The wine stain of blood had blossomed from her temple through her silvery locks. "Th-there was so much blood. So much. My mother was babbling how my father had gone too far and what were they to do."

Mary's fingers came up and stroked his shoulder, but he couldn't bear the attempt at comfort, not in this memory, not when he could still smell death and hopelessness. So he shrugged his shoulder away from her soft hand. He drew in a ragged breath and went on. "I ran to the girl. She was still breathing ever so slightly. But my father grabbed me and forced me from the room. I didn't know what to do. Who to tell. So . . . I told no one what I saw. But it didn't end there."

Tears—god-awful, womanish tears—stung his eyes. If he wasn't careful, a torrent of his grief would pour forth from the dam he had kept erected for so long. He swallowed back the acidic taste of sick before continuing. "The girl's father came to find her, to defend her honor. My father disposed of him."

Unable to bear it any longer, Edward opened his eyes and stared into the flickering fire until his pupils burned to the point of blindness. It would have been so much easier to believe that none of it had been real, but the pain of it carving out his heart tore apart any such consoling fantasy.

"You see, when the constables came to investigate the disappearances . . . this time, I knew what had to be done. I—I told them everything." He smiled a tremulous mockery of a smile. "I still recall my father's face. Sheer disbelief marred his countenance. I was his son and heir, after all. What son betrays his father?" He choked on the pain of it but forced himself to finish. "In the end, it was my testimony that condemned him. They kept the worst of it out of the papers."

Shaking, eyes wide, Edward could not exorcise the memory of his father's blackened tongue lolling out of his purple face, eyes bloodred and bulging. That hellish vision would never leave him.

"And your mother?" Mary asked quietly.

"She tried to destroy herself. She failed," he said factually. "She lives in the country." His voice broke and he had to wait several moments before he could finally confess. "Servants watch over her."

What else could he say? Nothing could soothe this moment into something bearable, but now he'd gone to the edge of memory and needed to put the last nail in his own coffin. "So that is who I am. Who I belong to."

"Edward, you are not your father." Her voice came like rain upon the parched earth. "Or your mother."

Edward threw back his head, wishing he could drown himself in the comfort of her voice. But there was no comfort for him now. Staring up at the wood-beamed ceiling, he let out a harsh sound. "But I am of their making."

She came up behind him and placed her curves against his, holding him, attempting to make them one. "How can you say so?"

"I didn't save her. I did nothing," he growled, his voice reverberating off the crystal chandelier. A tear slipped down his cheek and he dashed it away lest more follow. "I let my father push me out of that room. And—and if the constables hadn't come, I would have told no one. I would have allowed him to get away with it. What if he'd done it again—?"

He shoved back from the mantel, breaking their embrace. He turned to Mary, hoping wildly that even she might be able to explain his behavior. "How could I have done that?"

"You were little more than a child," she protested.

He shook his head at the feebleness of her argument.

How many others had tried to convince him thusly? "I should have stopped it." There was no excuse. And that was his hell. "I should have taken a pistol or fire iron or whatever it took to stop my father. I should never have kept his secret. Not even for a moment." Edward grabbed her upper arms and shook her, willing her to understand what he was. "I did nothing. *Nothing.*"

Mary grabbed hold of his biceps and commanded sharply, "You listen to me, Edward Barrons. You are no more to blame for what happened to that girl than I am for what happened to my mother."

His memories stuttered. What the hell could she possibly mean? The words were out of him now, but he felt no better. In fact, he felt coated in misery. Coated in a memory he had not fully allowed himself to visit except for in his dreams. "I failed that girl," he whispered as his throat began to close. "And now, I begin to think I will fail you."

Her fingers stroked up his arms until she clasped them around his neck. "You must let go of this guilt."

The feel of her was the only balm he had ever known, yet he couldn't quite bring himself to wrap his arms about her, not when he was finally seeing himself so clearly. "I can't."

"If you don't, it will obliterate what is left of you."

He was going to fail her. It was as certain as the setting sun. "Can you forgive and forget what your father has done?"

She narrowed her eyes slightly. "'Tis different. He never suffered for his crimes."

"When he has suffered, will you forget then?" He should keep these thoughts to himself. The bitterness, the anger—now that he had opened that prison in his head, all the torment seemed to be pouring out.

"Yes," she said vehemently.

He shook his head wildly. "No, you won't. This is what I am trying to explain. I don't regret testifying against my father. But what I do regret is never letting it go, of always trying to find more justice. If you can't move on from this, you will dream of him until the day you die because it is half of who you are. Revenge leaves you dead inside."

She cocked her head to the side as she reached up and attempted to smooth his brow. "I *will* move on with my life. Away from all that I have seen and done."

"Even though I wish it, you will never escape the past if you continue on this course. I was a fool to have not seen it immediately. For too many years I have lied to myself, but no more. Because I didn't let it go, the past owns me. So please listen."

Her face contorted with anguish. "Edward, after all you have done for me, after all this . . . I must ask again. Why are you doing this now?"

"Because you demanded to know what makes me the way I am. If you had not insisted, I would not have told you. But I see you on the same path, choosing to believe justice or vengeance will give you peace. It won't."

Her lips tightened. She tore her hands from him and thrust them over her ears as she lamented, "I will always hear your words now. The threat that I will never be free."

Edward's hands dropped to his sides, empty. "Forgive me."

"At long last, we have found something that can't be forgiven." Her fingers slipped away from her face as tears sprang into her eyes. She shook her hands, ridding herself of his poison. "You are stealing back the hope you gave me."

She had demanded to know his innermost hell, yet

he should have kept it locked deep down in the blackness of his unsalvageable soul. There was no more selfish bastard than he. "Please—"

A sort of panic whitened her already pale features as she backed slowly away from him. "This evening has painted me the greatest of fools. I always knew that it was not me you wanted or truly hoped to right. I was a means to some end of yours. But I was so wrong. Oh, god, I was wrong." Her voice pitched up. "I needed you for protection. You needed me for retribution of some kind. But in the end, Edward, we are only using each other. And you're right in this—it's time we stopped."

Chapter 22

The silence between them was full with her hope that he would negate her words, but he couldn't. Because in the deepest part of his heart, he was afraid that they would never be able to defeat their demons. No matter what they did. And she was correct. They had been using each other.

The hollows of her cheeks, which had begun to fill out over the past weeks, intensified and her violet eyes—eyes that had ripped up his heart—stared with vacant acceptance. "I had thought that perhaps you had seen some part of me that was beautiful. Some part of me to love, and for a long time now I have believed that I would never be worthy of love. That there was something so wrong with me that my father sent me away. That I was ruined beyond loving with what had been done to me. I want more than just an *arrangement*. You will never give me that. By your own admission."

More.

He didn't know how to give her more. He'd let her in for brief moments, confessing his past, but the pain of it was so great he never wanted to discuss it again.

Love meant pain. Hadn't his parents shown him that?

Oh, he'd had a sick alliance to his mother and father. Duty and kinship had drowned him in guilt for betraying them. But love? Love the way she meant it. He had never, nor likely ever would, experience it. "I am sorry."

It was not what she had so wished to hear. Her face creased and her chest heaved as she let out a broken sound. "I cannot stay here. I cannot. I—" Her breaths came in great waves of anguish. "We have lost our understanding."

Something rose inside Edward so fierce that it nearly blinded him. "I don't care if you are using me, Mary."

She lifted trembling hands, appealing to some invisible power before she fired out, "You should care. What are we if we are just using each other? Parasites. That's what we are."

Edward took a step forward, wishing he could hold her to him until all was at peace again. "It doesn't matter."

Her hands pressed to her temples. "Do you hear yourself?"

"Mary, whether you wish to hear it or not, whether you agree about vengeance or not, you belong with me. You belong *to* me. It doesn't matter if it's not the love you so desire."

"Yes," she sobbed, "it does." The pain on her face contorted into a calm determination as she drew herself up and dropped her hands to her sides. "Edward, the only person I *belong* to is me."

And with that, his Calypso darted from the room.

"I won't thank you, Powers," Mary clipped as her stomach twisted into a snake, coiling with determination and regret. The nauseous feeling didn't direct her back toward the house, from where Edward had no doubt seen them enter the stables.

The dank smell of hay and horseflesh and the heady scent of rain clouds surrounded them. Mary drank it in, dreading and simultaneously savoring her impending escape. Now she just had to rid herself of Powers and be gone.

The viscount towered above her, his blond hair glowing pure silver in the moor's moonlight. "And I can't help the gnawing feeling I am making an irreversible mistake."

Mary arched a brow, every limb, every essence of her tired and so bitter she could manage nothing more. All she longed for was to climb onto the waiting gelding and tear across the heath. "You? You don't make mistakes, my lord."

Powers's glacial eyes stared into hers with the power of some eternal being. "Let me go with you. Please, Mary."

Her breath puffed out white in the cold night. *Please?* "Powers—"

His usually so impassive face softened, showing her a face without a mask. "I'll never forgive myself if you go alone."

She eyed him carefully, sure this was some ruse. "I'd no idea you had such qualms of conscience."

Powers's gloved hand came up and paused just by her cheek. "There is much to me that I don't show the world."

Mary's skin prickled with the intensity of his gaze and the promise of his touch. The possibility of his hand cupping her cheek was harrowing enough, but it was his look that devoured her. There was no mockery, no promise of bite. Just the clarity of a man about to throw himself into the abyss.

"I realize now I must do this alone, my lord." Slowly, she lifted her fingertips to the charcoal sleeve of his riding coat, lightly pushing his hand away. "And Edward will need you."

Powers melted under her touch, the ice sliding away

from him. His big body closed the gap between them. His head bent down, closing several inches of the considerable distance between their faces. "He will hate me," he whispered.

"No. He won't. And I must go. It is right." The words tore at her throat—if they had had physical shape, she was sure they would have left her windpipe bloody, like flesh raked with thorns.

His strong hand closed over hers, his fingers as large as Edward's, as warm as Edward's, and as sure—but wrong. "I am not here with you now because it is right," he said.

"Then why?"

Powers's sensual mouth worked, the conflict on his face revealing he was just as much at odds as she. "Because if you two cannot be together, then perhaps . . ."

Without warning, Powers dipped his head down, his scent of erotic spices and leather surrounding her.

Mary froze, unable to believe what he was about to attempt. Just as his lips were about to caress hers, her wits barreled down upon her and she stepped away. With a determined growl, he caught her shoulders, keeping her firmly in place. She jerked her head to the side and his lips smeared across her cheek.

At the failed kiss, Powers hung his head for a moment, resting it against her forehead. Only the sound of his ragged breathing pierced the night's silence. "The unthinkable is happening to me, Mary."

It took everything she had not to slap him, for betraying Edward with such ease. "Have you lost what little sense you have?" she hissed.

"I set out to seduce you . . . To prove to Edward it could be done."

If she'd been a fanciful woman, she'd have sworn she heard her heart breaking. But she wasn't fanciful and she shouldn't have been surprised. Yet the pain sliced right to her bone. Still, she hoped . . . Perhaps Powers had done it entirely of his own accord . . . "Did Edward know?"

"Not in words, but I think he wondered."

She had known that Edward's soul was strangely bruised, had let her heart open to him in spite of that, but she had never considered he might have doubted her loyalty.

"Mary," Powers said, his breath teasing across her cheek. "I am coming to care for you."

She snorted. "That is a ludicrous thing to say especially after your previous declaration."

He lifted his head, his blond hair flicking over his furrowed brow. Hopelessness shone from his cold eyes. "I thought it would be so easy to defeat you . . . but every moment I spent peeled away my resolve. I found myself feeling not apart from you, but one."

Not apart, but one. Mary bit back the answer that she understood. "I can never care for you in that way."

"Let me come with you." His icy eyes were piercing in their intensity. "I will protect you. I know you. I know you as no one else can. And perhaps out of this, there could be love."

If she could have staggered away, she would have, but he held her with a fierce need. Now there was nowhere to run. Impossible though it may be, he was offering her what Edward never would. And the pain was enough to nearly break her. Her veins seemed to close, turning her blood to frigid liquid.

How had her life come to this? How had it come to such a painful decision in which, to save herself, she'd have to betray the man she loved? But there it was. Edward would never love her. Without him, she still needed revenge in order to be free and Powers would be a perfect ally for such a thing. She lifted her chin, ready to make the most treacherous deal of her life. "If you take me to my father, I will let you accompany me."

His grip hardened. "Absolutely not."

Her resolve tempered to something so hot she was amazed that she could endure the burn of it. "Then I go alone."

Powers pulled back and drove a hand through his wild hair. "Damn it, Mary."

"Please do as I ask. The man who helps me in this will always have my gratitude." She hated herself with every word. She was just as dangerous as Powers. She had become someone who would do anything, say anything to gain her vengeance.

Perhaps she'd been a better student than even Edward could have imagined. But she wouldn't regret it. Not now.

For the years she'd lost, beaten and broken in the madhouse, and for her mother, bullied and stolen from this world too soon, she'd proclaim words she didn't mean.

Powers's face turned grim, but he said nothing as he offered his hand to toss her up onto the saddle.

She slipped her knee into his cupped hands and grabbed the reins and a bit of the gelding's mane. She was in the air, flying up, and then she landed softly on the polished leather.

"Wait for me," he said.

Powers headed down the stable yard and chose a russet stallion. It took little time to saddle the horse; then he mounted it. Grim determination lined his eyes and mouth.

He returned to her and said, "Perhaps we are both mad to do this."

There was something unspoken, though. The word

"mad" stung, but Mary couldn't argue. She was ruled now by something far more powerful than she could ever have imagined. The need to avenge herself and her mother. And for that, she'd leave everyone else behind.

In Powers's haunted gaze there dwelled a broken hunger, and if she were a better woman she would have pursued it. But right now all she cared about was driving a wedge between herself and Edward so permanent that he would let her rot before coming for her again. For if he came for her, she didn't know if she'd have the strength to deny him again.

No matter that he wished to own her.

She let herself take one look back. Candlelight glowed forth from the windows of the house, beacons in a sad, cold world. Though Edward would never love her, he would always be with her. As long as he was alive. As long as she knew he was out there somewhere, standing upon the same earth as she, she would be content.

She sat silent, her back rigid while she snapped the reins. The gelding raced out under the low black sky full with the promise of slashing rain. As she cracked the reins again, the gelding beneath her surged faster, eating up the earth beneath its hooves. Riding away from her heart and its master in the house behind them.

Chapter 23

The torchlight outside the coaching inn sputtered under the torrential downpour, its glowing fire barely penetrating the ebony night. Barely lighting the road that led back to Edward. Arms limply at her sides, Mary glared out onto the soaked moor bordering Yorkshire. Loss pressed at her throat so crushingly she could barely swallow.

Powers's Northumberland estate was far enough from London that it would take a significant journey to reach their destination. They'd only made it to the Durham county line.

With a sigh of resignation, she turned away from the mud-slogged yard and entered into the long, tunnellike passage that led past the courtyard and through to the inn beyond.

Powers was negotiating accommodations somewhere within.

Frankly, she would have preferred to keep riding. If they'd thought the horses could have traversed the roads, she would have pushed forward.

Now that she knew what she wished to do, anything that stood in her way was infuriating. She'd waited long enough to confront her father. It seemed unreasonable that rain should hold her back now.

The dreary light and the rushes beneath her feet

gave the small passage a closed-in feel. She shivered. On such a night, the inn was most likely packed, but given the lateness of the hour, most of the occupants had turned to their beds. The stillness, punctured only by the drumming rain, was disconcerting.

Boot steps entered the passageway behind her. She was tempted to glance back, but she kept her gaze ahead, even as her skin prickled with an intense awareness and her own breath suddenly boomed to the volume of thunder in her ears.

Increasing her pace, she attempted to ignore her follower, but once the dull thud of footsteps continued down the passage, she could not. Rapidly, she assessed her options. She could run or scream for Powers, but he might not hear in this storm.

There was but one choice. Mary whipped around, confronting her follower. Despite the fear brewing within her, she forced herself to stand strong and throw her shoulders back.

A gentleman, his russet hair glinting copper, stood in the amber glow of torchlight. His long riding coat dripped with rain and he inclined his head slightly.

She didn't return the gesture. A deep foreboding slid through her. She turned back to the inn and increased her pace. His steps matched hers. Fear gripped her heart in its brutal fist.

Mary slipped her fingers around the ivory knife hilt at her waist.

"You didn't truly think you could run, did you?" the voice called behind her.

Anger . . . Anger so intense she could barely see wrapped her up and spun her around.

His eyes flared in surprise.

"I'm not running," she hissed.

"That will make this so much easier," he said non-chalantly. With one gloved hand, he slid a folded white handkerchief from his pocket.

Mary sucked in a slow breath, commanding herself to wait for him to draw closer. "Hardgrave?"

He inclined his head again. "You and I were always going to meet, Mary."

"Yes." She would keep still. She would not bolt or act too soon.

"Now come with me." Hardgrave smiled, a private joke in his own twisted head. "And all will be well."

"Well?" she mocked, shifting slightly, moving her weight to the balls of her toes. "Have you ever lived in an asylum?"

"I lived in St. Giles. Not much difference, I should think." Without warning, Hardgrave darted toward her, the handkerchief fluttering in his hand.

Mary countered his movement as she yanked out the knife Powers had given her. She didn't allow herself to think of anything but freedom as she took a balanced step and arced the knife up across his open chest. As she brought the knife back in the swinging figure eight pattern, she changed the balance of her feet, moving away from him with the ease of water pouring over stone.

Hardgrave winced and recoiled. He gaped at the twice-sliced material across his chest, his face broad with dismay. His head snapped back up and rain droplets sprayed into the air.

Panting now, Mary feinted right, then struck, intent on gutting the man who'd come for her.

Now aware of the skills of his opponent, Hardgrave slid back fast, then dropped to one knee and barreled his fist with an abrupt swing to the small of her back.

A scream tore from her throat as pain erupted in her kidneys. The blow knocked her facedown. As she flew toward the floor, she thrust the knife out so she wouldn't fall on it. Her knees slammed into the rush-covered stones. Her bones seemed to crack as her teeth clattered together. The world swung on its hideous axis as vomit teased the back of her throat.

"Mary?!" Powers's shout thundered through the passage.

She tried to twist around, but her skirts were caught about her ankles. "Kill him!" she screamed.

A shot cracked through the small space, accompanied by the acrid scent of gunpowder. Horror raked her with its merciless talons. Who had fired that shot? Disoriented, her blood pounding so hard she couldn't hear anything but its wild rush, Mary scrambled to get up. Her knees wobbled and she staggered as she stepped on the hem of her gown.

Before she could establish her footing, a gloved hand padded with a handkerchief slammed down over her mouth and nose. Another arm wrapped around her middle, dragging her back against a broad chest.

She struggled against the hold, arching wildly away. But that hand held down tighter over her face, and as she gasped for air, the strangest scent filled her nostrils. She gasped it in, her mind whirring with light and shadow as she tried to recoil and see Powers.

Tears stung her eyes as the flickering torchlight guttered away.

Where was Powers?

Her vision dimmed in rapid degrees. She struck out slowly, futilely. Her body moved with the aptitude of one swimming through seaweed-strewn waters. Even the panic that had so wholly gripped her faded away and her body relaxed. She began to float. A sensation she knew all too well.

She was being drugged.

Hardgrave picked her up off her feet as he fought for control. As he shunted her, she spotted Powers. His white-blond hair glowed golden against the dull rushes and his black riding coat lay flung about him like a broken angel's wings. There was no movement to his massive body.

She refused to let it register. That he was dead. Instead, even though her fingers were numb around the knife, she turned it in her palm, aiming the blade back. With one solid jab, she drove it into Hardgrave's flesh.

A grunt echoed behind her and then her wrist was in his grip. Her pale hand flew forward. She watched as it crashed against the wall, her fingers opening and releasing the knife. She didn't feel the pain of mashing flesh or grinding bone. She didn't feel anything except . . . at last, regret. She'd killed Powers and she would never see Edward again.

Chapter 24

"**M**y dearest Mary, we are so relieved to have you back in our keeping."

Mary longed to cower against the dripping stone walls of her cell and lose herself in the shadowy light of the windowless room. It was what she would have done when she'd been a prisoner here weeks before. But she was no longer the girl Mrs. Palmer had tried to destroy.

It didn't matter that they'd left her in isolation for almost a week with no company but the contemplation of what Mrs. Palmer was planning for her. And thoughts of the loss of Edward. She'd learned to pretend that she had never had a rending conversation with Edward. The illusion gave her a solace that allowed her to control her fear, honing it to a sharp steel edge. So now she squared her chin and replied, "Not as relieved as I."

Mrs. Palmer's brows rose slightly, creasing her usually implacable brow. "Indeed?"

Mary slid her bare foot across the damp stones, taking the step with a sort of swaggering confidence only the deadliest creatures displayed. "For now I need not travel to kill you."

A laugh rippled from Mrs. Palmer's throat. "Your delusions were always most amusing." She glanced back over her shoulder, the folds of her simple skirts swaying. "Matthew?" she called.

Sick little fingers wound their way into Mary's heart and she froze, relentlessly still in her thin, scratchy shift. He was dead. She'd killed the keeper. She'd plunged the rusty metal into his corpulent flesh. He'd fallen at her feet.

Mrs. Palmer cocked her head to the side as she folded her slim fingers before her, ladylike as ever. "You do recall Matthew?"

The wood door swung open on its creaking black iron hinges and Matthew lumbered through. With his size and girth, a slow lumber was all the lout could manage. The hate in his dim eyes promised retribution.

Mary found herself swaying backward as if she could somehow escape him, but all that was behind her was a stone wall at least two feet thick. And if she took a step back, it would be the first of many steps back to that broken girl she'd been before. She would never do that.

She dug her toes into the frigid stone floor, willing herself not to give away any of her hard-won self. But 'twas not easy as the stench of animal fat and unwashed flesh wafted toward her.

Matthew had not altered in the last weeks, nor had he likely bathed. His dirty brown hair lay in greasy tracks over his thick forehead and his dull brown eyes glared down at her with promise. A promise to exact revenge for her temerity in wounding him.

Mary gave a wry, mocking bob of a curtsy. "Matthew. It would seem the devil didn't want you quite yet."

The flesh under Matthew's eye twitched and he took a menacing step toward her, his black boot clomping. "Nah, Mary. He wanted me to fuck you for him."

Mary squared her shoulders, then slowly lifted her hand and summoned Matthew farther forward with a determined wave. "Come on, then. Let's see you make the attempt."

His animal eyes sparked with surprise. His wards normally trembled in his presence. They never challenged him. His confused gaze shifted to Mrs. Palmer. Something about Mary had changed. Even he, beast that he was, could see that.

"Mary, now that you've had time to contemplate your position"—Mrs. Palmer reached into the deep pocket of her skirts and pulled out a small tubular device—"we have a gift for you."

Mary shifted on her feet and focused on the little thing. "A *gift?*"

"Mmm." As Mrs. Palmer lifted the device, she flicked her finger against the tube, then pushed against a small handle at its base. "It is something new. Something that will help you accept your place in this world."

"I know my place," she snapped, her body pulsing with growing fury. "It isn't here."

A burst of liquid bubbled from the needlelike top. "Of course it is here. And we shall help you recall that. Very slowly."

Mrs. Palmer stroked the cylinder. "You've embarrassed me, Mary."

"You'll understand if I don't apologize," Mary mocked in a tone that resembled Powers at his most cutting.

Mrs. Palmer's nostrils flared slightly. "You've gained an impertinence in your time away from us. A pity, then, that you shall be spending the rest of your miserable life—short though it may be—in this little room."

Even though the walls seemed to close in around her, Mary cocked her chin up and refused to utter another word.

"I've written to your father, making him aware of

your untimely death. This news no doubt cheers him and it frees me to make you an example to the other girls at my own leisure."

Mary eyed the "gift" wondering how it would be used to make her such an "example." "What is that?" she asked.

"It is the newest invention in medicine. Perfect for someone of your temperament. It is a syringe. You see, it delivers the most remarkable of medicines. Morphine." Mrs. Palmer advanced slowly. "Far better than laudanum."

"Better?" Mary hissed. She wished she could lay the woman down and force-feed her laudanum until she choked.

"Let me simply say"—Mrs. Palmer gave an ingratiating smile—"that once I inject you with this, Matthew here could ride you like a May Day pony and you'd not complain."

Rising images of Matthew's merciless degradation of her body spun in her head. In the past, she'd have slipped away into terror, but now those sickening thoughts gave weight to her spine and determination to her desire to thwart them.

But there was something else. Something very serious. If this new medicine was related to laudanum, and they put that poison into her, she would never be free of the demon that screamed and clawed for escape. No one—not even Edward—would be able to help her then.

"I don't want it!" Mary roared. She had rid herself of that deviltry and never again would she touch it . . . even though, as if laughing at her proclamation, that torturous creature within her howled for it. *Take it*, it screamed. *Before you suffer through every moment of this.*

Drawing on the strength Edward had forged within

her, Mary balled her hands into fists and shouted with all her might, "No! I will not!"

"It is not a matter of what you want but of what you need," Mrs. Palmer stated with a hint of satisfaction. "And mad girls need their morphine."

Mary's nails dug into the soft flesh of her palms until she felt the skin give way. "*I . . . am . . . not . . . mad.*"

"Ah. But you are, Mary. And we cannot have you making our lives difficult. Indeed, Matthew must be sure that you are . . . submissive to his will."

"Too afraid to fight me on even footing?" Mary challenged.

Matthew bellowed with laughter, the mirth causing his thick middle to shake. "I loves a good fight, darlin'. But I get that from the other girls. You—" His eyes narrowed from their piggish rounds to the narrow slits of a snake. "I want you half dead. To remind you of your place—beneath me."

Mrs. Palmer shrugged, as if there was nothing more to be said, then gave her a sympathetic frown. "You know how this shall end if you struggle. Make it less painful. Simply extend your arm for me and you will forget."

Mary lifted her arms and folded them tightly over her chest. "Go to the devil."

Mrs. Palmer let out a sigh as she closed the distance between them. As soon as she was but a few inches away, she called, "Matthew, hold her for me."

Mary swung her gaze to Matthew as he strode forward, assessing what she must do. Mrs. Palmer didn't fear her, or she wouldn't have come so close. She was still accustomed to the frightened prisoner. Mary's thoughts came in fast succession and, before she could doubt herself, she cracked her hand against Mrs. Palmer's wrist.

The woman let out a sharp cry and Mary grasped the syringe from her.

Matthew reached to grab her, but as he did she swung forward and plunged the syringe into his arm. She eyed the little handle and instinctively pressed it down.

Matthew's eyes widened and he bellowed with pain. With his free arm, he grabbed on to her, latching her to his broad, fleshy chest.

His hairy forearm squeezed across her middle. She cried out as her ribs pressed inward, nearly buckling at the pressure. But even as he gripped her, she did not stop and forced her fingers to fumble for the club he kept hanging from his trousers.

As her fingers brushed the weapon, his hold began to lessen.

Mrs. Palmer stood gaping, her hands still outstretched, not quite believing what was happening.

At last Mary yanked the club free from his belt. Just as she did, Matthew's arm slipped free from her and he slumped to the floor. His big body thundered as it hit the stones. Mary lifted the club, ready to bring it down on his head, but before she did, she glanced at Mrs. Palmer.

Panic creased the woman's face. "Mary. Do not. Do not—"

"Destroy you? As you would have me?"

"I will help you."

Mary smiled. "Yes, you will."

She was truly free of her fear. She might be alone, but she was not afraid. Nothing was going to stop her now. Not Matthew. Not Mrs. Palmer. And most certainly not herself.

Mrs. Palmer's skin turned a sickly blue white. "You need me to escape."

Mary glanced from her captor to the bolted door. Matthew was sprawled, comatose, upon the floor, but there were other armed keepers downstairs. It was an impossible situation. It was not fear now that crept into her heart but the realization that escape mightn't be imminent.

Mrs. Palmer held out a slender hand. "Come, Mary," she coaxed. "Give me the cudgel. I see it upon your face. You know you cannot succeed in this."

Mary's fingers tightened around the wooden instrument. "Do not tempt me to dash out your brains, madam. Recall—according to you—I am quite mad."

Still, Mrs. Palmer didn't flinch as she said firmly, "Then let us go downstairs."

Downstairs was where the flaws in her escape would erupt. It was a horrible feeling, her sudden indecision. Perhaps . . . perhaps . . . if she took Mrs. Palmer down the back stairs . . .

But before she could give it a thought, footsteps thundered down the hall.

Triumph flooded Mrs. Palmer's face with a healthy flush. "You see, Mary? You cannot escape."

Edward charged down the dank hall, pistols in hand. Blood dripped from his knuckles, splattering into the damp patches upon the stones beneath his boots. A primordial rage pumped through him as he closed in on the door at the end of the long hall.

He did not hesitate as he lifted his booted foot and slammed it against the wood. The surface splintered and crunched. The squeal of the lock giving way screeched through the air and the door flew off its hinges, landing hard upon the stone floor.

The windowless room was a soul-sucking death trap. Pain emanated from the chamber as it did throughout the entire asylum. As his eyes adjusted to the obscure light, he met a sight he could not fathom.

Mary stood firm, half wild. Her hair was spiked about her face and a thin, ratty shift barely covered her lithe body. In her hand she gripped a hefty cudgel.

Her amethyst eyes were fixed on the open doorway. Dread tensed her beautiful features. And the hope that had sprung to life within her these last weeks had disappeared into nihilistic acceptance.

For that, someone was going to pay with blood.

Recognition dawned upon her face. "Edward!" she exclaimed as the dread faded away. "Oh, Edward!"

Though he longed to cheat the distance between them and draw her into his arms, her safety was far more important than his own dangerous desires. His gaze swung to the woman standing opposite Mary and then to the body on the floor.

He lifted his pistol, extended his arm, and pointed the muzzle neatly between the woman's eyes. "Mrs. Palmer, I presume."

The auburn-haired woman drew up her face, a face that might have been rendered by Raphael, not a gleeful satanic deity. "Sir, you are acting without legal means."

He cocked his head as if unsure what she had just spoken, but it was all he could do not to slide his finger a little and pull the trigger. "Legal? You dare speak of legal?"

The woman had the audacity to lift her chin and fold her hands calmly. A damned persecuted Madonna. "All those here are in my special care, approved by their guardians and the Crown."

Edward's blood raced icily through his veins. The hate he had felt but a moment ago distilled into something much more deadly than rage. Slowly he crossed to her, each step a warning.

At last, he paused before her, allowing the mouth of the pistol to press against her forehead. "Let me make plain. While your other prisoners do not have friends, Mary does."

The woman's breath seemed to stop entirely before she replied, "Her father is a very important man and will not be gainsaid by someone such as you."

"Then perhaps I should introduce myself. Edward Barrons, Duke of Fairleigh."

The muscles in her throat convulsed as she audibly swallowed. "Still it does not matter. Her father wishes her here and he is her guardian—"

"I have never hit a woman, but feel I am about to make an exception."

"Edward," Mary said tightly.

He did not move the pistol or look away from Mrs. Palmer's unrepentant face. "Yes?"

"I—wish—to leave—now," she choked out.

Edward nodded. "First . . . I think we shall have to tie this one up." Then Edward gestured with his chin to the body prone on the floor. "And that? What is that?"

"A keeper," Mary whispered. There was such hate in her voice that Edward's stomach curdled.

In a moment, he was transported back to his London house, Mary naked upon the floor begging not to be ravished. Quietly, he backed away from Mrs. Palmer and held the pistol out to Mary. "Take it," he growled.

Her cool fingers slid around the butt without question.

The moment she had the weapon trained upon Mrs. Palmer, any reason within him vanished, replaced by a ravenous need to vanquish. He threw himself atop the keeper's body and pummeled his fists into the man's fleshy face. He hit again and again, red blossoming in veiny lines over his vision. He barely saw the piggish face he beat, only felt the ever increasing urge to pound harder until there was no face left to pound.

The man's arms came up feebly, shoving at Edward's body ineffectually, but his weakness didn't stop Edward. Mary's weakness had not stopped this piece of filth from brutalizing her.

His bloody knuckles impacted again and again. As his breath rammed through him, he did not give pause, hitting left, then right and again and again. Hands pulled at his back, but he ignored them. Lost in the moment of hammering the man who had tortured his Calypso for so long, he ignored everything but the waning life beneath him.

Screams ripped from the man's throat, but it wasn't enough. Not when this man had so nearly destroyed Mary. Edward wrapped his fingers about the man's thick throat and pressed down on the esophagus.

Just as the keeper's face was fading into a satisfactory shade of blue, someone threw a punch at Edward's jaw. A punch hard enough to jangle his brain. Shocked, he momentarily loosened his hold. In that instant, whoever had attacked him hauled him off the beaten mound of flesh.

Panting, Edward blinked furiously, ready to wheel around and kill whoever had interfered with his vengeance.

"Enough, Edward," Powers's calm voice drummed through his brain. "Enough."

But it would never be enough. Nothing would ever be enough to save his Mary.

Chapter 25

Mary couldn't tear her disbelieving gaze from the bloody scene. Edward hung limp in Powers's arms, his face sprayed with blood and flesh. His coat and cravat were splattered with the stuff. And Matthew . . . He was barely recognizable as a human—fitting, since he almost certainly never was to begin with. His chest lifted up and down, proving he was almost as impossible to kill as a cockroach.

One thought blazed through her soul.

He'd come.

Edward had come. Mary drew in such a free breath it was as if she'd been in water since the moment she'd left him behind. In this moment, she could not fathom how she had ever left him.

Her hand trembled and she forced herself to steady and not accidentally pull the trigger. She darted her glance from Matthew's unrecognizable body to Edward and then to Powers. Powers staggered under the weight of his friend, dressed in his muddy riding clothes. His face shone a strange gray under the consumptive light, and beads of sweat slid down the sides of his usually pristine face. All she could muster was a stuttering "H-how?"

Powers hauled Edward to his feet and shoved the duke aside. And Powers, who always seemed so god-like, swayed on his boots. "Hardgrave is a . . . piss-poor . . . shot."

"You look half dead," she said, lacking any better reply. Relief swelled inside her at his resurrection.

"*Only* half."

A grudging grin parted her lips. "Fully dead would have been exceedingly bad."

"Indeed."

Edward glared from Powers to Mary, his eyes glazed. Then he lifted a hand and smeared the blood away from his face. "Still engaged in witty banter, I see."

Mary swallowed back a hasty reply. She was far too happy to see Edward's face to let words fly. He had every right to be angry, since she had gone off with Powers. But could he not see the light in her eyes at his arrival?

Edward didn't look at her as he strode toward Mrs. Palmer. Heedless of the woman's shrinking fear, he took her arm in his grip and twisted her roughly toward Matthew's gruesome body. With his free hand, he shoved her facedown so that she was but inches from the battered flesh. "Now, unless you fancy having your face rearranged in similar fashion, you will comply."

Mrs. Palmer nodded frantically. "A-anything you wish."

A slow, terrifying smile curled Edward's lips. "Good. You see, madam, I have just the place to keep you until the authorities can be made aware of your activities."

"What are you going to do?" Mary asked, wondering if Edward had crossed into madness himself.

Edward's brow rose as if his plan should be altogether obvious. "Put her with her prisoners."

Mrs. Palmer's eyes widened with glassy terror and she flailed against his hold. "You can't!" she shrieked.

Edward shook her until she was limp as a cloth doll. "I can."

With that, he marched her forward as she fought to keep her feet planted. In stuttering strides, he shoved her toward the door.

When Edward had maneuvered her halfway down the hall, Mary turned to Powers. "I—"

Powers shook his head. "He loves you."

Mary bit her lip. "I don't know."

Powers snorted, then winced. "That man would have raced across hell to save you. I couldn't save you on my own, not wounded. My god—you should have seen his face when I told him you'd been taken."

She hardly dared believe Powers. A wavering smile lifted her lips. "You're a good man."

He snorted. "Liar."

"Drunkard," she teased.

"True." His eyes batted open and closed. "Sorry it took us so long."

"You both came. That's all that matters."

"Had to send a note to Edward, then track you—"

"Shh. Shh. I am safe now." Her hands fluttered over his chest, not knowing what to do. "You're not dying, are you?"

"Good god, woman, have some faith." Powers rolled his eyes in exaggerated disdain. "A piddling little bullet would not kill me."

She smoothed back his damp hair from his ashen forehead "Forgive me," she teased, aware that his bravado only hid his hurt. "How could I have been so foolish?"

"Hmph. Well, perhaps if you kissed me—"

"Don't tell me you believe kisses fix everything," Edward said, his form suddenly blocking the dim light in the door.

"One might as well try," Powers replied.

Edward looked to Mary, the anger and danger gone. His gaze searched over her with a sort of desperation. "Are you all right?"

She nodded.

"Then perhaps you could kiss me," Edward said. "I do believe I need a bit of healing as well."

A trembling grin pulled at her lips. She rose quickly and crossed to him so fast they collided. Their bodies came together perfectly as his strong hands clasped her back.

She leaned her head back. "Get your healing, then."

Edward hesitated for one moment, a shadow somewhere still between them.

But none of that mattered now. Not when she'd almost lost him forever. He lowered his head toward her.

"Excuse me, but I'm still on the floor."

Mary blushed. She hated to interrupt their kiss, this moment, but she pushed gently at Edward's shoulders.

"He needs a doctor," she said simply. She'd come to care for the blond bastard who made no demands upon her already strained soul. If she'd had a brother, she couldn't have wished for any other.

"Who needs a doctor . . . when I have an angel?" Powers asked mockingly.

Mary snorted. "You'll be seeing angels if we don't get you help."

"Devils," Powers put in pithily. "Devils, my dear."

Edward arched a dark brow. "I'll make you see devils if you don't shut it."

Powers tried to shuffle away, but he was sweating considerably now and shivering slightly.

Edward bent down, his brow creasing with worry. "Fool has a fever."

Mary took in Powers's pallor in a new and more frightening light. "We must take him away. Now."

Edward pulled his hand back and swiped it over his worn face. "I never should have let him come. But he would not be gainsaid."

"He knew you needed him," Mary offered.

"*He* is still listening," Powers mumbled.

"*He* is fortunate I haven't killed *him* myself. Asking Mary for a kiss and all." Edward shoved his hands under Powers's armpits and hauled him up.

Mary backed away, watching in awe as Edward dug his shoulder into Powers's middle and hoisted the thickly muscled man as though he weighed no more than a slip of a girl.

Edward adjusted Powers carefully so as not to jostle his head or his wound, then started for the door. "Come on, then."

Mary nodded, but hesitated. Matthew was still alive, if not present in the world. She hated him with her entire being . . . but if she left him here he would die. "C-can we send for a physician to be sent here?"

"Mary—"

"Please," she heard herself beg. It was the most confusing thing, pleading for the life of Matthew, but . . . She'd killed him once, and his death twice upon her conscience didn't sit well. "I shan't be able to forgive myself if we do not."

Edward's face softened and a look of pure pain sliced across his features. "You've a beautiful soul, Mary."

Before she could even reply, Edward was striding down the hall. She understood him well enough to know that a doctor would be sent for. And that he would set this hideous asylum to rights.

A beautiful soul.

She stared after Edward's retreating form, strong and unbowed by Powers's impressive frame. She only wished that Edward could see that his soul was as beautiful, if not more so. Until he did, he would never be able to love. Not her. Not anyone.

An unbidden tear slid down her cheek and splashed against her fraying chemise. He had rescued her so many times, but it was he who would never be free.

"I am going to Duncliffe's tonight," Powers boomed most pathetically from the massive bed at the center of the room.

Edward fought back the urge to coldcock the man. Instead, he set his jaw and stared Powers down. "The hell you are."

"Y-you need me," Powers insisted as he attempted to shove himself up onto his forearms and into a sitting position. It took him several seconds, but at last he managed it.

Edward's butler would no doubt suffer a fit if he knew Powers was attempting to rise. The whole house had taken their return to London quite seriously, and the staff was in a flurry taking care of Powers, Mary, and, yes, Yvonne, who had managed to make it back to London in high dudgeon for being left behind.

Edward fought a beleaguered sigh. Fate had delivered a strange opportunity or perhaps curse in the form of an invitation to one of the season's most prestigious balls. Duncliffe always invited him to his events, but it had never occurred to Edward that he would have to face such a thing now. And Powers, of course, wanted to go. "You'll collapse before you get your trousers on."

A look of pure loathing tightened Powers's drawn features. In defiance, he swung a bare, hairy leg over the side of the bed. After he sucked in several breaths, he managed to shove the other free of the blankets. Both limbs dangled over the side of the bed in the childlike manner only fever could induce in such a masculine bastard.

"I am not taking you with us," Edward reiterated, though he was beginning to believe only beating the man over the head with a cricket bat or a bottle of brandy would keep him in bed.

It would have to be the brandy bottle beside the bed. He had no idea when last he'd used a cricket bat. He shouldn't even be taking Mary, but it was her choice, not his, as painful as it had been to accept that.

"You just want to be alone with her," Powers accused, his face mottling with a shocking dose of jealousy.

Edward thrust a hand through his hair, then wiped said hand over his face. "There is nothing more between Mary and myself."

Powers let out a snort so loud one might have thought his brains had exploded out the back of his cranium.

Standing firm, Edward said quietly, "There never can be, old man. Look at what I did to her."

Powers eyed him suspiciously, looking damn foolish with his bare legs peeking out from under the crisp white sheets and his arms shaking as they supported his considerable upper weight upon the down-filled mattress.

"You supported her and I . . . I abandoned her. She's yours," Edward added with as much conviction as he could place in words that ripped his guts out. In fact, he could feel a cold wind in the cavernous regions of his chest where his heart should have been.

"Mine?" Powers echoed blankly.

Folding his arms over his chest, Edward desperately sought some way to explain without baring what he had only so recently discovered about the real nature of his withered soul. "I can't have her."

Powers shook his head slowly, amazement lightening his fevered face. "Do you think her a sack to pass off to another?"

"No," Edward bellowed as he flung his arms to his sides, bunched his fingers into fists, and wished there was something he could punch. If he'd been alone, the wall or even himself would have done. Instead, he forced himself to uncurl his hands. "I— You see," he said, gesturing to himself. "Look at how enraged I become when simply discussing her."

"Forgive my apparent blindness, but I don't see what you are getting at."

"I thought I knew best. I have made so many mistakes. And all I keep doing is hurting her." He gulped back the ugly words that signified his own possessive nature. "I shall be leaving Mary here to be free, once I have completed my assistance toward her."

Powers cocked his brow with the same sort of disbelief one might make upon being informed that his best friend was not a man but an elephant. "Not that I don't enjoy the idea of you never being part of her life again, but I must point out that you are talking lunacy."

"For the first time in my life, I am speaking with utter sanity."

That silvery brow remained quirked in disdainful skepticism. "Go on."

It was clear Powers would not let him skulk off without some sort of explanation. Edward stared down at the burgundy carpet, brought home years earlier from the East. He finally managed, "I drove her to leave me. I put her at utter risk, by being so insistent she do as I wish. But that is who I am. I mold. I push. From the beginning I was so certain I knew what was best for her, and what occurred? She ended up back in that damned place. I am not good for her. For anyone."

That damned brow lowered, replaced by a look of horrified sympathy. "Old man, you are being ridiculous."

"Am I?" Edward shook his head.

"Edward—"

"Look at my family," he rushed, his chest rising and falling quickly as he admitted his inescapable future. "We destroy people."

"You would never—"

"I held a hard line when all she needed was my support and understanding, even if I disagreed with her. I drove her to revenge, and then I took it away. When she acted on her own, I let her go alone. What does that make me?"

For many moments, Powers stared at him, his icy eyes boring through any shield Edward might put up. Powers blinked, then looked away. "I know not what to say."

Edward shrugged, his shoulders as heavy and tired as an old man's. "There is nothing to say. But despite your failings"—he gave a reluctant smile—"many that there are, if she allows, you would take care of her far better than I."

"I—" Powers opened and closed his mouth, but no witty repartee issued forth.

None of this felt truly real. Edward kept forcing himself to speak even though he felt as if he were in a dream. "You will allow her to be herself."

Powers met his gaze and said with conviction, "I care deeply about her, you know."

Edward gulped back the torrent of emotions that battled up from his gut. He nodded sharply. If he spoke, he would curse Powers to Hades and back and then beat the life out of him for daring to love his woman. "Now. Let's hear no more about your accompanying us."

Retaliation boiled back up in Powers's face. "But—"

"I've relinquished her. Is that not enough?"

"No. I don't suppose it is," a soft voice said from the doorway.

Edward's spine cracked straight with dread. He did not turn to look, for he knew she was standing there. How much had she overheard? *How much?*

She walked slowly into the room, cradling her bruised wrist slightly, until she stood just between him and the bed. "Thank you for my freedom, Edward." She hesitated, her gaze sliding up to him from under her thick, sooty lashes. "Though it was never yours to give, now was it?"

Edward's entire body seemed to come alive in her presence. The raging beast within him demanded he roar that, *yes*, her freedom was his to give, for she belonged to him and him alone. "Of course not," he replied quickly. "It was merely a turn of speech."

The smile that tilted her soft lips was cold, the smile of a woman who had seen too much of the disappointing nature of men. "It is very kind of you to assist me in this. I know you didn't have to tell me about the invitation."

"I still wish you safe above all things and it is not my right to make decisions for you. I should have supported your wishes. The least I can do is to see you through this now."

Her brows tilted into a bemused expression. "Safety is a state which I believe is an illusion, but thank you. However, I prefer your assistance in revenge, rather than in my safety."

"You are still determined?" he asked, wishing she would change her mind but already knowing the answer. It had been tempting to conceal the invitation from her father, but that would have been his greatest betrayal of her. Mary deserved to choose her own path and make her own mistakes. Though every fiber of him screamed against it, he would assist her in her quest. He owed her that, at least.

"I am," she said, her chin lifting.

"You wish my assistance, too," added Powers as he struggled off the bed and into a standing position. His nightshirt draped morosely over his frame, hanging about his knees. Though he towered above Mary, he swayed on his feet and the color drained from his already ashen face.

Mary turned her bemused face to him, reached out a single hand, and pushed Powers slightly.

His eyes flared, his arms windmilled, then he tumbled easily back upon the bed.

"I think not." Mary stood over him, planting her hands onto her hips. "As Edward said, you will stay."

"It is not fair," Powers groused, righting himself and his nightshirt upon the bed.

Mary peered at Powers. "I suppose I could wait for you to heal, but I find I have given enough of my time to waiting. Tonight is the night to expose my father, thanks to the invitation."

Edward scowled. Though Mary's father had hired Mrs. Palmer and subsequently Hardgrave, it appeared the old duke thought Mary was dead. Duncliffe had been misled by his underlings, of that Edward had little doubt. Clearly he never would have invited the man who might very well assist his daughter in her revenge. "I have concerns—"

Mary speared him with a determined glance. "I will go alone if you do not feel comfortable."

"For god's sake." Powers groaned.

"No, for mine," Mary countered. "I long to see his face."

Edward nodded. What else could he do? He could only hope that he wasn't right and that tonight Mary would find peace.

She drew in a slow breath. "But first, there is something I need you to do for me, Edward."

"Yes?"

"I wish to see someone." A shadow crossed her face. "I do not know what shall occur this night, and I must see her before I meet my father."

"If that is what you wish," Edward said carefully. "And then?"

Mary squared her chin. "Tonight my father shall have to confess before all London that I am alive. It will be my revenge, seeing all society know him for the monster he is. It shall be most amusing to see him dance that dance."

As Edward stared at the woman who had managed to abduct his heart, he grieved his great mistake. For Mary's heart was hard now, the tenderness gone, compulsive revenge in its place.

And for that, he would never forgive himself.

Chapter 26

"**T**his is not a prudent plan."

Mary ignored the impassioned note in Edward's voice as they stood in one of the long halls of Edward's home. She stared at the closed door, her breath slowing, the whole world slowing. "I must see her."

"Why?" Edward demanded. "I've brought her for you because I can deny you nothing." He placed his hand lightly against her cheek, the gesture so soft it was as if he dared not even allow himself such a brief concession. "But tell me why."

His touch burned against her skin and she longed to turn her face into his palm, kissing it. She didn't. She wouldn't until she heard the words *I love you*. "Because I must know she is well. Because she is a soul lost to the same sea as I."

"I understand."

"Thank you."

Edward gripped the door handle and turned slowly. As the panel swung open, Mary clenched her hands into twin fists, a hint of fear swerving up her spine. Determined, she stepped over the threshold into the dark room, lit only by the flames in the fire.

At first she spied no one, seeing only the rich Oriental carpet and heavy furniture drenched in firelight. Then she spotted the shadow in the corner.

The woman stood in silence, her full skirts as motionless as the long veil over her face. "Step into the light," said the figure, "so that I may know it is you."

That voice. That voice had spoken to her a thousand times out of comfort, out of fear, out of sheer will not to die in a frozen room in a prison devised by the cruelest of God's creatures. Mary slid her foot forward and stepped into the warm glow of amber luminescence. "Shall we speak of Brighton? Of ices and running down to the sea?"

That figure let out an audible breath. "Mary!"

Joy swelled in Mary's heart. "Yes."

Eva flew across the room, her veil fluttering behind her, dark butterfly wings in the dim world. She whipped the fabric back, revealing her Madonnaesque face framed by curled dark hair. A porcelain other-world woman who now glowed with health. Eva's pale hands grasped Mary's, squeezing to the point of pain. "We have been looking . . . My god. Wyndham said you'd gone from the asylum—"

"Who is Wyndham?"

"My husband's friend."

Mary blinked. "Husband?"

"Yes." The strangest look of contentment softened Eva's face. "You recall Ian?"

Ian. That dark-haired man who had come in the night like a savior. She closed her eyes. She'd flung herself out of the coach, and as she landed on the hard ground she'd seen Eva screaming and Ian's face etched with horror and awe. He'd struck her then as the only kind man she'd ever known. A man who'd attempted to save her for Eva's sake. "He proved worthy?"

Eva smiled, an unreserved smile that blossomed in her gaze. "Oh, yes."

Mary swallowed back the touch of bitterness that she had not been as fortunate in love as her friend. "I am glad for you."

Brushing a hand over her slightly increasing middle, hidden by the fabric of the veil, she whispered, "And I am with child."

Mary let out a cry of joy. "Eva, everything has changed for you. I cannot believe how much and how many congratulations you deserve."

"There is one last thing, which you will never believe." Eva's face alighted with a beauty so pure it was painful. "Adam, my son, is alive."

A burst of shocked laughter passed Mary's lips. "Can it be true?"

"Yes, by a miracle of kind servants, he was protected." The joy faded from Eva's face. "But, Mary, it is your protection I now think of. We feared you dead. Wyndham did everything he could to track you but could find no sign." Tears sprung into Eva's eyes, replacing the joy. "I had resigned myself to praying to your ghost."

Mary caressed her thumbs over her friend's hands, assuring her she was indeed flesh. "I am not dead, though some would have you believe otherwise."

"Your father."

Mary drew in a sharp breath. "You know?"

"The information we've received has been small," Eva whispered, the words dangerous, even though they stood alone. "But since Ian and I knew you were the only daughter of a very important man, we were able to use birth and death records to discover your origins. And that your body has been lying in the cemetery these many years."

Mary shook her head at her friend's audacity. Not many would have gone to such lengths, especially when Eva's own safety hadn't been guaranteed. "You are very clever."

"Did you ever doubt it?"

"No."

Eva's brow furrowed. "I visited. The grave."

"Everyone seems to."

Though Mary's comment had meant to lighten the moment, Eva didn't respond in mirth. Rather she said, "I left flowers for your mother."

Mary's heart squeezed with pain, choking her with a sudden desire to cry. "Thank you. Thank you so much."

"Now you must tell me. You are leaving, are you not? This is why you asked for this meeting?"

Mary slid her hands away from Eva's and turned to face the fire. "I—I don't know."

"You must." Eva stepped closer, her skirts swishing against Mary's. "If your father finds you—"

Mary stared into the flames, the bright fire burning her gaze. "I go to see him this night."

"What?"

Drawing in a fortifying breath, she prayed her friend would understand. "He has invited Edward to his ball—"

"The Duke of Fairleigh?"

"Yes, and I am going to confront my father there."

Eva stood in silence. Then she said flatly, "And Edward . . . he condones this?"

Mary shrugged, not daring to voice that Edward thought she should take a different path. "It is what I must do."

Tentatively, Eva reached out and placed a light hand on Eva's shoulder. "I long to see you happy."

Slowly, Eva looked from the fire and held her friend's eyes. "This will make me happy."

Shadows danced over Eva's face. "I couldn't bear it if anything happened to you. Your father, he is—"

"Mad?"

Eva reached forward and stroked an errant lock

from Mary's face, the gesture reminiscent of one she would have made in the asylum. That of an older sister protecting her younger. "Madder than you or I ever were."

Mary said nothing. Not needing to. The truth hovered around them, an ill, portentous specter.

"Do you trust the Duke of Fairleigh?"

"I do."

Eva's tone gentled. "Do you love him?"

It was so tempting to lie. To pretend. But she never had been untruthful with Eva, nor would she begin now. Not when they'd both been given the chance to live outside asylum walls. "Yes."

"And he loves you?"

Mary winced. "No."

A frown pulled at Eva's soft mouth. "Are you certain?"

"Yes." The confession struck at her heart, bleeding it anew with the importance of accepting her position.

"When he came to find me . . . Mary, he cares for you greatly. It is the only reason I came. The only reason I believed he truly knew your whereabouts was because he spoke of you with a reverence that couldn't be denied."

"I—"

"He stands outside that door now, does he not? Ready to come to your aid if I should prove unworthy to be your friend?"

"Yes, but—"

"All the buts in the world cannot change how we feel," Eva said, her voice a melodious beat of truth. "The obstacles may stop us, but he loves you."

She wished she could believe Eva, but she couldn't dare to hope again. To be mistaken would send her down the broken road she'd turned her back on. "I needed to see you because . . . I do not know how this night shall end."

"And if you must leave, you wouldn't leave me without word?"

Mary nodded.

Eva swept her up in her embrace, holding her close, her arms wrapping about her like fierce wings. "Thank you. I have thought on you every day since the asylum. My heart not whole without knowledge of your safety."

Mary dared to rest her head on her friend's shoulder. Surrendering to the safety of the woman who understood what she'd been through. Not as Powers understood, or Yvonne, or even Edward, who had held her heart in his hands, but as one who had lived it, been through it, and survived.

Eva rocked them, slowly, a side-to-side motion as if they were children. "Your father is a dangerous man."

Despite herself, Mary's fingers tightened along Eva's back, fear sliding over her skin.

"You must be brave and you mustn't let him be victorious over you."

"I know," Mary whispered. "But I— What if I fail?"

"You cannot fail, my darling, because you are already free."

Chapter 27

Clare tossed the laudanum back into her mouth and swallowed in one quick commitment. She grimaced. It was bitter and she hated the feeling of being utterly lost after she'd drunk it. The stuff had been prescribed by her doctor at her husband's request. For her nerves.

At first, she'd attempted to dilute the tinctures, unwilling to give herself over to it. She'd tried adding water. But he was far too cunning, or perhaps she was simply not cunning enough. He'd immediately noticed the anemic color through the brown glass. Anthony also measured the bottle and was aware when she didn't take her dose.

Discovery was not worth the risk of defiance.

He'd threatened to have her examined, for duplicitous women were surely weak of reason.

In only a few short weeks' time, Clare had come to understand hate. At least her husband no longer waited in the room to make sure she was dressed properly. He had beaten such fear into her through word and deed that he was utterly certain of her compliance in dress. In truth, she complied with all his wishes now. With each new compromise, she felt her soul slipping away little by little. Soon, she would not recognize herself.

The laudanum left her soaring in a strange sort of bodiless way. She almost didn't care that they were to host a ball this evening and that she would have to pretend her life was ideal. As it was, she barely felt the weight of her silver and lavender gown, a gown he had chosen, one that did not suit her at all.

She had seen a similar gown in the portrait of his first wife downstairs and could not fathom why he would dress her thusly. In it she looked nothing like that exotic beauty whose eyes peered out from the oil painting with soul-stirring allure.

Though almost a decade's difference in style, the guests would no doubt observe the similarities in the frocks. Would they think it was she who was attempting to match the beauty of the first Duchess of Duncliffe?

Minding her step, she swayed from the room, aware she might need to reach out and touch the wall if she should stumble. But she didn't mind. Once the laudanum took its hold, her entire body drifted in a beautiful daze. Truly, she would not resist the substance any longer. Life with her husband was so much more pleasant when she'd drunk her medicine. Everything was more pleasant . . . even the feel of her skin as it tingled with a strange dullness that also manifested a simultaneous awareness. She smiled to herself at the incredibly odd but magnificent sensations.

Just as she entered the hall, she spotted her husband, a man she now knew to be nothing more than a tiger in a human body. What with his fierce white teeth, teeth that could tear one's flesh, he was a rippling predator that stood vibrant at his own door. His suit was so perfectly formed to his strong frame one might have questioned his actual reality in the world of mere mortals.

Hmm. She swayed slightly and blinked, catching herself before he might notice her stumble. Yes. Perhaps he was not a tiger but a forbidding, bloodthirsty deity come down to torture females and any who might attempt to defy his commandments.

Such swirling, vivid thoughts came only in flashing moments under her laudanum doses, but they still seemed so vitally true.

"Are you ready?"

She nodded, extending her wrist dripping with the diamonds and opals he'd given her yesterday. With deceiving gentleness, he folded it into his grasp and led her down the hall. Staring straight ahead, Clare focused on the swish of her skirts and the hoops beneath them.

This evening, the height of London society would pause before her as they entered the ballroom. A laugh teased the back of her throat, but she quickly suppressed the mad little sound. How terribly amusing. They would all be entering her prison, happy little inmates, and yet . . . they would have no idea she was jailed. Not one of them.

The red silk gown clung to Mary's bodice like tendrils of shimmering blood. 'Twas an apt color. Tonight she would reveal her father for the inhuman, bloody monster he was. She fingered the knife resting within the discreet slit made into the folds of her skirts. Powers had taught her to use a blade, and Edward would protect her at any cost. But if she found herself alone and in danger, now she could defend herself.

"You will stay by me," Edward intimated as he gripped her white-calfskin-gloved elbow with surprising firmness, drawing her from her thoughts. The large, buzzing mass of the *ton* separated for him, allowing the young duke and his lady to pass across the wide black and white marble floor of the foyer without even slowing their regal gait. Edward was a prince among men tonight. There was no questioning that he had been born to power.

Self-assurance and entitlement emanated from his entire being. Every woman in the large entry leading to the central staircase coveted him with the fawning desire of a troop of alley cats in heat.

The men also stared. Envy laced their intense gazes as each and every one of them knew they would never be able to compete with Edward's title, finances, or physique. Her spine straightened, her stance proud knowing that *she* was on his arm this night.

Edward took the first stair, pulling her slightly. "Mary? Are you listening?"

The red silk and gold-fringed turban wrapped about her head, which hid her shockingly short hair, brushed her neck as she nodded. "I promise."

And she meant it. Edward would be at her side when she finally brought the culmination of her tutelage to bear. She knew Edward hoped for just a confrontation. A moment of truth in which she could face her father and force the facts out before all of London. But she couldn't predict what she might do when she finally set eyes on her father.

Poor Edward. But it would matter not. His intention to leave her as soon as revenge had been delivered had been conveyed only too clearly that afternoon, even if he had not wished for her to overhear. Once her father was brought to justice, Edward could move on.

She was so grateful that, in the end, even though Edward didn't agree with her plan, he had decided to accompany her. He gave her so much strength.

As they swept up the grand staircase, followed by a tittering horde of London's most important families, Mary's heart sang with a sort of hideous anticipation. Each step unfurled the memory of her father at the top of the stair and her mother plunging down them, her silk gown twisting about her body. Yes, she could recall every moment that had led to her mother's death at the bottom of the stairs. The same stairs that she now soberly climbed.

Not even the bright glow of the crystal lamps could dim that infringing memory.

When they reached the first landing, she froze. Something was there that hadn't been when she was a child.

A portrait, taller than Edward, mounted in a gilt frame hung at the top of the landing. Any who ascended would see it.

Immediately, she snapped her fan open and brought it to her face. The portrait showed a woman in a lavender gown, her black hair curled and artfully arranged around her elfin face. Amethyst eyes stared down upon her as if the woman were beckoning Mary to be a part of her secret world.

She could not breathe. Not under the siren gaze of her mother.

Edward caught sight of the portrait and his step hesitated. "Impossible," he said so quietly it was almost inaudible.

She kept her fan close to her face as she tore herself away from the landing. Many people here had indeed known her mother and she did not wish to play her hand too soon. "Please. Let us move on."

Edward led her up the remaining stairs to the first floor, which, too, was crowded with the full skirts of ladies and the ornamental swords of the officers. Once again, as soon as Edward was noticed, the thick parade of guests began to move apart to allow the duke through.

As though it were the most common thing in the world, Edward escorted her through the gawkers to the entrance of the ballroom. He gave his title and instantly his name was boomed out into the burgeoning ballroom, accompanied by *"Miss Smythe,"* her own amusing alias for the evening.

As they swept through the arched doorway, Mary placed her fingers lightly upon the top of Edward's extended white-gloved hand. She attempted to glance about, but before she could even take in the ballroom she had played in as a child, she was in the receiving line.

"Are you ready to reveal yourself?" Edward asked so low she almost did not hear him amid the muddle of conversation and the sugary notes of the orchestra.

She was going to rip her father from the pinnacle of society and she could barely wait. "I have been ready since the day he killed my mother."

Edward met her eyes. The look in his own black orbs was the stuff of murderous gods. He might not agree with her, but at this moment no one could have been more ready to aid her.

As they followed the other couples before them, Mary spotted her father.

The room stilled and the sound dimmed until she heard nothing but the insistent slam of her heart.

The perfumes of the many guests melded into one noxious scent and her stomach turned, but as she drew in a slow breath her resolve solidified so intensely she almost savored her progress forward.

In the last years, her father had not changed. His jetty hair was brushed back and oiled away from his strong face. Once, she had loved that face with all her childish heart.

He was smiling graciously at the couple before them, offering his hand, bowing as though he were a benevolent being come down to shower his graciousness upon them all. But she knew the true nature of that withered organ beneath the snowy waistcoat.

The woman beside him was a diminutive blond in a gown that bore a striking resemblance to her mother's in the portrait. Her face was a mask of fear, and her eyes . . . Her eyes were glazed in a way Mary knew all too well. A burst of sympathy for the young woman only added fire to her conviction.

As the room came into sharp focus, Mary's entire body simmered with anticipation. Her eyes widened with the bright colors of the silk wall hangings, contrasting with her father's austere dress. The silence that surrounded her erupted with the voices of all around her and the return of the orchestra's sweeping waltz.

Suddenly, her father was greeting Edward with a staid smile upon his handsome face. Edward appeared just as any grateful guest should, bowing his head only slightly to a fellow duke. And then Edward was gesturing toward her.

The racing of her blood did not diminish as she slowly stepped before the Duke of Duncliffe. With deliberate ease, she lowered her fan and sank into a curtsy.

Her father's smile remained fixed for a moment, but then it began to die a slow and painful death. The muscles seemed to collapse as his features paralyzed with disbelief. He stared down at her face, his eyes blank, then flaring to life with the most shocking emotion . . . *love*. Wild, rabid love.

"Esme!" he exclaimed before he reached down and grasped her fan hand with his own. Those fingers clasped hers with fervor, massaging against the glove as if to assure himself she would not disappear.

She could not seem to move as her father's eyes darted over her face, devouring its planes and contours. Then a most alarming thing happened. His reason vanished as did his love. Pure terror shone from his orbs. "Forgive me," he choked out.

Anthony Darrel, Duke of Duncliffe, fell to his own knees before her.

The guests' chatter faded into an abrupt silence. As dominos fall, gaze after gaze turned toward them until even the orchestra's playing stopped abruptly, punctured only by the errant bow of a violin.

"You must forgive me," her father begged.

It would be so easy to torment him. To play the ghost, but that was not the lie she wished for herself and her mother. All she longed for was truth. "Why should I forgive you . . . Papa?"

His face creased into a map of confusion and then dawning lit his eyes. "N-not Esme." He swallowed quickly but did not rise from his knees. "Of course not, my darling pearl."

Tears sprung up in his blue eyes and suddenly her father appeared twenty years older than his true age. His shoulders sagged and the skin of his face slackened. "I miss your mother so much."

This is what he had to say? After years of misery? After he'd sent her away to a madhouse? He missed her mother? She wanted to retort with savage sarcasm that if he missed her so much, perhaps it had not been wise to shove her to her death. Those words she managed to keep back. She had other words to say, after all.

The terror that had briefly seized the older duke slipped away as he murmured, "I was informed of your death."

"A lie." Her lips moved numbly, the whole situation dreamlike, surreal.

Unbelievably, a warm smile lifted her father's lips. "Thank god."

He yanked her forward, pulling her against his smooth cravat and waistcoat as he pressed a kiss to the top of her head the way one might do to a small child. "You are returned to me."

Mary pushed away from him, his very proximity enough to send her insides reeling with nausea. "Why did you do it?" Her throat burned with the demand. "How *could* you?"

"Sending you away . . ." His voice broke before he sucked in a breath. "It was the only thing to do. I did it for your protection."

"Protection?" she echoed. Mary felt no tenderness and she could not help but wonder if this was some performance, like all the other performances he gave to society to hide his true nature. "You sent me to a madhouse."

He nodded but seemed to slowly disappear into memories, his eyes dazed. "I feared you would be mad. I feared you would be like . . . your mother."

Exclamations and gasps filtered around her from those watching, but Mary paid them no mind as she focused on rending every truth from his hateful heart.

Both his hands swallowed her single one up, sending a pulsing ache through her bruised wrists. He leaned toward her. "Say you forgive me. Say . . . say we can begin again. When I heard you died, my heart broke for I never was able to say good-bye." His large hands, cool and dry, rubbed against hers like old, rumpled paper. "Do you know what that is like? To never say good-bye?"

It took all her strength not to tear her hands from his or to give in to the small girl within who so desperately longed for a father's love. "I do."

Relief eased his sagging shoulders. "You understand, then?"

She narrowed her eyes. "Oh, I do understand, for I never said good-bye to my *mother.*"

He blanched but showed no remorse. "Neither did I."

Fury stung her heart and seized her body at his callous reply. "Because you pushed her down the stairs!"

Another titter of gasps and cries surrounded them, but Mary didn't care if their audience devoured their conversation whole. She hoped they would finally see her father for the cold creature he was . . . but perhaps her father still longed to keep his facade firmly in place?

The Duke of Duncliffe blinked and his breathing slowed slightly. "I didn't push her, Mary. Don't you recall?"

She stole her hand from his unbearable touch. "You did."

"No," he countered passionately. This time, a genuine horror lit his once regal face. "I t-tried to catch her. I begged her not to drink so much wine. I begged!" His strong, rough voice pitched up into the shocking whine of one who could not be comforted. "But she would not listen. She would not act the proper wife."

A flash of memories thundered through Mary. Her mother, a crystal goblet in her hand. A laudanum tincture in another. Her mother had almost always carried a glass of champagne or rich red wine. The images fell upon her swiftly, innocent pictures suddenly meshing into something sinister. "No," she protested. "That is not true."

Her father's face creased with grief. "It is. I tried to save her. I did everything in my power to correct her unfortunate shortcomings. I swore I'd save our daughter before she, too, became mad."

"By sending me to hell?" Mary said so calmly she didn't believe she had actually spoken.

"Perhaps it was a mistake," he began. "Perhaps—"

"A mistake?" she repeated. "My life was a living nightmare and all because of your own failings as a man."

"I am not a failure," he snapped, the old anger beginning to rise. "And you will forgive me, as a dutiful daughter must."

She leaned forward and hissed, "You are a failure and I will never forgive you. My mother will never forgive you. No one will *ever* forgive you!"

That rationality which always clung to his exterior evaporated into rage. His fist clenched and hauled back as if he would strike her, but before he could swing, his eyes flared suddenly. The left side of his face drooped and his mouth opened and closed several times in wordless speech while his blue eyes blazed with panic. Abruptly, his entire body jolted; then he tumbled forward.

"No!" she screamed as his body pummeled into hers and then slid to the floor. "No!" she screamed again, not believing he would deny her revenge even now.

Drool slid from the corner of her father's mouth and he lay without moving. His wide eyes stared, pleading for help.

Anger throttled through her, singeing Mary's body. She leaned over him, letting her face linger only inches above his before she cursed him. "You will never be forgiven. *Never!*"

"Mary!" Edward demanded.

Hands grabbed at her upper arms, but she shoved them away as she continued screaming, a relentless chorus of her own hate. "I will never forgive you!"

But her father didn't move or recoil. He remained locked in his pained position, his eyes blinking and his mouth working furiously. No sound came from that mouth and she suddenly wished that he could say something, anything to make her years of pain all vanish. As a sob tore from her throat, she collapsed upon his chest. Her fingers wound into his black evening jacket and an inhuman cry wrenched from what seemed to be the very center of all that she had ever been or could ever be.

The wailing would not stop as she pressed her face into the stiff folds of his cravat. She sobbed for her mother, for the man she had always wished her father had been, for her own broken life devoid of love. Nothing penetrated the great wave of sorrow. Nothing ever would. Of that she was sure.

Even as hands finally grabbed her upper body and hauled her off her father's still-breathing form, she shook and heaved with tears and anguish she could no longer keep caged.

Edward swung her up into his arms, cradling her against his chest. She should have felt safe in that embrace, but she knew it was a temporary comfort. Something that would vanish. Just like everything else she had ever loved, he, too, would go. Had he not said it?

There was one more thing to sob for. And she did. She let the pain come over her, swallow her, and spit her out. Perhaps if she gave herself over to it, if she did not fight the pain any longer, she would no longer be under its spell.

Chapter 28

"**I** shan't be able to carry you, you know," Yvonne pointed out to Powers as they slid along the back streets of St. Giles.

Powers let out a snort. "I've fallen in worse places."

Yvonne peered at the slimy pools on the gritty cobblestone. Her lip pulled back in disgust at the image of Powers lying facedown in one of them. "Hard to believe."

Powers gave a tight gallows smile. "Come, my dear madam. One needn't be so condescending, given your own familiarity with these alleys."

She made no reply. Once, she'd known every place suitable for a quick piece. A professional necessity. Things had not changed overmuch in the last twenty years except the rookery seemed to be even more crowded than it had been in her day.

The din of fiddle and drunken men, women, and children from only one street over could be heard in the silence of this cutthroat path. It struck her as shocking that such a place should be allowed to continue festering, germinating the worst of London's crime. Thank the heavens she was free of it. If she had not gotten out, she'd be dead now . . . or so pox-ridden that only the poorest, sickest of men would have paid for her cunny.

But she was not here for those memories. Oh, no.

She'd returned to St. Giles for an altogether more agreeable circumstance.

They continued down the narrow alley, the lack of moonlight making the narrow space as black as molasses. Death lurked at every doorway and cross alley they came to. It might come from anyone, including the smallest child, in this part of London.

Still, she would not pass this opportunity. And as they made the next left turn toward the Merman's Tail, Yvonne fingered the pistol in her pocket. Her own skin crawled with worry for her companion and, as a consequence, for herself. Powers was truly in no condition to be following, but she could not have gone alone, and he deserved this moment just as much as she.

As they stepped out into the busier, gaslit street, Yvonne hesitated, then jerked her attention back to Powers. His skin blended ominously with his blond hair and each step sent him lurching. Anyone who studied him with any particularity would see him as an easy mark.

Without giving it another thought, Yvonne grabbed his arm and slung it over her cloaked shoulder. "A room, you say, me luv?"

She grinned up at him and started tugging him across the shit-and-trash-covered street. They wove through the stench of unwashed whores and their slightly cleaner pimps with cash in one hand and bottle in the other. And of course there were the drunken customers of gin and slit.

As they made their way around the cart of a hot-chestnut seller, Powers's uneven step appeared to be that of a man deep in gin going after a bangtail who would likely fleece his pockets as well as tickle his cock. In other words, a common enough sight. And though she loathed it, 'twas easier to recall the swagger

of a whore and the businesslike attitude of one escort-
ing a client toward a hasty screw than to risk going into
the red-light inn as her more educated self with a sick
lord on her arm.

They sauntered into the Merman's Tail, her now
blackened slippers kicking lightly at the straw strewn
over the filthy wood floor. She squinted through the
smoke until she spotted the greasy-haired, one-eyed
porter. "A room, pet, if ye please," she said in the accent
of her childhood and former career.

"'Ow long?" he demanded as he turned slowly and
opened a small cupboard hanging upon the cracked
wall.

"Half hour, luv." She dug in her pockets to find the
coin, but before she could pull it out Powers smacked
her hand away.

"Not you, sweetheart," he slurred. "I pay."

The porter smirked, revealing cracked yellow teeth
covered in the scum that grows from years of inatten-
tion. The patch over his absent eye stretched ominously
as he waggled his wiry gray brows. "You got yourself
a gent."

"I 'ave that." She winked at him, knowing full well
he'd expect a cut of whatever she rifled out of Powers's
coat.

"Now give us the damned key, my good fellow,"
Powers drawled, his lips moving exaggeratedly.

The porter's soot-caked fingers scrabbled among the
iron keys before picking one. "Number six, my dear.
Nice room. Just the thing for your fellow."

She nodded, businesslike. "Ta very much."

"Hurry up," Powers demanded in the perfect tones
of a petulant lordling.

"Ah, luv, don't you worry now," she soothed. "I'll
show you a lovely time."

"Better," he said before he let out a wet belch.

Yvonne's brow shot up, surprised that Powers could assume the role of slumming client with such ease. It gave her the suspicion he'd played the role before and not in jest.

She pulled him toward the stair, tightening her grip about his waist, wishing he wasn't quite so big. "Will you be able to handle yourself?" she whispered.

"Don't be ridiculous." He sneered, though the sweat beading his brow belied his arrogance. "I will wait outside and ensure no one disturbs your '*appointment*.'"

They started up the narrow stair. The walls leaned in, crooked. Paint peeled off them, the very image of skin sloughing off a diseased old woman. Each step creaked with their weight, but soon enough they were up to the hall and heading toward a very different room from the one the porter had intended.

A fatty candle sputtered and spun its twisted illumination along the small way, bathing them in dim, dirty light.

Yvonne slowed her steps until they were silent, as silent as the viscount's. Considering he was a man of such large frame, she was shocked to find that she was making more noise with the rustle of her gown than Powers was with his entire being. *How the blazes did he do that?*

Halfway down the hallway they stopped before a black-painted door. She swallowed back the sudden saliva that pooled in her mouth.

"You're sure," Powers murmured. "I could—"

She shook her head sharply. This was one thing she had to do herself.

Powers hefted his arm from her shoulder, then slid a dagger from some hidden pocket and placed it firmly in her hand. "Don't waste time."

Yvonne nodded, astonished at how the silver weapon weighed her palm down. Without another thought, she lifted the catch in slow, silent degrees and slipped into the room lit only by the street's lights.

The shallow breathing of deep sleep drifted toward her and Yvonne focused on the man lying on the narrow cot. Anticipation laced through her body, sweeter than any drug. It also prickled her senses with such a clarity she thought her skin would not be able to contain her insides.

In three short strides, she crossed to the head of the cot and stared down at the man who had shredded her soul and beaten her body to the point of death.

The planes of his brutish face were hard even in slumber and his bronze hair was dull, the color of old blood in the night. With each rise and fall of his chest, she found herself recalling the blows he had rained upon her face and body. But even more so, she could not escape the cruelty he'd spread in the world. How many other women had been broken and, worse, left utterly friendless?

Yvonne leaned over his body and placed the tip of the dagger at his jugular, savoring the soft give of the skin without breaking it.

"Mr. Hardgrave," she called softly.

For such a dangerous man, he was a shockingly deep sleeper—perhaps entrenched in his importance, he had gained a sense of invincibility. 'Twas why Powers had found his location so easily, she guessed.

Carefully, she pressed the dagger just far enough that a ruby tear slipped from his throat.

His eyes snapped open, two glinting ovals.

Yvonne stared into those eyes. "Hello, Mr. Hardgrave."

He said nothing for a moment as his eyes attempted

to flick toward the weapon at his throat, but no doubt the stinging pain told him that one move would see him dead.

Blinking furiously, he lay absolutely still. "Look 'ere. Surely, we can come to an agreement someways?" he rushed, his learned accent abandoning him.

She cocked her head to the side, eyeing that ruby tear trickling down his thick neck. "Agreement?"

"There must be something I have that you want."

"I recall I once offered you an arrangement."

Fear tensed his features and his pupils turned to pinpricks. "Madam, I was just doing my job. It was my duty—"

Yvonne arched a brow and leaned low over him so that she could whisper just above his lips. "And this is my *pleasure*."

In one swift slice she raked the blade against his vein and across his throat. The flesh severed, exposing slippery, glistening sinew. Blood sprayed up, splattering her face.

She didn't wince.

A strange gagging sound ruptured from his mouth and he shuddered. His hands stretched out to grab her, but Yvonne jerked back.

She waited as the life leaked out of his body and onto the filthy pillow and bedding. She should have felt some semblance of regret, but she didn't. Vindication was all she felt as his last breath puffed from his slack mouth and the gaping hole in his neck.

No woman would ever suffer at his hands again. This was a good deed done.

After the last guest had vacated the Duke of Duncliffe's London home, Edward stood in the foyer, wondering how in the hell the night had turned into such a disaster. It had taken far more of his commanding voice to evacuate the guests than he should have liked. London's curiosity had been piqued and by morning the entire city would know that Lady Mary, daughter of the Duke of Duncliffe, was most certainly living and that her father had been the instrument of her disappearance.

He glanced up the wide stair to the woman who was the center of all this. Esme Darrel smiled down upon him, the seductive quirk of her lips promising and playful. What a woman she must have been. How he wished he had met Mary's mother. At least now she would be able to rest easily . . . But as he studied the portrait he could have sworn sadness marred her amethyst eyes. Eyes exactly like his Mary's.

The unease in his chest was hard to bear. The sight of Mary sobbing over her father ripped him asunder.

He had been afraid this would transpire. After coming so far in her quest for revenge, there was no further that she could go. He cursed himself for ever putting the idea into her head.

One emotion superseded his exhaustion and shock: *fear*. It was not an emotion to which he was accustomed and the way it dried his mouth and kept his thoughts at a frantic pace was most unwelcome.

Edward kept his gaze fixed upon Esme, wishing she could speak, wishing she could advise him in how to set all to rights. But her enigmatic visage revealed nothing. How he longed to rail at her that he had done all he could . . .

But she would tell him no, would she not? She would say there was one more thing he could do.

And he had to do it now. Without allowing himself to second-guess his instinct, Edward turned from the portrait. As though Esme was guiding him, he strode down the hall behind the stair leading to the duke's private receiving room. The room he'd tucked Mary into when her father had been taken to his chamber. But with each stride to the woman he loved, fear chinked away at his hope. Had he lost his love to revenge?

He *loved* her.

It was an emotion he'd thought himself incapable of, but in that moment when she shattered under her father's apoplexy, he knew that the wildness in his heart was not just possessiveness but fearsome love. He would have swept her away and cradled her in his arms forever if he thought it would have saved her this pain . . . from her father, from anything.

And that was the subtle message floating from Esme's portrait. It was the one and only thing he could do to finally make amends for his sins and to bring peace to all who had been tormented. Love.

Without hesitating, he opened the oak-paneled door carved with acorns and oak leaves.

It was a strange room. A parlor of sorts, but decorated in ivory and teak with almost no ornament, something completely in contrast with the current style.

The skirts of Mary's gown peeked out, bloody crimson over a luminescent silk fainting couch. Her hands were placed calmly over her tightly corseted middle and she was propped up by several pillows as she stared into the hearty fire.

"I should never have let you do it," Edward said suddenly.

Her face remained in profile focused on the flames before her. "Edward, you and your *let*. You know you could not have stopped me just as you cannot give me to Powers."

"If I had known . . . what would happen— How he would speak to you and then—"

"It was my choice to see him." Mary stared fixedly ahead, her pale skin tinted gold in the firelight.

"I should have found another way. I should have saved you without risking—"

"I wished for revenge more than saving. I made that very clear. I wouldn't listen to you or to Eva." Mary dropped her head back against the pillows and stared up at the ceiling as though they were the celestial heavens and not Adam's plasterwork.

Anger and his newly discovered love consumed Edward with such intensity he couldn't stop himself from storming across the room and grabbing her. He forced her to look up at him, twisting her body upon the couch so that she hung in his grip and faced him. "None of that matters anymore, Mary. The revenge? Our struggle? It is done. I believe we can let it go."

Her eyes flared under his fiery emotion. Slowly, her fingers slid over his biceps, gripping hard. "How can you say so? I—"

"Love," he cut in. "Love is how we are free. Until I met you, I was dead. But then, day by day, being with you, living with you, I have been awakening to happiness."

Tears glazed her wide eyes. "Edward?"

"I nearly destroyed you with my—" He choked on his own shame. "My need to play out a justice that was served years ago and my inability to forgive myself."

Her brows drew together in distress. "Oh, Edward. No—"

"Yes," he burst out. "I gave you my own self-loathing and bitterness. How could I have done that to you?"

Tears tumbled from the corner of her lids, down her pale cheeks. "You don't need to say this."

"I do." His own voice was a rough, half-broken thing to his ears. "Look at how far I've driven you, all because I was afraid to give you love. But I realize now that I am not my father. His actions were his own. I don't have to pay for them anymore. And I can celebrate life now. With you."

Her own face twisted as more tears slid from her eyelids. "I wanted to be free from my father, from it all—" She gasped. "I was so sure confronting him would end it."

"I have been trying to find freedom all my life. Freedom from my own father, from my memories, my mother . . . but most of all myself. You have given me myself again, Mary, and because of that I have the greatest gift that could ever be given."

She shook her head slightly. "I could never give you all that, Edward. I am a broken person. I—"

"We are all broken, Mary, but together . . . you and I are whole. Yes, we used each other in the beginning. But now it is so much more. Out of pain came love." He clasped her up against his chest. Burying his face into the nape of her neck, he said with utter conviction, "You have given me the gift of learning to love. I love you. I love you with all my being. I love you so much, I would do whatever needed to be done to whisk you from this house, revenge, and what the past has done to us."

"I—I never dared believe—" Her face pressed lightly against his head and her lips kissed his hair. "Oh, Edward, how I love you. I have loved you now for some time. From the first moment you called me Calypso I knew you were unlike any other man. That you were special."

Edward pulled back ever so slightly so that he might see the truth of it on her face. "Can you forgive me?"

She beamed up at him and her tears now were tears of joy. "Cease asking. The mistakes we have made, the hurt we have caused, it was all a part of our path to love."

"Promise me. Promise me that if ever I act the ass again, you will not hesitate to tell me and remind me that when I am an ass I am betraying our love."

A shining laugh bubbled from her lips and her eyes sparkled with joy. "Certainly, my love, if you promise to do the same for me."

"Together, then. We shall be whole."

"Yes," she said with such assurance it could never be gainsaid. "You are my other half as I am yours."

"Then kiss me."

And to his disbelieving heart's delight, she did. As her lips touched his, drinking him in, he felt true freedom for the first time in his adult life and it was more glorious than anything he ever could have imagined.

Chapter 29

Clare sat in the corner, silent, wondering how it had been possible for her stepdaughter to so quietly enter the chamber and sit on that bastard's bed.

Clare kept her head back, propped against a cushion, watching through slitted eyes as the beautiful young girl, an image of her mother, laid a hand on her father's still one.

The girl, Mary, leaned over the half-dead duke, and even from across the room Clare could hear the remarkable "I forgive you" come from Mary's mouth. Her hand reached up and gently touched her father's slack cheek. "For all of it. And now . . . we are both free."

Then, without a backward glance at the devil, Mary rose, smoothed her hands down the front of her crimson gown, and quietly left the room. Leaving Clare with her husband.

Slowly, Clare pushed herself up from the silk chair, her lavender gown heavy like death's hand. She had not changed, not even when the doctor had departed. The duke's death was not certain, but nor was his life. The doctor had intimated that the night would see whether he stepped from this world to the next.

The sudden feeling that overtook her moved Clare toward the bed. It was remarkable that her stepdaughter's sudden presence this night should prove to be the means by which she could be freed from her prison. But free she would be.

She took even steps upon her slippered feet, her mind remarkably sharp without her usual dose of laudanum. Though she could already feel the hunger for her medicine building within her, she ignored it. She stood beside the high bed. To her amazement, her husband's eyes were open and he was staring upward. His breath came in slow, shallow takes. "Your Grace?" she murmured.

He blinked, aware of her presence.

She leaned forward and took one of the pillows from beside his head and held it carefully in her hands. "I should like to make you more comfortable."

His gaze flicked to hers and he looked upon her with trust and the sure knowledge that she was his dog. A dog that would never hurt its master, no matter how often it was beaten.

With a muted cry, Clare lurched forward, shoving the pillow against his face.

He struggled feebly, his impaired body shuddering but unable to truly fight back. Clare stared at the simple headboard made from some wood she'd never heard of, nor knew whence it came. She stared at it until her husband struggled no more.

When she was certain the last breath had gone from him, she lifted the pillow. Disbelief and fury filled his eyes even in death. Shock that she had betrayed him and fury that she had exceeded his control. In the end, it had been a simple choice, she realized as she carefully lifted his head and placed the pillow beneath it. Her life or his. And she would no longer sacrifice herself to his power.

Without remorse, she pressed his lids closed, then calmly departed that room forever. Just as she would soon depart this prison of a house.

Yes, Mary had forgiven her father, but somehow she doubted the girl would be overly sorry to hear of his death. As she walked down the hall to the stairs, she paused before the portrait of the woman who had come before her.

Though it might have been a trick of the light, she could have sworn that Esme's beckoning smile softened to one of gratitude. "You're most welcome," Clare replied to that benevolent face, then floated down the stairs, happy at last.

"I am so sorry," Mary said softly.

Powers hesitated by the mahogany sideboard, his fingers splayed over the polished wood. "You love him."

Mary folded her hands together, wishing she could reach out to the man who had become so dear to her. She refrained, knowing her touch would break his strength. So she stood by the windows, all too aware of the spring sun pouring in through the panes, a contrast to Powers's disappointment. "I do. I have done for some time."

"I see." Powers mouth worked with some unsaid piece of drollery before he quickly went about pouring himself a drink from the grog tray before him. "And he loves you."

"Yes," Mary said, wishing there were some way she could relieve his pain.

He took a long swallow of whiskey from the snifter in his palm. "And even if he did not . . . you wouldn't have been able to choose me?"

Though it blistered her tongue, she admitted, "No. I would not have done that to you."

A dry laugh rumbled from him. "Done that to me?"

Mary shifted on her kid slippers, wishing she did

not have to hurt him. "You deserve someone to love you."

Powers blew out a derisive sound through his nose. "My luck with love is so entrenched in misfortune I might as well hang myself."

Mary blanched. "Please don't say such a thing."

He tossed back the remaining contents of his glass and smiled weakly at her. "Of course I don't mean it, my dear. I am far too vain to ever cut short my life."

"And you are recovered?"

"From my fever?" he asked, as if this was the least of things to recover from. "Yes."

"I am relieved." She couldn't help the smile that blossomed on her lips. She smiled so much now. "You have been such a good friend to me."

"We shall always be friends." He swallowed sharply, the muscles in his throat contracting. "Shall we not?"

"We shall. For who else could understand the demon inside me?"

"Then love has not freed you of it?" he mocked.

"You know better than any, that while love might give one the incentive, only one's self can ever conquer the demon."

"You've grown irritatingly wise," he drawled.

"With someone's own wise help," she countered playfully, yet meaning it with all her heart.

"Hmm." He thunked the crystal glass down, then turned fully to face her. "I wish you happy, Mary. You realize, in this whole world, only Edward loves you better than I."

"I know."

"But I think I must go away for a while."

Mary considered protesting, but knew it would do no good. She nodded. "Do not stay away too long."

"From you?" His gaze, always hard, softened. He

studied her face as if committing every plane to memory. "Impossible."

Mary did not rise to his defensive words, but instead she closed the distance between them and took his large hands in hers. She went up on the tips of her toes and kissed his cheek. And then, without another word, he strode quickly away from her and out the door.

Mary stood silently in the room, wishing with all her heart that he would know the happiness that she had only lately discovered. And soon. Somehow, deep in her heart, she knew he would. For only a man who had felt so much pain and sorrow could deserve the greatest of loves.

"Do you think he will be all right?" Edward asked as he walked through the door and to her side.

Mary nodded. "After some time has passed."

Gently, he cupped her cheek. "And to think I almost gave you away to him."

Mary scowled teasingly. "Ha."

Edward gave her a cheeky grin. "You always would have done as you willed."

She pressed her face into his palm, savoring the strong warmth. "Mmm."

He caressed his thumb over her lower lip before angling her face up to his. "And your will now?"

"To cherish you as long as I have breath."

He lowered his head slightly, his lips lingering over hers. "And after?"

"And after." She slid her arms around his waist and pulled his body full against hers. "Always."

Epilogue

It was astonishing what a difference a year could make. Thanks to Edward's influence, Mrs. Palmer's establishment had been permanently closed. The woman had been imprisoned after society learned about the extent of her duplicity.

Matthew, recovered, now languished in a prison hulk.

Yvonne, one of the greatest madams London had ever known, had retired from the world's oldest profession to open a school for prostitutes so that they might learn some other gainful means of employment. Since it was run by a former prostitute and not some hellfire-breathing reformist, the school was a remarkable success.

Mary's stepmother had proved most surprising, heading a charitable committee for the establishment of several homes where women suffering abuse could find shelter and support. She'd become quite a power in society.

And Mary herself?

A smile tilted her lips as she reclined in bed.

Her husband offered her a steaming cup of hot chocolate, his eyes brimming with adoration. "Our daughter is going to have quite the sweet tooth."

Mary took the cup and savored the heat seeping into her hands. "And what makes you certain I am not carrying the future Duke of Fairleigh?"

"Because of the glow in my heart. Her name is Esme. She told me."

"She told *you*?"

Edward nodded, his black hair flopping boyishly as he eased down onto the bed beside her. He nestled in carefully, wrapping his body about hers so that he could cradle her swelling belly. "She did indeed. She intends to be trouble but very loving."

Mary laughed softly, so alight with love for her husband and unborn child she almost couldn't fathom how hopeless her life had once been. "I suppose we deserve nothing less."

"She shall be loved as no other child."

Mary shifted and placed her hot chocolate down on the table beside the bed. "Edward, have I told you that I loved you today?"

"Three times," he quipped as he slid his hand up the base of her throat, then around to cup the back of her head gently.

"Then let me say it again."

His lips lingered over hers, and as she whispered, "I love you," he pressed his mouth to hers.

"I love you, too."

She slid her arms around her husband and allowed him to carry her away with his passion, and the knowledge that no matter how hopeless one might believe things to be, there would always be love to light the darkness.

Read on for a sneak peek at
a tale of redemption and love,
Máire Claremont's

THE DARK AFFAIR:
A Novel of Mad Passions

Available from Headline Eternal in March 2014.

London
1866

Lord James Stanhope, Earl of Powers, was going to kill the ridiculous Irishwoman standing before him. In slow degrees. He was going to kill her for daring to mention his wife. For daring to even whisper his daughter's name. He was going to rip her to bloody pieces for insinuating that he, the son of the Marquess of Carlyle, was insane.

"My lord?" she asked, her voice rising above the howling, barking voices scattered throughout the warrenlike rooms of the asylum.

James blinked. The shadows of the single gas lamp danced over her. His mind abruptly skittered. Skittered to the swish and sway of her pressed gray skirts. The way they molded over her hips and the tiny form of her corseted waist. Astonishing. She was such a tiny thing. Barely coming up to his shoulder. Perhaps she stood as tall as his sternum. Perhaps.

Yes. One of the fairy folk.

Oh, god. He shook his head, but the motion felt as defined as movement through muddied water. What had he been thinking? Oh, yes. He'd been angry with the petite creature. Furious. But now? He swallowed and the room swung on its axis and his body whooshed through the air. . . . And yet he didn't fall. He stayed upright on his boots, planted, despite the treacherous feeling of being adrift. He opened his eyes as wide as they would go and grunted against the unpleasant rolling sensation. "What did you say?"

She stepped forward, her soft crimson hair glinting in the half light. "I'm askin' only that you allow me to call you by your given name, my lord, not for the personal history of your opium exploits."

Christ . . . The way her mouth worked as she spoke . . . Her rich, lilting voice sounded as if she was fucking every single word. . . . Even her pink lips were lush. Soul seducing erotic art. Gorgeous. Slightly pursed. Not for a kiss but in disapproval. He arched a single brow, determined to put her in her place. A damned difficult thing, considering he was the ward and she the interrogator. And the fact that his brain seemed entirely at its own command with very little rhyme or reason to his thoughts didn't aid him.

He hadn't taken any opium in days, but he still felt in the throes of it. It was most distressing. "Powers," he said tightly.

She sniffed. That pert little nose, free of a redhead's cursed freckles, tightened with her own irritation. "That is your title. I ask again that you permit me the use of your name."

In the shadowy light, her skin appeared translucent. He wondered if he reached out and put his hand on her, would it rest on mortal flesh? Or would it slide through her, ghostly female that she appeared to be? "My name was for one woman." Why was it so hard to speak? He swallowed and slowly articulated, "And you are not she."

She cocked her head to the side. Her curls, which

had been smoothed back into a tight coif, slipped free at her temple, dusting her high cheekbones. "And you shan't make me an exception?" She smiled. A pixie, winning, devil's smile. "Lovely lass that I am?"

He smiled back. "I'd sooner rip your arms off."

Her cinnamon brows lifted, a stunning imitation of his own disdainful gesture. "Indeed? And wouldn't that be a great shame, fond as I am of my arms?" She licked her lips . . . not a seductive gesture by any means, for there was nothing suggestive in her controlled demeanor, which exuded propriety from the tips of her booted ankles, up her charcoal frock, to the starched white collar ramming her neck straight. "Don't you see, I wish us to be on equal footing. And if you are unwilling to be gentleman, I shall have to be unwilling to be a lady."

An image of her white body sprawled out naked on the stone floor flashed before him, her pristine gray skirts thrust up about her waist, white legs parted, stockings embracing her thighs. He was going to worship her. Bury his face into her sweet, hot folds. The desire that shot through him was so strong, he could barely countenance it. Yet this woman, she appeared as marble. Perfect. Smooth. Pale as porcelain yet hot. She wouldn't be cold to his touch. Oh no. She'd be wild and hungry and warm, opening herself to his tongue and caresses.

"How fascinating," he said, finding his voice despite his strangely whirring thoughts and wondering if a woman such as she could ever possibly descend to his lack of gentility. "I'd love to see you not . . . the *lady*."

Her cheeks flushed, yet all the same her eyes narrowed around her startling gaze. Good Christ, her eyes were the wicked color of West Indies waters. Waters that had driven men to piracy. Perhaps her eyes would drive him to plundering. Whatever course, he was going to make those eyes heat with fire . . . and once the fire was lit, she would do whatever he bid. She would free him from this prison of madness. A prison he didn't belong in.

"Your mind is in the same gutter in which you were found . . . James."

James.

A pain so deep it lacerated his heart jolted him out of his swaying inaction. He darted forward, his long legs eating up the space, driving her backward without even touching her until she collided with the stone wall behind her. He thrust his hands out, slamming them on either side of her head against the wall. The rigid surface thudded harshly under his palms as he pinned her between his body and the stones. To her credit she didn't flinch, despite the fact he towered over her.

That anger that had driven him forward kept him from weaving or losing his focus as he whispered out his warning. "Call me James again and you're dead."

Only his wife was allowed to call him James. Only his wife. And she . . . Sophia . . . Sophia was gone. Once, there had been another woman—a woman just like him—lost on the road of opium he'd thought might say his name. But that had been a mistake. She belonged to someone else. So no one would ever call him James again.

Certainly, not this chit of a woman who dared enter his cell and treat him like an insect in a box to be speculated over.

"Luckily, I've secured my place with the angels and have no fear of dying." Her chest lifted up and down in quick breaths, her corseted breasts pressing against the imprisoning fabric of her bodice, defying the calmness of her words. Her gaze locked with his eyes, strong, calm, unafraid . . . and intrigued. "You on the other hand seem bound for hell's gate."

"Hell and I are good friends," he growled softly, letting his lips lower until he was but a breath away from her soft siren's hair. "We're always open to new members."

Boot steps shifted on the other side of the bolted thick iron door. His gaze twitched in its direction for a moment. The keepers were out there sensing his misbehavior. Ready to enter en masse and beat him into submission. Usually, it took at least three of them to subdue him.

And yet he knew that out of all the places he could have been sent to, this was one of the best. It galled him he was here at all.

Even with his body so intimately close to hers, she didn't call out for the keepers or order him strapped as the others had done. By now . . . all the men his father had employed to put him in his right senses had run, locking his body up with cuffs and manacles whilst he raged. He let his gaze trail over her face, lingering on those plump lips. . . . He couldn't recall the last time he'd had a woman. Months, at least. He'd given them up long before he'd been put in this cell. He couldn't stand the emptiness of those fucks. But this one . . . There was something undeniably unique, as if she might strike him with her governess's stick, then kiss away his hurts.

She tsked lightly, ignoring his intimidation and attempts to shake away her poise. "What you are doing now? 'Tis only securing yourself in this place." She glanced up, her gorgeous eyes darting about the dank cell, with its damp interior and inadequately proportioned bed. "Is that what you wish?"

He hesitated, considering her words. He wasn't mad. He wasn't. And yet his father had placed him here. For his own good, so the old man had said. A small snaking voice whispered through his head that yes . . . perhaps he was mad. Madder now than any mercury-muddled hatter. The thought shuddered through him, leaving him brimming with fury and pain that this had happened to him. "Your wishes are not my concern."

"Ah, but they are." That careful gaze probed him without mercy. Pushing against his barriers, determined to breach him. "Without my say, you shall wither in these rooms."

Who the hell did she think he was? He slammed a palm against the wall, unwilling to be handled. "You can't keep me here."

She blinked once, but then cocked up her chin, defiant. "I can."

He swallowed hard, and blinked rapidly. The ability to focus his thoughts under her onslaught of information was unraveling. Quickly. The need to get rid of her, to make her leave him here so that a woman of such beauty and poise wouldn't see him in such a disgusting state, sent him drawling, "Sod off."

Apparently the insult was of no new occurrence, for her countenance remained untouched. "Now, you're not actually thinking such uninspired drivel assists you?"

How long had she been doing this that she didn't care he treated her thusly? How many men had insulted her? Attacked her? Fucked her body in their minds? The very notion was galling to him. In fact his insides tensed, burning with a sudden violence to destroy all those men. Even in his strange state. But he didn't wish her to know that he cared. That he was capable of caring about someone else's welfare. "I don't give a damn."

She tilted her head back, the tight weave of her locks bumping against the slick stones behind her. "I don't believe that. Not for all the holy saints in the heavens above." She hesitated. "You don't know who I am, but I know you. You're a good man."

He snorted.

"It's the only reason your father convinced me to come."

"More fool you."

She shook her head. "Ah no. I'm not the fool."

"Are you insinuating I'm a fool?"

She pressed those perfect lips together before saying. "You've forsaken yourself and the man you are."

He sucked in a sharp breath, hating he didn't know what she was speaking of. "How do you know me?"

Her gaze softened. "You sent three thousand pounds to Ireland. To the west."

Blinking, he thought back. It wasn't possible that such a thing would make her think so highly of him, was it? "And?"

She sighed. "Do you not know how many you saved? Just with those funds, you made it possible for my family to care for the starving."

He yanked his gaze away from her earnest one. "It was only money."

"It was everything," she said firmly. "And I won't let you forget it."

"You don't have the power to let me do anything."

"There I must disagree with you. Your father has given me that power. For now."

His fingers curled, nails scraping lightly against the unforgiving surface. He desperately wished to reach out and touch something as beautiful as her hair. How would it feel? To touch something beautiful again? To have something beautiful let him touch it?

Now, the way she looked at him, as if he weren't the very dregs of society sparked something deep within side him, urging him to believe. But he couldn't. He'd gone too far down the road to ruin to ever come back.

"I can help you," she whispered.

headline
ETERNAL

FIND YOUR HEART'S DESIRE...